PRAISE FOR
OFF THE GRID: FBI SERIES

#1 NEW YORK TIMES BESTSELLING AUTHOR
BARBARA FREETHY

"PERILOUS TRUST is a non-stop thriller that seamlessly melds jaw-dropping suspense with sizzling romance, and I was riveted from the first page to the last...Readers will be breathless in anticipation as this fast-paced and enthralling love story evolves and goes in unforeseeable directions."

— *USA Today HEA Blog*

"Barbara Freethy's first book in her OFF THE GRID series is an emotional, action packed, crime drama that keeps you on the edge of your seat...I'm exhausted after reading this but in a good way. 5 Stars!"

— *Booklovers Anonymous*

"What I love best about Freethy's books are the characters and the depth she puts in them, the story can be as good as ever, but if you don't care about the characters you can't help but be unbothered by the events unfolding. RECKLESS WHISPER has so many twists and turns that I read it in one sitting.....a must read for everyone, I don't want to ruin anything so I will just say.....WOW"

— *Booklovers Anonymous Blog*

"You will love RECKLESS WHISPER. From the first sentence of the book until you end, you are on a suspense filled ride. I loved it and couldn't put it down."

Janel – Goodreads

"LOOK OUT! There's danger up ahead. Off the Grid is a labyrinth. Each tale pulls readers deeper into the abyss. DESPERATE PLAY amplifies the chill factor. Freethy intensifies the fear as the danger level rises. Unpredictability is a seductive aphrodisiac. Barbara Freethy uses it in a way that will chill, thrill and appeal."

Isha Coleman — Goodreads & I Love Romance Blog

"DESPERATE PLAY is definitely a page turner! Once you think you have something figured out, something else happens and your trying to figure out what's going to happen next. The question is can you love and trust someone after they lie to you so many times?"

"It's been a while since I have had the fun of reading a brilliant romantic suspense book – Perilous Trust gets me back into this genre with a bang!"

"A uniquely seductive, gripping and exhilarating romantic suspense that is fast paced and action packed...Barbara Freethy is the ultimate seducer. She hooked me and slowly and keenly reeled me in. I was left in a trance. I just cannot wait for the next book."

"This was my first time reading Barbara Freethy and I loved Perilous Trust from start to finish. Right from the start the tension sets in, goodness, my heart was starting to beat a little fast by the end of the prologue! I found myself staying up late finishing this book, and that is something I don't normally do."

"The suspense and action continued throughout the whole novel really keeping the pacing going strong and the reader engaged. I flew through this story as Sophie and Damon went from escaping one danger into having to fend off another. I'd definitely recommend Perilous Trust to anyone who likes suspense romance or even contemporary romance. Its fast paced, entertaining and filled with sexually tense moments that would appeal to any romance lover!"

"Perilous Trust was a well-written story with lots of twists and turns. Who's bad? Who's good? Who killed Sophie's father? There's also lots of hot and steamy romance! I'm looking forward to the next installment! 5 Sexy Stars!

Also By Barbara Freethy

Off The Grid: FBI Series
Perilous Trust (#1)
Reckless Whisper (#2)
Desperate Play (#3)
Elusive Promise (#4)
Dangerous Choice (#5)
Ruthless Cross (#6), *Coming Soon!*

Lightning Strikes Trilogy
Beautiful Storm (#1)
Lightning Lingers (#2)
Summer Rain (#3)

The Sanders Brothers Series
Silent Run & Silent Fall

The Deception Series
Taken & Played

The Callaway Series
On A Night Like This (#1)
So This Is Love (#2)
Falling For A Stranger (#3)
Between Now and Forever (#4)
Nobody But You (Callaway Wedding Novella)
All A Heart Needs (#5)
That Summer Night (#6)
When Shadows Fall (#7)
Somewhere Only We Know (#8)

The Callaway Cousins
If I Didn't Know Better (#1)
Tender Is The Night (#2)
Take Me Home (A Callaway Novella)
Closer To You (#3)
Once You're Mine (#4)
Can't Let Go (#5)
Secrets We Keep (#6)

Standalone Novels
Almost Home
All She Ever Wanted
Ask Mariah
Daniel's Gift
Don't Say A Word
Golden Lies
Just The Way You Are
Love Will Find A Way
One True Love
Ryan's Return
Summer Secrets

DANGEROUS CHOICE

Off The Grid: FBI Series #5

BARBARA FREETHY

HYDE
STREET
—PRESS—

HYDE STREET PRESS
Published by Hyde Street Press
1325 Howard Avenue, #321, Burlingame, California 94010

Printed in the United States of America

Cover design by Damonza.com

ISBN: 9781944417505

One

The church bells rang through the small village of Cascada in the hills of Colombia, overlooking the Suarez River Canyon. The bells called the believers to Holy Thursday Mass at St. Catherine's. It was the official kickoff to Easter week, otherwise known as Santa Semana.

In this picturesque village, there was no shortage of believers. There was also no shortage of violent criminals, many of whom lived hidden away in the rolling hills surrounding the town and conducted their business in Medellin, only an hour away. But on Holy Thursday at almost four p.m., everyone became a child of God.

FBI Special Agent Diego Rivera left the hotel he'd arrived at thirty minutes earlier. He'd only had time to drop his bag and ask directions to the church, which proved to be unnecessary since hundreds of people were heading to Mass. As he joined the throng of tourists and locals walking through the centuries-old plaza with its cobblestone streets and colorful Spanish Colonial buildings, his practiced gaze swept the surroundings, searching for potential trouble. But there was a festive feeling in town. It was early April, almost Easter, a time of rebirth. People were talking, laughing, in the late afternoon sunshine, as if they didn't have a care in the world.

He couldn't quite get into the holiday spirit. He'd been seeking answers to questions he'd had for eighteen years, and now a tip had led him around the world, to this pretty village. He hoped he would not leave disappointed, as he had so many times before.

As he walked through the streets, he noted signs of modern life: an internet café, a new urgent care center, and an electronics store. But there were also signs of the past: an open-air vegetable and fruit market, a couple of goats grazing through a nearby yard, the squawk of chickens from a coop behind a café, and boutiques with hand-crafted artisan goods and clothing. 7

According to the front desk clerk at his hotel, a young man by the name of Enrique, Cascada had been founded in the seventeen hundreds and named for an amazing gold waterfall that shimmered in the sunlight and fell into a pool that allegedly provided healing properties. A story in a major travel magazine six years earlier had quadrupled the tourist dollars, and now there were only rare months when the hotel rooms weren't full.

An older woman caught his attention, her long brown hair drifting down her back, and his heart skipped a beat. Then she turned around, and her features were those of a stranger. She wasn't his mother. But he couldn't help wondering if his mom had left her hair long all these years, if she'd walked these same blocks, if his younger brother had played in the fountain in the square like so many of the local kids.

Or maybe they'd never been here at all. Perhaps this trip would be another waste of time.

He forced the cynical thoughts out of his head. Until he knew one way or the other, he wasn't going to speculate. He'd been actively searching for his mother and brother since he'd graduated from college. But they'd been out of his life eight years before that, eighteen years in total.

Their trail had gone very cold. There had also been a lot of false clues, wasted trips, dashed hopes, disappointment, and frustration in the last decade. He was afraid today would bring more of the same, but the remote location gave him a small hope. Perhaps this was exactly the kind of place one would come to if they wanted to disappear.

And disappear was exactly what his mother had done.

It was almost impossible to believe that even with all his resources at the FBI, he hadn't been able to find her or his brother.

But now he had a lead. It had come from Special Agent Tracy Cox, a woman with whom he'd spent an impulsive night a year earlier. That night had been a mistake, but Tracy had caught him at a bad time, and they'd drunk a lot of alcohol. He'd told her way too much about himself, and their very brief fling hadn't ended particularly well when she'd suggested another night and he'd said no.

They'd managed to work through it; they were friends, he supposed. Although, he wasn't really sure why she'd suddenly decided to help him in his search. But a clue was a clue. Her motivation for providing it was something he'd deal with later.

His phone buzzed, and he pulled it out of his pocket, moving over to the sidewalk as he checked the text. It was from his boss, Roman Walker, asking when he'd be landing in DC. He'd just finished up a two-month counterterrorism assignment in Brazil, where they'd managed to uncover two active cells and stop the flow of weapons to that group.

He replied that he needed a few personal days but would probably be back by Wednesday. That gave him a little time to figure things out. And he had plenty of leave on the books. He'd been working sixty-hour weeks for months.

Slipping his phone into his pocket, he headed down the

street once more. He wished he'd arrived earlier. It might be difficult to see Father Manuel before the Mass, but hopefully he could grab him for a few moments.

When he got to the church, he headed toward a side door rather than get bogged down with the people crowding the front steps.

As he moved down a side hallway, he saw an older priest engaged in a very heated conversation with a woman whose golden-blonde hair stood out in a village where dark hair and dark eyes, like his own, were the norm.

The woman wore white jeans and a flowing sleeveless floral blouse, a pair of high-heeled wedge sandals on her feet. She had a large tan bag hanging over one shoulder, and her long hair moved in silky waves as she shook her head and interrupted the priest.

Despite the fact that they were speaking Spanish, he thought she might be American.

He took a few steps closer. They were so involved in their conversation, they paid no attention to him.

"Por favor, please," she begged.

The priest, who was tall with thinning gray hair and appeared to be in his late seventies, patted her arm and spoke in a hushed tone, so quiet Diego couldn't hear what he had to say.

The woman uttered a desperate, hopeless sigh, but when the priest motioned her toward a side entrance into church, she reluctantly moved in that direction.

As the priest started to follow, he hurried down the hall. "Padre," he said. "Father Manuel?"

The older man paused, giving him a sharp look. "Sí?"

"I'm Diego Rivera. I understand you might know my mother, Camilla Rivera, or she might go by the name Camilla Lopez," he added, referring to his mom's maiden name. "Do you know where she lives? Where I can find her?"

"Camilla? You don't know?" The priest's dark brows furrowed together.

"Know what?" A bad feeling twisted his gut.

"I'm sorry to tell you, but—"

Before Father Manuel could finish his sentence, an altar boy came through the side entrance, motioning to the priest that it was time for the Mass to begin.

"I must start the service. We will speak after that," Father Manuel said.

"I only need a minute," he started, but his plea went unheard as the priest disappeared into the church.

His stomach churned as he followed him inside.

The priest had told him he was sorry...*that hadn't sounded good at all*. He hoped it just meant that his mother had left town, and he didn't know where she was anymore.

When he entered the church, it was standing room only. He walked down the side aisle toward the back, sliding into an empty space next to the confessionals and right behind the beautiful and stressed-out blonde. She turned her head, giving him a sharp look. Her eyes were a deep sea-blue, and his body tightened as their gazes met. She offered a slight nod, but not a hint of a smile. Then she directed her attention toward the altar where Father Manuel began the service.

As the service progressed, his gaze moved around the church, noting several men who looked like bodyguards standing near the front pews. As one shifted, he saw a gun at the man's hip. He wasn't surprised. While the village was a tourist mecca and the residents extremely devout, the nearby farm lands were a haven for coca growers, fueling Colombia's cocaine market.

As the priest raised his hands in the air in prayer, a gunshot blasted through the church.

Stunned, he watched as Father Manuel fell backward against the altar, blood spattering across his chest. A second and third shot came amid screams of terror.

He pulled the woman in front of him down, as more bullets sprayed from the choir loft. Some of the men he'd noticed earlier by the front pew started firing back, but he couldn't see who they were shooting at.

"Oh, my God! Oh, my God!" the woman in front of him screamed, her eyes now wild and panicked.

"We have to get out of here." He grabbed her hand, and she clung to him, as they ran toward the side door at the back of the church. There were many others also trying to escape, and he feared they'd be trampled or gunned down before they could get outside, but somehow, they made it.

When they reached open air, the woman gave him a terrified look.

"We have to keep going," he said, pulling her along with him as they ran across the grass and down the block. Seeing the cemetery ahead, he plowed through a thick line of trees, entering the cemetery through a gate. There was a mausoleum at the back of the property and the building could provide cover.

They dashed through rows of graves, moving around the mausoleum, where they ran into a brick wall too high to scale.

"We're trapped," she said in a panic.

"We're safer here than in the street," he replied, peering around the wall.

"What's happening?" She put her hand on his back as she tried to look over his shoulder.

Before he could reply, a white van went screaming down the street, away from the church. Police cars were coming from the opposite direction, sirens blaring.

"Was that the shooter?" she asked. "Is he gone?"

"I don't know." He turned to face her. "Let's give it a few minutes."

She gave a tight nod, her breath coming short and fast. "Father Manuel?"

"It didn't look good."

"I was supposed to talk to him after the service." She shook her head in confusion and despair. "He said he would help me. Now he's dead. It doesn't seem real. Why would anyone want to shoot that old man? He's a priest, for God's sake."

The same questions were rocketing through his head. And like this woman, he'd been hoping to get vital information from Father Manuel after the Mass.

"Was it one person or more than one who was shooting?" she asked.

"I couldn't see. The shots were coming from the loft above us."

"People were shooting back."

"I saw that. Probably local cartel members. We may have ended up in the middle of a turf war. This part of Colombia is rife with drug trafficking." He paused. "What's your name?"

"Tara—Tara Powell," she said, her voice shaking.

"You're American?"

"Yes. And you?"

"I'm also American. I'm Diego Rivera."

"Like the painter?" she asked in bemusement.

He smiled. "Yes. My mother had a fascination with his paintings. I, unfortunately, have no skill when it comes to art."

"Oh," she said, as she tucked her hair behind her ears.

"You looked upset earlier—when you were speaking to Father Manuel. What was he helping you with?"

Surprise flashed in her gaze. "You saw us talking?"

"I was in the hallway waiting to speak to him. I didn't want to interrupt your conversation. It looked emotional. You seemed upset."

"I was upset. I spoke to Father Manuel yesterday. He had told me to come back today, that he could help me, but then he was unwilling. I don't know what happened, why he changed his mind. He said we'd speak later, and I had to wait. Now..." She shook her head. "Whatever he was going to tell me died with him."

"What was he helping you with?"

"It doesn't matter now. The police are at the church. It's

okay for us to leave, don't you think?"

"In a minute. In this part of the world, sometimes the police aren't always the good guys."

"I know. But in this case, I think they are. I hope they are." She pulled a silver heart across a chain at her neck, her fingers nervous and twitchy. "I can't believe someone would kill a priest in a church. They must not believe in godly retribution."

"I wouldn't think so," he agreed. "When did you arrive in town?"

"Yesterday."

"Vacation?"

A guarded look came into her eyes. "Not really."

"What does that mean?"

"You ask a lot of questions."

"I'm a curious person. What was the priest helping you with?"

"It's personal. What were you talking to him about?" she countered.

"That was personal, too."

She blew out a breath. "Do you think Father Manuel was targeted, or did someone just want to shoot up the church on Holy Thursday?"

"It felt targeted."

"Do you think a lot of people were killed?"

"I don't know. I hope not."

He looked around the wall of the mausoleum. The street beyond the cemetery was empty now, but as he watched, an ambulance sped by on its way to the church. *Was that for the priest or someone else?*

"I want to go back to the hotel. I want to get out of here," Tara said, a desperate note in her voice.

He was about to tell her she could go, when his gaze caught on a nearby headstone, and Father Manuel's last statement to him rang through his head. *"I'm sorry to tell you..."*

A statement that was often finished by words like...your loved one is dead.

"The cemetery," he said aloud, moving around the wall, caught up in the unspeakable idea running through his head.

"Are we leaving?" Tara asked.

"I have to see if she's here."

"Who's she?"

Ignoring her question, he strode down the first row of graves, reading the headstones as quickly as he could.

"What are you doing?" Tara asked again, as he came back in her direction.

"I'm looking for a name," he said shortly.

"Can that wait? Or you know what? You do that, and I'm going back to the hotel."

He couldn't answer her. His gut was twisting with agonizing fear. He jogged down the next row and the next, regaining hope with each grave that maybe he was wrong, that Father Manuel hadn't been about to give him horrible news.

And then he saw the name *Camilla*, and he stopped abruptly.

He read her name with a growing sense of horror and disbelief. *Camilla Lopez Salazar* was etched on the stone with the words Madre Amada—Beloved Mother. He didn't recognize the Salazar part of her name, but her birthdate was the same as his mother's.

As he read the date of her death, he was hit by another wave of shock. She'd died fourteen years ago. *Fourteen years ago!*

He'd been seventeen when she passed away. He hadn't even started looking for her then.

The pain cut through him like a knife, and he fell to his knees, his breath coming hard and fast.

"Diego?"

He stared through dazed eyes at Tara, who had left her hiding place to regard him with great concern.

"Who is buried here?" She tipped her head toward the headstone.

He looked back at the grave. "It's my—my mother." He could hardly get the words out. In all the outcomes he'd imagined, he'd never thought she was dead. Never. And she'd died before she'd turned fifty. *What the hell had happened to her?*

"This is your mother's grave?" Tara asked in shock. "You didn't know she was buried here?"

"I didn't know she was dead," he said flatly. "I've been searching for her for a very long time. But she died years ago. All this time, she's been here, this small cemetery, a world away from where we lived. Father Manuel started to tell me something was wrong, but he didn't get a chance to finish. Now I know what he was going to say."

"I'm sorry," Tara said quietly.

He shook his head in anger and regret. "If I'd started searching for her earlier, if my father hadn't been such a complete ass, if my grandmother had had the guts to stand up to him...maybe..." He drew in a hard breath, the reality stabbing him again, like a knife to the gut. "I can't believe she's dead." He suddenly noticed the fresh flowers on her grave. Someone had placed those recently, maybe only a few days ago.

Who?

Could he dare to hope that he hadn't lost everyone?

As he got to his feet, he saw a shadowy figure moving through the trees. For a split second, he thought maybe it was Mateo...

But he didn't recognize the tall, thin man in jeans and a hoodie sweatshirt.

When the man caught sight of them, he pulled out a gun.

Diego shoved Tara out of the way as the bullet bounced off the headstone. Then he grabbed her hand once more, and they ran through the cemetery, slipping through a thick crush of trees on the far side that thankfully provided some cover.

Several more shots rang out, some coming dangerously close.

They ran into the wild, unincorporated hills behind the village, trying to lose themselves in the brush. The shots eventually stopped, but Diego kept running for another twenty minutes, not coming to a halt until they were halfway up a hill, a mile or two away from the church. From their vantage point, they could see the village, the cemetery, the police cars lined up in front of the church. But there were enough trees and rocks around to keep them in the shadows.

"Why was he shooting at us?" Tara asked, her breath coming fast. "I thought the shooter from the church had left."

She'd done well keeping up with him in her sandals. She'd stumbled a few times, but he'd dragged her back to her feet.

"So did I," he said grimly, meeting her questioning gaze. "Maybe there was more than one shooter, and the other stayed behind. He might have been surprised to see us in the cemetery. We caught him off guard."

"And he decided to shoot us? Why? It doesn't make sense."

It didn't make sense.

Had someone tracked him to Colombia, to the priest, who'd been his one chance at finding his mother? But why? Who would care about his personal family history?

As his gaze moved back to Tara, he thought about her intense conversation with the priest and wondered if the shots were about him at all. "Are you in trouble, Tara?"

A mix of emotions ran through her eyes. "Why would you ask me that? Do you think he was shooting at me?"

"You tell me."

"Maybe the shooter was after you," she countered. "Maybe he's tied to your mother." She licked her lips. "The real question is—what are we going to do now?"

Two

Tara asked a good question. He looked at their surroundings. If they continued on this path, they'd be entering a wilderness area, and they weren't dressed or prepared for that.

"We need to get back into town without anyone seeing us," he said, gazing back at her flushed face, her bright, worried eyes. "Once we do that, we should be able to get information on the shooting, the motivation behind Father Manuel's murder, and if there are any known suspects."

"Are we getting that information from the police? Are we going to tell them what happened to us?"

He hesitated. "I don't know. We'll have to play it by ear."

"Maybe Enrique can fill us in. He's the desk clerk at the Palomar Hotel where I stayed last night. He's very friendly. He said he grew up here. I'm sure he'll share what he knows."

He'd found Enrique to be friendly, too. In fact, Enrique had been quite interested in why he was in town. He hadn't shared his real reason with the clerk. He'd simply said he was on vacation. Now he wondered if Enrique was just a genuinely hospitable, friendly person, or if he was keeping track of the guests for a different reason.

"Diego?" Tara pressed. "Should we go back now?"

"Let's wait a few minutes. The sun is going down. I wouldn't mind a few more shadows."

"In that case..." She sat down on a flat rock and removed one of her sandals, shaking out some small pebbles. "That's better. These aren't exactly running shoes. I have a couple of good blisters going."

"You did well to keep up."

"I think you willed me to keep up. You had a vise grip on my hand," she said, as she put her shoe back on.

"Sorry about that."

"Don't apologize. You probably saved my life. I don't know if I would have made it out of there if you hadn't moved so quickly."

"I'm just glad we got away."

"Me, too. I can't believe I've been in the line of fire twice in one day. I've never even heard a gunshot until today. Now, it's echoing through my head like an unrelenting drumbeat. I can't seem to shut it off. I feel like I've stepped into another dimension—a very unlucky one."

"You weren't hit, so your luck is actually pretty good. And the drumbeat will lessen. Give it a little time."

She stared back at him. "Sounds like you're not unfamiliar with that beat?"

"Today wasn't my first time."

"Diego..."

"What?" he asked, seeing the wary suspicion in her gaze.

"Your mom's grave. What's the story? Why didn't you know she was dead?"

"Because she disappeared eighteen years ago. I was thirteen at the time. According to the date on the headstone, she died four years after she left me. I would have been seventeen then. I never knew."

The finality of her death hit him hard, making him

struggle to take his next breath. His mother was dead. He was never going to see her again, never talk to her, never hear her laugh. There would be no heartwarming reunion. His gut burned with anger and sadness.

"I waited too long to look for her," he continued, running a hand through his hair. He wasn't sure why he was telling this complete stranger his personal business. The only excuse he had was that he was rattled.

But he was an FBI agent; he needed to get his head together, compartmentalize the way he'd always done. He needed to work the problem, and right now the problem was not his mother: it was the shooter in Cascada, who had not only shot his source, but had also come after them in the cemetery.

"She just disappeared?" Tara pressed. "Why?"

"It's a long story."

"We seem to have time. Maybe you could give me the condensed version."

"It's private. You should understand that, considering you don't want to tell me what your conversation with the priest was about."

She shrugged. "Have it your way."

Silence fell between them, then he said, "Look—I really need you to tell me what you and Father Manuel were speaking about."

"Why?"

"Because we have to figure out who tried to kill us, and whether it's tied to you or to me. I told you about my mother. Now it's your turn."

"You told me very little."

"I gave you something, so talk."

She gave him a disgruntled look, then she let out a breath and said, "Fine. I went to Father Manuel because I was hoping he might have seen my friend, Bethany. She's missing. The last time she was seen was in Medellin, and she was getting on a bus to Cascada. So, I came to the town to look for her. Enrique suggested I check in at the church. He told me every visitor goes there, and Father Manuel has many friends in town he could contact on my behalf. I went to the church yesterday and I told Father Manuel the story. He asked me to come back today, which I did, but suddenly he wasn't willing to help me. I don't know why. I felt like he was holding back, as if he was scared to tell me the truth."

He didn't know what he'd been expecting her story to be, but it wasn't anything close to what she'd told him. "I'm sorry about your friend. How long has she been gone?"

"I haven't heard from her in almost three weeks. I spent the first week calling her every day and begging her to call me back. I checked with her friends. They hadn't heard from her, either. Her employer told me she went on an unexpected trip, but I didn't believe she would go on vacation and ignore all my calls. So, I decided to come to Colombia and look for her myself."

"How did you know to come to Colombia? Does your friend live here?"

"No, she doesn't. She's a tour guide for Allende Tours. They run one-week and ten-day excursions to Colombia, among other places. And Bethany had just finished a tour in Medellin the last time I spoke to her. She told me then she was coming back to the States in two days. That's why I got worried when I didn't hear from her."

"And you jumped on a plane and came to Colombia—a place you'd never been?" he asked doubtfully.

"Actually, I was in Colombia at Christmas. Bethany arranged for me to try out as a potential tour guide at her company. I work as a high school Spanish teacher during the year, but in the summers I'm free to travel. She thought it would be the perfect summer gig for me. And I loved the idea. I'm supposed to start with my first tour in June. Now I don't know. I'm bothered that Allende doesn't take my concern seriously."

"She hasn't been gone that long. And if she told them she

was taking a trip…"

"I know something is wrong. I know Bethany," Tara said with a stubborn glint in her eyes. "And when I arrived in Colombia and called her again, her phone was dead. It didn't even go to voicemail anymore."

"How did you find out Bethany was seen at the bus station?"

"I went to the police in Medellin last Monday. They weren't particularly helpful or interested, but they did do a cursory scan of the local bus stations, and they told me that a security camera had captured an image of Bethany boarding the bus to Cascada the previous Wednesday. I decided to take the same bus. There were two stops along the route. I got off at each station and showed her photo to anyone who would stop and look, but no one recognized her."

"This was a week ago?"

"It was three weeks ago that we spoke, but eight days since she got on the bus. I've narrowed the timeline, but that hasn't really helped. Bethany is a social media addict; she posts photos every day, but there hasn't been one single picture in the last eight days. Nor has her phone number ever come back into service." Tara drew in a deep breath. "I'm afraid something terrible has happened to her."

"I understand why you're concerned. What about her family? Have you checked in with them?"

"I'm her family. Bethany grew up next door to me. Her dad died when she was born, and her mom passed away when she was sixteen. She moved in then with me and my parents. She's been more than a friend to me; she's been a little sister. There's no one else to look for her besides me. I have to find her."

The desperation he'd heard earlier was back in her voice, and now he understood why. He also thought there was good reason for her fear. Young women disappearing in this part of the world was always cause for concern. "Maybe I can help."

"How?" she asked sharply.

"I'm an FBI agent."

Her brow shot up in surprise. "Seriously? Then how come you don't have a gun?"

"Because Colombia doesn't allow foreign agents into their country with weapons, and I wasn't planning on getting into trouble. I'm not here as an agent. This was a personal trip. But I can talk to some people. I have some connections in this part of the world."

"That would be great." Hope lit up her blue eyes, and his gut clenched for a different reason. *Tara really was a beautiful woman.* Distracting himself from that thought, he pulled his phone out of his pocket. "I don't have a signal. But when we get one, I'll make a call."

"I would really appreciate it. I didn't get far with the police in Medellin or here in Cascada."

"Wait—you went to the police here in Cascada?"

"Yesterday, when I first arrived, but they were also of no help. They said unless there was actual evidence that Bethany had arrived in Cascada and gotten into trouble, they couldn't do anything. Enrique said she hadn't checked in at the Palomar. I went to other smaller hotels and had no luck."

"So there is no evidence she was in Cascada?"

"Father Manuel had seen her. He recognized her picture yesterday. But today he had nothing to say. I think..." Her voice drifted off.

He knew what she thought. "That someone hurt her and then threatened the priest."

Agony ran through her eyes. "I don't want to believe that. It's the only conclusion I can come to. If there is anything you can do to help me, I will be forever in your debt."

He didn't really want her in his debt, and he still had his brother to find. But it was hard not to want to help Tara. She was fiercely devoted to her friend and willing to fight as hard as she could for her. How could he turn away? "I'll do what I can," he said finally.

"Thank you, Diego." She swallowed hard. "Do you think

Father Manuel is dead because of me? I really don't want to believe that my questions led to his murder. Enrique told me that the priest had baptized and married almost everyone in town. Who would have wanted to kill him?"

"I don't know. We need more information."

"Which is why we need to get back to town." She stood up.

"We'll get there. Did you ever consider how much danger you were putting yourself in by coming here alone?"

"I considered it. But I didn't have another option."

"What do your parents think about this fearless quest?"

She frowned. "They think I'm vacationing in Mexico, that it's my spring break. But I actually took a leave from my job. I couldn't tell them where I was really going. They'd only worry about me and also about Bethany. My dad has heart problems; I didn't want to add to his stress. Since they live in Santa Barbara now, we don't see each other in person very often."

"Where do you live?"

"San Clemente. It's a beach town about an hour south of LA."

"And Bethany? Where does she call home?"

"She has an apartment in West Hollywood. She lives about an hour from me. I know you probably think I'm stupid for doing this. I've certainly been told that by a number of people, and I've had the same thought myself. But I didn't know what else to do. I couldn't sit at home and do nothing."

"I think you're a very brave and loyal friend," he said. "And a little stupid."

She gave him a small smile. "Well, thanks for giving me some credit. I'm sorry I was being cagey before. I'm really on edge and after what happened at the church and the cemetery, I'm afraid to trust anyone, but now I'm trusting you, and I hope I haven't made a huge mistake."

"You haven't. I already saved your life twice."

"You were saving your own, too," she pointed out.

"True, but I'm not going to hurt you, Tara."

"I'm counting on that. Shall we go back?" She glanced at her watch. "It's almost six. It's been over an hour and a half since the shooting."

"Let's do it," he said, watching as she squared her shoulders and lifted her chin. She looked like she was going into battle. She had guts. He had to give her that. But he knew she was also terrified, and not only for herself, but also for her friend. He had a feeling she had good reason to be scared.

It had been a relief to tell Diego her story. She'd been holding in her worry about Bethany, having to pretend to her family and her friends that everything was fine, that Bethany was just living her adventurous life. It was possible that was still true, but her bad feeling was getting worse by the minute.

The shootings at the church and the cemetery felt surreal, as if they had been a terrible dream. But the sight of Father Manuel's blood-stained robe ran through her head, and she knew it wasn't a dream. The godly old man was dead. And she really hoped it wasn't her fault.

She cast a glance at Diego, who was striding a few steps in front of her. He was a tall, attractive man with dark hair and compelling brown eyes, tanned skin, a strong jaw, and a powerful, agile body that had allowed him to drag her halfway up a mountain without breaking a sweat. He had a commanding presence, and it was clear he was used to being in charge and calling the shots. She had no problem with that if he could help her find Bethany.

He seemed willing to try, at least at the moment.

Would that change when the finality of his mother's death sank in? He hadn't had a chance to come to terms with that. And clearly there was a lot more to his story than he'd shared with her.

It occurred to her that Diego's conversation with the

priest, and his dead mother, could be tied to the shooting, too. Not to mention the fact that he was an FBI agent. Maybe that had made him a target in this country, where drug cartels ran the villages. She wondered if Father Manuel had known Diego's profession, or if he'd just presented himself as a man looking for his mother.

How had Diego decided to come to Cascada? What clue had brought him to a remote village in the Colombian hills?

She had a lot of questions, but the last thing she needed was to get distracted. Bethany was her only concern, not this very attractive and somewhat mysterious FBI agent. She would take whatever help he was offering, but beyond that she really didn't need to get any more involved with him.

Diego's steps slowed as they neared the village. The hotel was located in the middle of the main plaza, and as they came down from the hills, she could see tiny flickering lights in the square. "What's all that?" she muttered.

"Looks like a candlelight vigil."

"There are a lot of people near the hotel. How are we going to get inside without anyone noticing?"

"At this point, a crowd is a good thing."

"It doesn't feel that way. We can't identify the shooter, but they might be able to identify us."

"Hopefully they're not anywhere near our hotel. Here's what we're going to do—we're going to walk quickly, but we won't run. We don't want to look like we're worried about anything."

"I'll try, but I just want to get there already."

"Stay close. In fact..." He held out his hand.

She hesitated for one moment, wondering why she was clinging to a man she'd met a few hours ago. But she needed his calm, confident strength right now, so she put her hand in his.

They walked briskly toward the front door of the hotel. No one seemed to be paying them much attention. There was a somber mood hovering over the entire area. Earlier in the day, the plaza had felt like a party stage. Now, it felt grim. There were people crying, holding each other, and hundreds of candles burning down to their wicks as a trio of men played a weeping song of sadness on their guitars.

When they entered the hotel, there were guests huddled around a television in the lobby, watching the local news. There was no sign of Enrique. A middle-aged woman now stood behind the front desk, helping an elderly couple check out.

"Let's take the stairs," Diego suggested. "What floor are you on?"

"Three. What about you?"

"Four. We'll stop at your room first."

"Okay." They made it up to the third floor without running into anyone. She pulled out her key and inserted it into the lock.

"I'll go first," Diego said, pushing the door open. He flipped on the light and then turned back to her. "Wait here."

Despite his order, she stepped through the doorway, gasping when she saw the state of her room. It had been completely trashed. Her clothes were everywhere. The dresser drawers had been completely pulled out and tossed on the floor. Even the bed had been ripped apart, the mattress slashed with a knife. She shivered at that thought.

Diego came out of the bathroom. "Whoever was here is gone," he said, pushing the hotel door shut and turning the bolt.

"Isn't it a little late for a lock?" she asked, dazed by what had happened.

"Get your things together, and then we'll go."

"Go where?"

"Away from this place."

She wanted to leave. She wanted to run as fast as she could. "But...Bethany. She might be here in Cascada."

"I know you want to find your friend, Tara, but we need to dig into her disappearance from another location. We can try from Medellin. It will be easier to hide in a bigger city."

"That makes sense, but I still feel like I'm letting Bethany down. She could be close by. If I leave now, I might never find her."

"If you don't leave now, you might not be alive to find her," he said bluntly.

She sucked in a breath at his words. "That was harsh."

"Sorry, but that's the truth." His glance swept the room. "What do you think they were looking for?"

"Looking for?" she echoed.

"This was a search, Tara. It wasn't random vandalism."

"I have no idea."

"Did Bethany leave you something or send you something in the mail before she disappeared?"

"No."

"When you went to Medellin, where did you look for her?"

"At the apartment that the tour group makes available for guides when they're in between tours."

"Did you take anything from there?"

"No. There was nothing to take. Bethany's things were gone. There was no trace of her."

"Well, someone thinks you have something."

His statement swirled around in her head. "Maybe I was the target at the cemetery."

"Why don't you pack? I'm going to make a call." He took out his phone. "What's Bethany's last name and birthdate?"

"Cooper. She was born April 25. It's almost her birthday. She's twenty-six years old."

"Where was she born?"

"Los Angeles. When we were growing up, we lived on Green Street in the Los Feliz area. Her mom's name was Joan." She knew she was rambling, but she wanted to be as helpful as possible.

"Okay. And the tour company name is Allende?"

"Yes. Their offices are in Newport Beach, California."

"All right. I'm going to step into the hall. I'll be right outside the door. You pack."

She wondered why he required privacy for his call, but now wasn't the time to ask. She needed to put her things together, so they could get out of here before anyone came back.

Three

———➤➤◀◀◀———

Diego walked down the hall to the window. From his vantage point, he could see the square, where the vigil was in full swing. His mind was spinning with a dozen questions and theories.

Was Tara the target of the shooter at the cemetery? Had her questions gotten Father Manuel killed? Or was there more than one thing going on?

His mind returned to the cemetery, to his mother's grave, to the flowers that had been placed by the headstone. *Who had put them there? Mateo?*

Someone in Cascada had known his mother, had cared about her. It would make sense that it was his brother. His mother had been dead a long time. *Who would take the time to place flowers so many years after the fact?* It had to be someone close to her, like her son. Although, it could be a husband. She'd clearly married someone else after his father. *Had she had more children? Had she forgotten all about him?*

His father had told him she had done just that every time he asked about her. He'd always had the same answer: *If she wanted to see you, she'd see you. She made her choice.*

He hadn't believed that. Even as a teenager, he'd wondered if his dad had kept his mother away from him. He'd accused him of that a number of times, especially in the first year after the split. His father had hit him in the face the last time he'd asked. He'd been fourteen. The next month, he'd been shipped off to military school.

But now he wondered if his mother had ever tried to see him, or if she'd simply started over with Mateo and eventually a new family.

He really wanted to stay in town and search for his brother. But he didn't know if the shooter had been after Tara or after him. Until that was clear, he needed to make smart decisions. To do that, he had to get more information, and he was going to start with the person who had sent him to Father Manuel.

He punched in Tracy's number. As far as he knew, she was working out of Chicago, which put her one hour behind him, making it about seven thirty there.

"Diego? What happened? Did you find your mother?" Tracy asked, her voice quick and sharp.

"Yes," he said. "I did."

"Oh, my God, really? I wasn't sure if it was a good lead or not."

"Where did you get the tip?"

"I told you before—I had a source. I put out feelers on your mom, and he pointed me in the direction of the priest. Did you meet your mother? Did you talk to her?"

A rush of pain stabbed his heart once more, but he couldn't let himself get caught up in emotion now. "No. I didn't talk to my mother. She's dead. She's buried in the cemetery near the church."

"What?" Tracy asked in shock. "I—I'm so sorry, Diego. I had no idea."

"I need the name of your source and a way to contact him or her."

"I understand that you're upset, but I can't give you his name. And I don't see the point. Why do you need to know? It sounds like your search is sadly over."

"Not exactly," he said, not wanting to bring up Mateo. He didn't think he'd ever told her about his brother, but the night they'd spent together was hazy in his mind.

"What do you mean?" she pressed.

"I went to see the priest, but we didn't have a chance to talk before the Mass. I was in the service with a few hundred other people, when a shooter in the choir loft took Father Manuel out."

"Wait. What? The priest is dead?"

"Yes. I think there may be other casualties as well."

"That's really shocking. I thought I was sending you on a simple trip to talk to a priest. I had no idea you'd end up in a shooting. Do you think it was tied to you? Were you the target?"

"Not sure. After I got out of the church, I ran through the cemetery. I was at my mother's grave when the same shooter or someone else shot at me again. That's why I need to know who told you to send me to Father Manuel. Because there's a chance someone set me up."

"There's no way this was a setup, Diego. I'm sure the priest had other enemies, or it was a random attack on Holy Thursday. Who knows? There could be any number of reasons why the shooting occurred," Tracy argued.

"In the church, yes, but not so many in the cemetery." He didn't bring up Tara, because he didn't want to distract Tracy.

"Look, Diego, I'm sorry. But my informant did me a favor, and I promised to keep his name confidential. I can't go back on my word. You know what it means to protect a source. You've done it yourself."

He blew out a frustrated breath, knowing she was right, but not liking it.

"Diego—are you there?" she asked.

"I'm here."

"I really am sorry that you couldn't speak to your mom. When did she die?"

"Apparently, a very long time ago."

"Do you need help getting out of Colombia? I assume you're coming back to the States. I can meet you somewhere."

"I don't know what I'm doing yet. I'd like to find out if anyone in this town remembers my mother."

"That makes sense, but considering the situation, it sounds dangerous. Are you sure there isn't anything else I can do? I was hoping that this lead would make things less awkward between us. I know that I didn't have the best reaction when you said you didn't want to continue on with anything, and I feel badly about that. I'd like to think we could be friends. Go back to what we were before that night last year."

He didn't think they'd really been friends before that night. They'd known each other at Quantico, but they'd been mostly rivals back then. "I have to admit I was wondering why you'd decided to help me."

"It was a peace offering. I care about you, Diego. The story you told me about your mother stayed in my head for a long time. I wanted to help you, so I started asking around."

"It's just strange that you came up with this tip, when I've been making inquiries for years without any luck."

"I obviously had different sources," she said lightly. "At least let me call our legal attaché in Bogota."

"I'll call Lucas myself," he said, having worked with Lucas before.

"I'm sorry I can't give you my source. Please call me if there's anything else I can do."

"I will." As he ended the call, he frowned. He didn't know what to make of her reluctance to put him in contact with her source. They weren't working a case. This wasn't a criminal matter. But obviously he was missing something. That bothered him.

Had he been set up? Was he supposed to die in the

*church? Is that why someone had come looking for him in
the cemetery? But why would anyone lure him to the
remote village where his mother had been buried just to
take a shot at him?*

It didn't make sense.

Lifting his phone again, he punched in the number for
Lucas Marengo. As the FBI's legal attaché at the US embassy
in Bogota, Lucas was responsible for coordinating
communication between law enforcement in both countries.
He'd worked with Lucas before—when they were both
stationed in Argentina for a time, and he knew Lucas had the
ability to cut through bureaucratic red tape faster than anyone
else.

"*Buenos noches,*" a man answered.

"Lucas—it's Diego."

"Oh, man, it's been awhile," Lucas said. "How are you?"

"I need some help."

"What's going on?"

"Two things. An American woman by the name of
Bethany Cooper has disappeared. She was last seen eight
days ago, getting on a bus in Medellin bound for the village
of Cascada. Her phone is dead. She hasn't been online, and
her friend is very worried about her."

"I can see what I can find out. I know a police officer in
Medellin. Are they looking for the woman?"

"Not according to her friend. Apparently, Ms. Cooper
works for a tour company and informed the owner she was
going on vacation. There's no evidence of foul play, but the
friend is convinced that something happened to her, and
based on what I know, I'm concerned as well. However, I'm
not in Colombia on official business. And I'd rather not run
this through my chain of command. It will bring forth
questions I don't care to answer."

"Got it. What else can you tell me?"

He rattled off the rest of the details that Tara had given
him in regard to Bethany.

"Do you have a photo?" Lucas asked.

"I can get one. I'll text it to you."

"I'll see what I can find out. You said there were two things. What's the second?"

"There was a shooting in Cascada tonight. A priest was killed in the church. I need to know if there are any suspects, any known motives."

"Why? Were you there?"

"Yes, I was. I don't know if I was the target, but I'm laying low at the moment. It's possible that the shooting could be tied to the missing Ms. Cooper as well. Her worried friend talked to the priest at the church right before he was killed."

"It sounds like you've landed yourself in a hornet's nest," Lucas drawled.

"It does feel that way."

"Is this number good for you?"

"I'll probably switch out when I leave Cascada. I know it's late in the day, but—"

"But I'll get right on it," Lucas said. "Call me back in a few hours."

"I will." He'd no sooner hung up with Lucas when the door to Tara's room opened. He walked down the hall as she rolled out her overnight bag, her large purse still slung over her shoulder.

"I'm ready," she said.

"Let's stop at my room, and then we can go."

They walked upstairs to the fourth floor. As he inserted his card key and opened the door, he was happy to see that his room was untouched. It was in exactly the same condition as it had been when he'd left. His carry-on was still packed and sitting by the bathroom door. He'd only dropped his case and used the restroom before he'd gone to the church.

"This confirms they were after me, not you," Tara said heavily.

"Whoever searched your room was definitely interested in you, but we don't know if it's tied to the shooting. By the way, I need a photo of Bethany. Do you have one on your phone?"

"Of course." She opened her phone and clicked on the camera roll. She flipped through several photos. "This one is from Christmas."

He took the phone to look at the pretty brunette with laughing green eyes. She was holding up an ugly Christmas sweater.

"I gave her that sweater. It's a tradition in our family," Tara said, a sad note in her voice. "Bethany felt like she was one of us when we included her in the ugly sweater contest every year."

"This will work." He texted himself the photo, then handed her back the phone. Then he sent the photo to Lucas.

"Who did you send that to?"

"Lucas Marengo—the FBI legal attaché at the US embassy in Bogota. He has connections with law enforcement. Hopefully, he can get some information for us."

"That sounds positive. Do you think I'll be able to find her, Diego?"

He really wanted to answer the plea in her voice with a positive statement, but missing women in this part of the world were rarely found in good condition.

"I guess your hesitation is my answer," Tara said, a worried gleam in her blue eyes.

"I'm going to do everything I can to help you."

"Why?" she asked abruptly. "You don't know me. We're not friends. You came here to find your mother. Why would you want to get involved in this?"

"Because you asked for my help. Because we got shot at together. That's a bonding moment. Maybe we're not friends yet, but we're definitely not strangers."

She gave him a faint smile. "You got shot at because of me. You'd be safer with some distance between us."

"And you'll be safer if we stick together, so we'll do that, at least for now."

"You're a natural-born protector, aren't you?"

The question hit him hard. "I wish that were true, but I haven't been able to protect a lot of people."

Her gaze met his. "You're referring to your mother."

He nodded. "And a few others."

"Don't you want to talk to someone about your mom before we leave town? If she's buried here, someone probably knew her."

"I don't think it's safe for us to walk around the village right now. And I don't want to leave you alone."

"I appreciate that, but you're helping me, and I want to help you. It's too bad Enrique isn't working tonight. He'd probably point us in the right direction. You'd need to find someone who has been in town since before your mom died. Maybe the older woman behind the desk downstairs would know something."

"Maybe." He hesitated, then said, "My mom wasn't the only one to disappear out of my life. She took my little brother with her. Mateo is five years younger than I am. The last time I saw him he was eight. He'd be twenty-six now."

"And you think he's here, too?" she asked.

"It seems like a good possibility."

"We definitely need to find Enrique. He's about twenty-five, close to your brother's age. He told me yesterday that there's a popular bar called Ventana's about a block from here. He goes there after work a lot. I'm not sure if he'd be there tonight, but we could try it. If he's not there, maybe one of the bartenders would know your brother. If he lives in this town, he has probably been there."

"It's risky," he said slowly. "I need to get you out of Cascada. I can always come back and look for Mateo another time."

"You're here now. The bar is close by. It's worth a try. And hopefully the shooter from earlier isn't in there tossing back shots. He'd be hiding out somewhere, right?"

"I would think so, but I don't know, Tara. It's one thing to risk my life. I don't want to risk yours."

"If you don't want to take me, go by yourself. I'll wait here."

He liked that idea even less. "No, we should stick together. Let's put our bags in my car, then we'll go to the bar. We'll ask a few questions and then hit the road."

"Okay. That sounds like a plan."

It did. He just wasn't sure it was a good plan.

Ventana's was packed with tourists and locals, but the atmosphere was still on the somber side. There was a soccer match playing on the television screens over the bar and some intense games of pool going on in an adjacent room, but there was no music, no laughter, just a lot of quiet conversations.

Diego spotted Enrique almost immediately. The good-looking young male was sitting at the bar, speaking to a female bartender. There was an empty stool next to him.

"There he is," he said, taking Tara's hand.

"I see him," she said, tugging her hand out of his. "I don't think we should act like we're together. It will seem odd. I checked in alone. Why don't I take the barstool, and you stand on the other side, like you're ordering a drink? Enrique flirted with me when I checked in. He might tell me more than he'd tell you, especially if he tries to hit on me."

She made a good point. "All right. You go first."

Tara walked across the room and slipped on to the stool next to Enrique, giving him a charming smile.

He had to admit he was impressed at how good she was at putting her fear aside to do what she needed to do. Looking at her now, flirting with Enrique, he could hardly believe she was the same woman he had dragged halfway up a mountain as they ran for their lives.

He moved into position on the other side of Enrique. There was plenty of room at this end of the bar, and Enrique didn't even give him a glance, his gaze locked on Tara's pretty face.

"I can't believe what happened today," she said to Enrique. "I'm still shocked and scared. I was almost afraid to leave the hotel. But I felt like I needed to be with people."

"You were at the church?" Enrique asked.

"Yes. It was terrifying. I've never seen anyone killed before. That poor man. I don't understand why someone would want to kill a priest."

"I know," Enrique said heavily.

Tara looked up as the bartender came over to take her order. "I'll have a glass of chardonnay," she said.

"Tequila is better," Enrique said. "Let me buy you a shot."

"Well, all right. That does sound good."

The bartender hit Diego up next. He ordered a beer and looked at his phone, just in case Enrique glanced in his direction.

"Have you heard any reason behind the shooting, Enrique?" Tara asked. "Do you know if the police have a suspect?"

"I've heard a couple of theories."

"Like what?"

"I don't know if I should say."

"Oh, please tell me. I really want to understand what happened."

"Well, one suggestion is that it was someone from the Pedroza organization. They're a drug cartel that operates mainly out of Cartagena and Medellin, but they've been looking to take over this region from the Salazar family. The Salazars were at the church, and Father Manuel has been a very close friend of the family."

"So the shooting was between rival cartels?"

"Possibly. The second theory is that the attacker came from inside the Salazar family. There has been some rumored dissension in the ranks. But that seems less likely. The

Salazars have been here for decades. They have a couple of large estates outside of town. They take good care of the community. They built a new hospital two years ago. They repaired the church after an earthquake last year, and Father Manuel has baptized every Salazar from the oldest to the youngest for the last fifty years. So why would anyone in the family want to kill him? Although..." Enrique dropped his voice, as he leaned forward. "The priest has heard every confession every Salazar has ever made. It's possible he heard one too many, and that got him killed."

"By someone in the family?"

"Who knows? It's not uncommon for brother to go against brother when power and money are at stake." Enrique paused. "This country—it is beautiful, but it is also deadly. I love my homeland, but sometimes it breaks my heart. Today is one of those days. Father Manuel married my parents. He baptized me. He was a good man."

"I'm so sorry, Enrique," Tara said.

"Did you speak to him about your friend as I suggested?"

"I did. He had asked me to come back today, but when I spoke to him, he didn't seem to have any new information. We were going to talk again after the Mass."

"Now I am the one who is sorry for you. I know you are very worried."

"I am."

"You should go home. Back to America. Someday I would like to go there. Where are you from, beautiful Tara?"

As Enrique's words slurred, Diego thought the young desk clerk had already had a few too many drinks. But when the bartender delivered their shots, Enrique slammed his down before Tara could even raise her glass.

"I'm from California," Tara said. "You would like it."

"I think I would." He tipped his head to her glass. "You are not drinking?"

She raised the shot glass to her lips and drained it down. Then she shivered. "That was strong. But I needed it. There's something else I want to ask you, Enrique."

"No." He shook his head. "No more questions. They will lead us both into trouble. You must leave here. Your friend is not in this village. You should go home before you end up like Father Manuel." Enrique slid off the stool. "I must go. Take my advice before it's too late." As he moved to leave, his gaze fell on Diego. "Senor Rivera?" he said in surprise. "I didn't see you there."

"Enrique," he said, with a tip of his head.

"I am glad to see you are well. I wasn't sure if you got caught up in the shooting. I know you were headed to the church."

"Fortunately, I wasn't hit."

I'm sorry you had such a rough start to your visit. Perhaps tomorrow you can go to the waterfall. It will be crowded. Many will seek its healing powers after today. But it will be worth the trek."

"I'll keep that in mind."

"Adios," Enrique said, as he took his leave.

Diego took the stool Enrique had left vacant.

"Why didn't you ask him about your mother?" she inquired. "You had the perfect chance."

"Because of the conversation you just had with him."

She gave him a quizzical look. "What does that mean?"

"I saw the name Salazar earlier today—on my mother's headstone. Camilla Lopez Salazar. She married into a drug cartel."

Tara's eyes widened. "Well, maybe not all of them are criminals. Enrique said they also built the hospital and have done good things here. Your mother could have been involved in that. Her husband—I guess it would be her husband who gave her the name—he might be a farmer or a builder or something else."

He appreciated her effort to defend a woman she'd never known. He swigged down a few long draughts of his beer. "I'd like to think that, but who knows?"

"Maybe you need a tequila shot."

"I'm good. I've heard enough. Let's get out of here."

"Are you sure?"

"Yes." Knowing that the Salazars operated a criminal organization, and his mother clearly had some tie to the family, made him cautious. It was possible Mateo was also tied up in the cartel. He needed to get more information and then he would come back.

He followed Tara across the room, watching a few men take notice of her. He quickly caught up, putting a proprietary hand on her arm. She threw him a quick, questioning glance.

"We need to look like we're together now. Trust me."

"Okay."

He moved through the door first, wanting to make sure there was no hidden danger.

But he'd only taken a few steps outside when a man rushed him, a fist coming at his face too fast to dodge.

He stumbled backward from the force of the blow, hearing Tara scream as she wrestled with another man.

As his attacker came at him once more, he sidestepped, grabbed the man's arm and twisted up behind his back in a way that drew forth an agonized scream of pain. Then he smashed the guy's head into the wall.

The man fell to the ground, and he turned toward Tara's attacker.

As he moved forward, Tara landed a solid kick to the man's groin, and he followed up with a series of blows to his face, until the man sank to the ground. He looked up and saw several people watching them, but no one seemed eager to call for help or get in the middle of their fight.

He and Tara ran down the street to his rental car. They'd stashed their bags there on the way to the bar, and, thankfully, it was less than a hundred yards away. They jumped inside, and he peeled away from the curb as Tara fastened her seat belt. He drove as fast as he could toward the main highway, hoping they wouldn't get stopped by the local police, who would probably be on the Salazar payroll.

"Is anyone following us?" Tara asked, as she turned her head to look out the window.

"I don't think so, but I'll feel better when we get farther away from here. Are you all right? Did he hurt you?"

"No. I'll probably have a few bruises tomorrow, but that's all. What about you?"

He could feel his eye swelling, but it could have been a lot worse. "I'm fine."

"You don't look fine. You're going to have a shiner."

"That will make me look sexier, right?"

She shook her head in bewilderment. "How can you joke at a time like this?"

"Because we got away." He shot her an admiring glance. "You did well, Tara. You held your own. Where did you learn how to fight like that?"

"A self-defense class at the community center. The guy always said go for the groin, so I did."

"Good call."

"I just never thought I'd actually have to fight like that. I've never hit anyone in my life. Oh, God, I can't believe what happened."

"You're okay." He put a comforting hand on her leg, sensing she was now about to fall apart. "Breathe."

"I'm trying. I—I don't know what to think. What if those guys had had guns or knives? We could have been shot or stabbed. We wouldn't have been able to escape."

"They did have guns. They weren't ordered to use them. They wanted us alive."

"They were going to kidnap us? Why? What would they want from us? I'm not rich. No one can pay ransom. Is your family wealthy?"

"I don't believe ransom was the focus. They might have just wanted to kill us somewhere less public."

She gave him a baffled look. "But they killed Father Manuel in front of hundreds of people."

"Good point. Then they might still think you have something of value. I keep going back to the fact that your room was searched."

"I don't have anything. And it's hard to believe someone wants to kill me. I'm a high school teacher from San Clemente. I'm a nobody."

"But you're in Colombia now, looking for your friend, and apparently making someone very nervous with your inquiries."

"Which means Bethany really is in trouble." She drew in a breath and let it out. "You were right, Diego. It was a mistake to go to the bar."

"It wasn't a mistake. We found out more about the shooting and the Salazars." His hand tightened on the steering wheel as his thoughts went to his mother and brother. *Could his brother possibly be involved in the shootings?* God, he hoped not.

"I think you're the one who needs to breathe now," Tara said, giving him a concerned look.

He forced himself to do just that and hoped as they sped down the highway that no one was coming after them. He had a feeling they'd already used up whatever luck they had.

Four

---><>><<<---

Tara rode the waves of adrenaline until her pulse slowed down and her breath flowed more naturally. The highway was dark with only the occasional light every few miles and very little traffic. There hadn't been any headlights behind them the past ten minutes, which made her feel better, although the remoteness of the highway did not. It was another fifteen miles to Medellin. A lot could happen between here and there.

She appreciated Diego's calm confidence. Thank God she'd run into him in the church. He'd saved her life three times already, if she counted the church. If he hadn't decided to come to Cascada to look for his family, she might not have survived. She might be dead or missing...just like Bethany.

Diego's comments about her having something kept going around in her head. If Bethany had gotten into trouble, if she had wanted to stash something away, where would she have put it? *Could it still be in the apartment in Medellin? Would she have left it with anyone else?*

Bethany had made at least six trips to Colombia in the

past year. And every time she'd always tacked on vacation days for touring. *Who knew where she'd gone or who she'd met during those times?* Bethany was a friendly, outgoing woman with an adventurous streak.

They were certainly different in that regard. She considered herself friendly, but not on Bethany's level. And she certainly wasn't adventurous. The tour guide job had appealed to her, because she'd felt like she was playing her life too safe, too boring. She'd been looking forward to the summer, to expanding her perspective, to getting out of her comfort zone.

Well, she was definitely out of her comfort zone now. She'd blown that to bits.

And she had no idea what to do next. She was worried about herself and even more worried about Bethany. She could be in terrible trouble. She might even be dead.

That thought made her suck in air, drawing a concerned look from Diego.

"Don't think about what is happening to her," he advised.

"How did you know that's what I was thinking?"

"Because it's what I'd be thinking."

That made her feel a little better. In fact, it was a massive relief to speak to someone who wasn't trying to talk her out of her worry. "Thank you, Diego."

"For what?"

"For not making me feel like a fool for worrying about a woman who told everyone she was going on vacation and kept that vacation going a little longer than expected."

"Well, I've had a front-row seat the last several hours, and I think you have every reason to be concerned. But I will say one thing…if Bethany was snatched off the street, I can't see anyone taking the trouble to search your hotel room, or to try to grab you. Why wouldn't they let you find nothing and then go home? Why raise your curiosity? There's some motivation we don't understand, but it's there."

"You're right. It doesn't make sense."

"What's Bethany like?"

"She's a happy person, outgoing, funny. She's also impulsive, free-spirited, and she tends to fall for guys who aren't always that good for her."

"Like someone working for a drug cartel?"

"I don't want to think that, but maybe. I did consider the fact that she might be with a guy somewhere. She did mention someone awhile back, but she didn't tell me his name or anything about him. I asked some of her friends who worked for the tour company, but while a few of them thought she had a boyfriend, nobody knew who he was. I know that's not very helpful. I'm completely frustrated by my lack of information. I hope your friend can find something out for us."

"I hope so, too."

"I'm curious about something. How did you come to be in Cascada at this particular time? You said you'd been searching for your mother and brother for more than a decade. What changed?"

"I got a tip from another FBI agent—Tracy Cox. She apparently asked around on my behalf and found a source who suggested I speak to Father Manuel."

"Who was the source?"

"She won't tell me. I called her while you were packing. She insists that she must maintain her confidential agreement with this person."

"Is that unusual?"

"In this case, it is. We're not working on something for the bureau; this is personal."

"So why the secrecy?"

"I don't know, and it's bothering me," he admitted. "The whole situation is a little off."

"How so?"

"Tracy and I have had some odd moments in our relationship. We trained in the same class at Quantico, but Tracy was always on an opposing team. We were rivals. And she was driven to win at all costs. She was ruthless and very sly, and I often thought she cut corners. After we graduated, we went our separate ways. I didn't see her for a long time, but then a year ago, she looked me up while she was on vacation in Rio. I was in Brazil at the time for work. I'd had a bad turn on an assignment when she showed up. A fellow agent had been badly injured, and I was worried about him. I was drinking pretty heavily the night Tracy appeared. One thing led to another."

"You slept with her."

"Yeah. It was not a good decision. But it was one night. I thought she understood that, but the next morning she made it clear she was looking for more. She said she'd always had a thing for me. Not that I'd ever known that."

"Well, men can be clueless."

He shot her a small smile. "True. But honestly, we hadn't talked in years. In fact, I really thought she disliked me. I have a very close group of friends from my Quantico days, and she was jealous of our bond. When she showed up in Rio, flirting and acting like we were good old friends—it was confusing. But I blame myself for not having the sense to stay away from her."

"What happened after your awkward morning-after conversation?"

"She left. We exchanged a few texts about six weeks later. She wanted to smooth things over. I said there was nothing to smooth, and we were good. Many months passed. Then a few days ago, she comes up with this big lead for me. Apparently, while I was drinking in Rio that night, I spilled my guts about my mother, and Tracy decided to see if she could find her. I'm not clear on her motive."

"Well, I am. She wants you back and figured this was a good step. You're obviously someone she can't forget." Tara wasn't really surprised by that. Diego was a very attractive guy and not easily forgettable. She had a feeling she'd remember him for the rest of her life. Although, their situation was a lot different. As he'd said, getting shot at together was a bonding experience. "What else did you talk about tonight? Did you tell her about me and Bethany?"

"I did not."

"Why not?"

"Lucas is in a better position to help us locate Bethany here in Colombia. I'm going to stick with him for now."

"I am grateful for any help I can get. I've obviously made a huge mess of things by shooting off my mouth everywhere I went."

"I don't know what else you could have done, Tara. You had to ask questions. But we are where we are, and there's something else you can do now."

"What's that?"

"Go home. I can put you on a plane in Medellin. I can work on this without you."

She immediately shook her head, not liking that idea at all. "No way. I can't leave yet. I'm not ready. I want to go back to the apartment in Medellin and see if I missed anything. I want to hear what your contact has to say. Then I'll decide if it's time to go home. I know there's danger, but I'm hoping with your help, we can figure out where Bethany is before anyone takes another shot at us."

"That would be great," he said dryly.

As they passed another mile marker, her thoughts moved from Bethany and her problems to Diego's story. "Diego, I know it's your business, but will you tell me what happened to your family—why you were separated from your mother and brother?"

He didn't answer right away, and she thought he was going to repeat what he'd said earlier, that it was too long of a story to get into.

Finally, he said, "I was thirteen years old. It was a hot summer night. I remember that I couldn't get cool. I also couldn't sleep because my parents were arguing. They'd been fighting a lot for weeks. And I was afraid they were going to get a divorce. That would have been better than what actually happened."

"Which was what?"

"My father came into my bedroom. He was furious. His face was beet red, and he was sweating like crazy. He looked like a crazy person. There was a wild light in his eyes. He was an intimidating man even on his good days, but that night, I was scared. He was big and strong and out of control. I didn't know what was wrong. He tossed a duffel bag at me and told me to pack it—we were leaving. I kept asking him why, and where we were going. He just said we had to get the hell out of the house. I wanted to know when we would be back, and he couldn't tell me. I asked for my mom. He said she wasn't going to talk to me."

"That's awful. Why wouldn't she talk to you?"

"I don't know. She was in her bedroom. Maybe he locked her in. Maybe she didn't want to say good-bye. I have no idea. But when I left the house, I didn't see her." He paused. "I did see Mateo. He must have woken up when he heard all the yelling. He stood in the hallway in his Ninja Turtles pajamas, and he started to cry when my dad told me to say good-bye to him. I could barely get the word out before my dad shoved me out of the house. I didn't even have shoes on."

"God, Diego. That's awful." Her heart tore at the images Diego's story had put into her head. How terrifying and sad for both him and his brother.

Diego cleared his throat. "We drove away and went to a hotel. The only thing I could get out of my dad that night was that my mother was a liar and a cheater, and he was done with her. It took a couple of weeks to get the rest of the story."

She knew what the story was. "That your mother had an affair and Mateo wasn't his child?"

He flashed her a look. "You got to that truth faster than I did."

"Well, I'm not thirteen and in terrible pain. Please tell me you saw your mother at some point."

He shook his head. "No. We returned to the house about a week after we had left, and she wasn't there, and neither was Mateo. Their things were gone. My father told me to forget about her. I kept asking him where she was. I asked everyone else in the family, too. My dad's stepfather was the only one who tried to help, but my dad immediately shut him down. I got nowhere with my grandmother, either. She wouldn't tell me a thing. My father had total control over her. I kept hoping my mother would get in touch with me, that she would find a way to see me when my dad wasn't around. Every day I came out of school, I thought she'd be on the other side of the fence waiting, ready to tell me how much she missed me. But she was never there. If she tried to see me, she must have been blocked by my dad."

"I'm really sorry. I can't imagine going through any of that."

"After a while, I got mad at my mom, too," Diego continued. "Why didn't she try to talk to me? Why didn't she find a way to get to me? If she really loved me, she would have done that. I became a really angry teenager. I got into fights. I drank. I took up smoking. I did everything I could to make my father realize he needed to bring my mother back. But instead, my dad shipped me off to a military prep school. Once there, I tried everything I could to get myself kicked out, but my father's power was once again too much for me. At some point, I stopped fighting, and to my surprise, I actually started to like the structure of the school. My life had been chaotic and unpredictable for so long, it felt good to know exactly what I had to do every hour of the day."

"What happened after prep school?"

"I went to West Point. I had turned myself around by then and I had a couple of teachers who helped me get recommendations, and I got in. After I graduated, I served for five years. It was during that time I started searching for my mother. But according to the date on her headstone, she was already dead by then. I waited too long."

His voice was riddled with pain, and she felt an enormous wave of compassion for him. "You were dealt a bad hand, Diego. But there's still your brother. He wasn't buried in that grave."

"I hope to God he wasn't buried somewhere else. I have to believe he's still alive."

"You'll find him."

"I don't know about that. Even with all my FBI resources, I couldn't find my mom until Tracy came up with this tip out of left field."

"Well, you know more now. You can start with the Salazars. If your mother married into the family, her son went with her."

"Which makes me wonder who he is now."

She couldn't answer that question. "Whoever he is, he's still your brother." She thought about his story for a moment. "Did you tell your father you were coming down here?"

"God, no. I barely speak to the man."

"I can see why. I'd like to strangle him for what he did to you."

He gave her a sad smile. "Join the club. It's a very popular one."

"It's one thing for him to divorce your mother and even to disavow your brother, but he had no right to rip you away from them. They were your blood, too."

"I agree."

"I'm going to help you find Mateo."

"You have enough on your plate, Tara."

"We can do both. We'll find Bethany, and then we'll find Mateo. Who knows, maybe their paths crossed."

"Who knows?" he echoed. "I will find Mateo. I won't stop until I do."

"I feel the same way about Bethany."

"We could both die trying."

"I know," she said. "But let's try not to."

It was after eight when they arrived in Medellin, and the tall buildings and city lights made Tara feel as if she'd finally made her way back to civilization. Medellin was known as the City of Eternal Spring because of its year-round moderate climate. It was also known for its booming coffee, textiles, and orchid industries. With two universities, there were plenty of young people and a vibrant nightlife, which made Tara wonder why Bethany would have wanted to leave and spend time in the quiet, sleepy village of Cascada. There was far more to do here.

"I feel better," she said, as Diego drove toward the downtown area, the bustling traffic slowing their progress. "With more than two million people in this city, we should be able to disappear."

"Agreed. We need to find a hotel."

"The most popular area for tourists is El Poblado. That's where the tour groups go, plenty of restaurants, bars, and hotels. I actually stayed there when I arrived last Monday. We could go to that same hotel."

"We definitely don't want to stay where you stayed before."

"Okay, well there were plenty of other choices."

"Why didn't you stay at the tour apartment."

"I'm not officially an employee. I have all the codes and access to the rental schedule for the apartment, but it felt weird to stay there, so I didn't." She opened up the internet on her phone. "I can look now. I have a signal."

"No. Shut it down. Turn off your phone," he said abruptly. "I should have told you to do that hours ago. I wasn't thinking."

His crisp words brought back the fear she'd spent the last hour trying to get rid of. "You think someone is tracking my phone?"

"It's a possibility. We need to stay under the radar. But I

do like your neighborhood suggestion. Do you remember how to get there?"

"I think so," she said, giving him what she hoped were good directions. In preparation for her tour, she'd spent a lot of time researching areas in Medellin and figuring out how to get around and where to go.

Eventually, they made it to El Poblado. At the sight of a six-story, name-brand hotel, Diego turned in to the parking garage. He stopped at the gate to get a ticket and then drove down two levels before pulling into a spot by the elevator.

They grabbed their bags and took the elevator to the lobby level. While Diego checked in, she looked around the lobby. There was a bar and grill off in one corner, and her stomach rumbled at the thought of some food, but she wasn't sure she was ready to sit in a public restaurant after what had happened when they'd left the bar in Cascada.

"I got us a room," Diego said, returning to her side.

"One room?" she questioned.

"We need to stay together. You can trust me."

"Good, because I've been trusting you for the last few hours."

"And you can keep on doing that."

She followed him over to the bank of elevators where a security official was checking keycards, and she was happy to see that layer of security. Their room was on the fifth floor. It appeared to have been recently remodeled and offered two full beds, a dresser beneath a flat-screen TV hanging on the wall, and a small table with two chairs by the window.

While Diego checked the bathroom and closet, she walked over to the window. The hotel was surrounded by restaurants, bars, and retail shops. There were plenty of people walking the streets and she could hear the faint beat of music coming from a nearby nightclub. Come tomorrow, the area would be even busier, especially with so many people getting ready for the upcoming Easter celebrations.

"Everything looks normal," she said, as Diego came up

next to her. "It almost feels like the last several hours were a dream—make that a nightmare."

"I wish they were. But you can't let down your guard, not even for a minute."

"I was just trying to cheer myself up."

"I get it, but lying to yourself won't be helpful."

"You don't like to sugarcoat things, do you?" she asked.

"All the sugar in the world doesn't turn bad into good."

As she met his gaze, the purple and black swelling around his eye made her realize that he was probably in some physical pain as well as emotional pain from finding out about his mother. "Maybe sugar won't help, but how about some ice for your shiner?"

He shrugged off her concern. "I'm fine. Don't worry about it. Are you hungry?"

"Starving. The steaks sizzling on the grill downstairs smelled like heaven."

A faint smile creased his lips. "I thought so, too. Why don't I go down and get a to-go order?"

"We could order room service."

"I'd rather not have anyone coming to the room."

"All right." There was a menu on the table next to them. As she perused it, Diego read over her shoulder.

She felt a little too aware of his presence, of the fact that they were going to share a room tonight. She'd met him a few hours ago. And here she was trusting him with her life. *Was she being a fool?* On the other hand, she probably wouldn't be alive right now if it wasn't for him.

"See anything you like?" he asked.

She could have answered that question in a couple of different ways, but she forced herself to focus on the menu. "The carne asada looks good."

"You can't go wrong with marinated grilled beef. I'll get the same. Anything else?"

"Avocado corn ensalada."

"Got it. Some wine?"

"I'll stick to water."

"I'll go downstairs and put in our order."

"You don't want to use the phone?"

"I'm going to see if I can find a store to pick up a prepaid phone," he said. "Bolt the door after I leave and don't open it up for anyone. If someone tries to get in, call the front desk immediately. I'll knock three times when I come back, so you'll know it's me."

His words sent more uneasy feelings through her body, but she told herself he was being extra cautious. After he left, she turned the dead bolt. Then she put her suitcase on the bed closest to the window and unzipped it. After kicking off her sandals, she pulled out a pair of leggings, a soft, comfy sweater, and thick socks that would cushion the blisters on her feet. Then she went into the bathroom to change.

As she stared at herself in the mirror, she saw brutal evidence of the day she'd had. Her face was very pale, her eyes still dazed and shocked by everything she'd experienced, her hair a tangled mess of waves, and she'd bit off the lip gloss she'd put on before going to the church. There was also a bruise on her neck from where the man outside the bar had grabbed her. But she was alive. And that was all that mattered.

That thought was immediately followed by worry for Bethany.

But she didn't have enough energy to get herself all worked up again. It was too much. Too overwhelming. Too terrifying. She just had to keep taking steps to try to find Bethany and not think of what condition Bethany might be in when she found her.

Although that resolve seemed almost ridiculously stupid.

Was she really going to keep asking questions after everything that had happened? But if she gave up, who would look for Bethany?

She clearly needed a more strategic approach. Hopefully, Diego's associate would be able to come up with information that could help them get to the truth.

She wondered how long Diego would work with her. He had his own search to conduct. His story about his father ripping him out of his bed and tearing him away from his mother and brother was horrific. She couldn't imagine her own dad doing such a thing. Nor could she imagine her mother not trying to get in touch, not finding a way to see her.

Diego had been looking for closure for a long time, but the closure had come with knowledge of his mother's death, and she didn't think he'd really had a chance to process that.

He still had his brother to find. Hopefully, Mateo would be alive.

But who was Mateo now? Was he part of the Salazar family? Was he a criminal? How was his FBI brother going to handle that?

Shaking her head at the relentless pressure of questions that could not be answered, she changed her clothes, and returned to the room.

She couldn't get on her phone, and she should probably check with Diego before turning on the laptop computer in her bag, which left the television for a distraction.

Picking up the remote, she sat down on the edge of the bed and flipped through the channels, grateful she was fluent in Spanish, so she could follow along.

She paused on a local news channel that was showing a photograph of the church in Cascada. The reporter was giving details of the shooting. The only fatality was Father Manuel. But six other individuals had been wounded. Two were in serious condition. The others were in good condition. All were expected to survive. There was no one in custody and no suspects.

How could that be?

How could no one have seen the shooter?

Or maybe it wasn't about not having seen him; perhaps it was about not wanting to identify him.

Five

━━▶▶◀◀◀━

Diego put in an order for food at the hotel grill, then was lucky enough to find a phone store still open two blocks away. He picked up two prepaid phones and paid cash for them. Then he returned to the hotel. When he entered the lobby, he opened the packaging for one of the phones and started it up. Then he punched in Lucas's number.

"It's Diego," he said, when Lucas answered. "I picked up a burner phone."

"Good idea. Where are you now?"

"Medellin. Tara and I got jumped outside of a bar in Cascada. We had to make a quick exit from the village."

"Damn. Are either of you hurt?"

"No. We're fine. But I'm obviously concerned."

"As you should be."

"What do you have for me?"

"Let's start with the church shooting. One theory is that the Pedroza organization wanted to send a message to the Salazars, that they could get to anyone they cared about at any time, and the priest was the symbol of that. Others speculate that there is infighting among the Salazars and that the priest sided with the wrong individuals."

"I heard similar rumors in Cascada. What can you tell me about the cartel?"

"They've been a player for decades in Colombia. They have a strong distribution network in the US. It's believed they work with another criminal enterprise out of New York."

"New York," he muttered, wondering if his friend, Wyatt Tanner, who had worked undercover in the Venturi organization, might know about the Salazar operation in that area.

"Yes—they're also in Chicago and Los Angeles. At the head of the Salazar organization is Caleb Salazar. His younger brothers Juan Felipe and Santoro are also involved in the family business, as well as multiple cousins, nephews, nieces—it's a big family. We did hear that the fifteen-year-old daughter of Franco Salazar and his wife Louisa was injured in the shooting. Franco is a doctor and not believed to be involved in the criminal side of the family, but you never know."

"Will she be all right?"

"It appears so. The other victims included an elderly couple by the last name of Valdez, both in their late eighties, a thirteen-year-old altar boy by the name of Joseph Bettencourt, and a twenty-nine-year-old male Adam Moldano, who is believed to be employed by the Salazars to provide security for the family."

"Did you hear any mention of a Mateo Salazar or a Camilla Salazar?"

Lucas thought for a moment. "No. Those names don't ring a bell. But as I said, there are a lot of Salazars. Caleb is in his sixties and has had three wives, all of whom produced children for him. Both of his brothers, Juan Felipe and Santoro, are married with children. There are also many cousins, including Franco, James, Tomas, Louise, and Irina, who may or may not be married and/or have children. I don't know all the members of the Salazar family."

He hoped his mother and Mateo were part of the family that wasn't directly involved in the drug business. "Okay. What about the woman I asked you to look into?"

"My contact in the police department in Medellin confirmed that they are not looking for Bethany Cooper. There's a record of a missing person report filed by Tara Powell. But nothing further has been done as there's no evidence of a crime. The tour company that Ms. Cooper works for stated that she's on vacation, and they have no idea why her friend is so worried about her."

That went with what Tara had told him.

"I also did some research on Ms. Cooper. She appears to have one checking and one savings account, neither of which has more than a couple of thousand dollars in it. The last time her credit card was used was at the Medellin bus station where she purchased a ticket for Cascada. There's no hotel check-in, no bank withdrawal, no evidence of her existence after that date. I pulled security footage from the bus station and saw the image that the police showed your friend. Unfortunately, she wasn't seen leaving the bus in Cascada, because they don't have any security cameras where the bus lets off."

"All right. That's basically what we knew, but I appreciate you checking."

"I'll keep digging, but Ms. Cooper is currently a ghost. What else can I do for you?"

"I need a weapon, Lucas."

"I can arrange that. But it will be tomorrow morning."

"That's fine."

"I'll text you. Stay safe, my amigo."

"I'm going to try."

As he ended the call, he thought about the information Lucas had given him regarding the Salazars. He punched in a number for Wyatt Tanner, one of his best friends from Quantico. Thankfully, he had Wyatt's number memorized.

Since he often changed phones in his job, he made it a point to keep track of numbers in his head.

Wyatt answered on the second ring with a wary, "Hello?"

"It's Diego."

"Well, it's been awhile," Wyatt drawled.

"I know. How are you? I heard something about you falling in love with a rocket scientist."

"Astrophysicist," Wyatt corrected. "And Avery is great. We moved in together last month, and we'll be tying the knot in the fall."

"Congratulations. There will be a few weddings this year with Bree and Nathan getting hitched this summer."

"Yes, and who knows who else is next. Hopefully you can make the wedding. Once I get a date, I'll let you know."

"I will try to be there."

"Now, tell me what you need."

"Hopefully, a little information, if you have a minute."

"Sure. How can I help?"

"Are you familiar with the Salazar cartel out of Colombia?"

"Absolutely. They ran some of their drug business in New York through the Venturi organization. I met Juan Felipe on two occasions. He's one of the top guys, although his brother Caleb was at the helm back when I was undercover. I'm not sure if that's changed."

"Ever hear of a Mateo Salazar?"

Wyatt thought for a moment. "I don't think so."

At Wyatt's words, Diego felt a rush of relief, but he couldn't entirely buy into the story he was telling himself—that Mateo was not part of the Salazar crime family.

"Do you want me to reach out to one of my CIs?" Wyatt asked.

"That would be helpful. But I need to be up-front with you. Mateo is my younger brother. I recently discovered my mother married into the Salazar family. She passed away years ago, but I don't know what happened to Mateo. I'm thinking he might have grown up in the cartel."

"Your mom is dead? I'm sorry to hear that."

Wyatt was one of only a handful of people who knew his past. While at Quantico, they had had to investigate each other to find their potential weaknesses, their vulnerability, and that's when he'd shared his story. Aside from Wyatt, Damon, Parisa, Jamie, and Bree, he'd kept his history private until he'd shot off his mouth to Tracy a year ago.

"Thanks," he said. "I'm still looking for Mateo. I'm currently down in Colombia."

"I wondered where this call was coming from. How did you get to Colombia?"

"Surprisingly enough, I got a tip from Tracy Cox."

"Tracy? I didn't know you kept in touch with her."

"I don't usually, but she knew about my search, and she came to me with a lead. However, she's refusing to name her source, which is very suspicious, because when I got to Cascada, the town she sent me to, I ended up in the middle of a church shooting. And I found my mother buried in the cemetery next door."

Wyatt let out a low whistle. "That's crazy."

"Tracy swears she wasn't setting me up, but I have a bad feeling."

"Bree can't stand Tracy. They had some run-ins back in Chicago when Bree was handling that kidnapping case."

"I remember hearing something about that. At any rate, Tracy aside, I need to find Mateo. I came down here in between assignments and I'm technically on vacation. I really don't want to fill in my team about my family, especially if there's a chance Mateo is operating on the wrong side of the law."

"Got it," Wyatt said. "Let me see what I can find out."

"I would appreciate it. I know I haven't been the best of friends the last year. I haven't helped out in any way. I was undercover for a long time and I was out of touch."

"We all do what we can when we can," Wyatt said. "And

we're still a team, even if we're spread across the world. By the way, did you get the information on Rowland?"

He frowned. "I got the warning from Bree, but I still can't quite imagine that Jamie's father is out to get revenge on us. It doesn't seem possible."

"There's a lot of smoke, Diego; we just haven't found the fire yet."

"Maybe there's nothing to find."

"Or maybe your personal troubles are a sign that you're next."

"What are you talking about?"

"The lead from Tracy came out of the blue."

"I don't know how Vincent Rowland could have given it to her. He's retired."

"And yet you'd be surprised how engaged he is in FBI business. He shows up everywhere we turn: New York, Chicago, LA. Parisa had a run-in with him last month. Keep your eyes open, Diego."

"Believe me, they're always open, but especially now." He didn't know what to think about Rowland, but right now he was the least of his problems.

"I'll see what I can find out on Mateo," Wyatt continued. "Have you looked for him through our databases?"

"Not with the last name Salazar. I've also been running from bullets the last few hours."

"I don't think you've told me the whole story."

"I haven't. Here's the short version. I was able to escape the shooting at the church with a woman, Tara Powell. She was in Cascada looking for her missing friend. Since the incident at the church, Tara and I were shot at and later jumped outside a bar. We barely got away."

"And these events are tied to your search for your brother or for this missing woman?"

"That's not entirely clear."

"What's the missing woman's name?"

"Bethany Cooper. She's a guide for Allende Tours. Lucas

Marengo, the bureau's attaché in Bogota has been in contact with the police in Medellin, who don't believe Ms. Cooper is missing. According to her tour company, she's on vacation, and the police don't care to dig any deeper. But she was seen getting on a bus in Medellin to Cascada, which is where Tara and I were yesterday. Tara asked a lot of questions in the town while she was looking for her friend. Her hotel room was searched. I'm pretty sure this Bethany Cooper is in trouble, maybe with the Salazars, who run that part of the country."

"This gets more complicated by the minute."

"I know. I'm still putting pieces together. Everything has happened really fast."

"Well, I'm happy to do what I can to help."

"If you have time."

"I recently wrapped up a case with Flynn, so I do."

"You're still working on his task force?"

"Yes. It's going well so far. If you ever want to talk to him, let me know. We operate enough off book to make it interesting."

He smiled at that. Like himself, Wyatt had always preferred being undercover. Wearing a suit and tie had never come naturally to either of them. The rest of the team he'd formed at Quantico was a mix of overt and covert. Parisa was often under whereas Damon and Bree often played it straight up. He had no idea what kind of agent Jamie would have been if he hadn't died during training, but he was quite sure Jamie would have been fearless.

The idea that Jamie's father Vincent would hold them responsible for Jamie's death didn't make sense. It had been almost five years since Jamie had died, and there had been a thorough investigation. *If Vincent wanted payback, why would he wait until now?*

Diego shook that thought out of his head, preferring to focus on the problems he had right in front of him. "I'll keep the task force in mind," he said. "But right now, I want to find my brother."

"And if you find him, and he's part of the Salazar organization..." Wyatt let that question hang.

"I'll worry about that after I find him."

"Maybe it's better not to look, Diego."

"It might be. But I can't do that."

"I had a feeling you were going to say that. I'll be in touch. This number good?"

"For now. If I switch things up, I'll let you know." He ended the call and slipped the phone into his pocket, then headed to the restaurant. Their steaks should be ready by now.

⸺◆◆⸺

Tara was pacing around the hotel room, worried as the minutes ticked by, and there was no sign of Diego.

Shouldn't he have been back by now?

What if something had happened to him?

She'd only met him a few hours ago, but already she had come to depend on him, probably too much, but it was what it was.

A knock came at the door, and she caught her breath, waiting for two more knocks. Another rap came, then another. She walked over to the door and checked the peephole. Seeing that it was Diego, she unbolted the door and opened it.

He came into the room with two bags in his hands, and they smelled wonderful.

"That took a long time," she said, locking the door after him.

He walked across the room and set the bags on the table. "The restaurant was busy. I also made a stop and picked this up." He handed her a prepaid phone. "I got one for myself as well, so we can stay in communication. I already programmed both phones with our numbers."

"I have to admit I feel a little better having this. When you were gone for so long, I really wanted to call you."

He gave her an apologetic look. "Sorry about that."

"It's fine. You didn't do anything wrong. I'm just nervous."

"I can't imagine why," he said with a smile. "Hopefully, you're also still hungry."

She took a seat at the table, as he unpacked the containers of food, her stomach rumbling at the delicious smells of grilled, spicy steak. "You'd think I wouldn't be able to eat with all this stress, but I feel like I could eat an entire cow right now."

"Hopefully, the filet mignon will suffice. It's the crash after the adrenaline rush." He took the seat across from her. "Don't be surprised if you fall asleep the second you finish eating. The body can only be on high alert for so long."

"I'm not sure my adrenaline has slowed down yet. I keep waiting for the other shoe to drop."

He nodded. "Understandable. I called a few of my contacts while I was waiting for our food. Unfortunately, there's no news on Bethany, but everything you told me regarding the Medellin police was accurate. Lucas reiterated that the local police don't feel a need to investigate Bethany's disappearance since her employer is confident that she's on vacation."

"Bethany is supposed to be leading a tour starting next Thursday. I can't imagine why Allende Tours isn't concerned about whether or not she'll show up for that."

"Who does Bethany report to?"

"Tony Allende. He manages all the guides. I spoke to him in his office before I got on the plane for Colombia. He told me not to worry. Bethany likes to travel in between tours. I couldn't argue with that, but I also felt that Tony didn't want to think that there could be a problem. Their business is dependent on their good relationships with foreign governments. They don't want to have a problem in

Colombia, so I think they're pretending not to see one."

"That makes sense. What else can you tell me about the company?"

"It was started by two sisters—Erica and Gretchen Allende—about ten years ago. They're in their forties. They were born in Rio de Janeiro but moved to the States with their family when they were teenagers. They traveled extensively in South America and worked at various hotels before opening up Allende Tours. I met Erica while I was interviewing. She's a sharp, ambitious woman. Tony Allende is their cousin. He's about thirty-five, I think. There are probably five or six admin-type employees in the LA office and about twenty tour guides who lead tours primarily in Mexico, Central and South America."

"You said they have an apartment here in Medellin?"

"Yes," she said, taking another bite of her steak. "They have apartments in six or seven cities that the tour guides use in between jobs, so they don't have to fly back to the States. I think the Allendes also sometimes use the apartments when they're traveling." She opened the bottle of sparkling water he'd bought her and took a sip. "Is any of this information helpful?"

"I'm not sure yet. Was Bethany close to anyone at work besides Tony?"

"I wouldn't say she was close to Tony. They butted heads a lot. But she had to talk to him because he was her boss. As for other friends, there's a woman named Rachel Cedano that she spent time with in between tours. Rachel is in Patagonia this week. I did talk to her, but she said she hadn't spoken or heard from Bethany in more than a month."

"What about boyfriends?"

"Bethany dates—a lot. And as I mentioned earlier, she did suggest that there was a guy, but I don't know more than that. She doesn't always tell me about her romantic adventures, especially if they are with questionable men. She thinks I'm too judgmental and I probably am. But Bethany is two years younger than me, and I've thought of her as my younger sister. After her mom died, and she came to live with me and my parents, I took it upon myself to watch out for her. She was wild back then, and I often bailed her out of trouble. She loved taking risks, and I avoided them at all costs."

"You're painting a picture of a somewhat irresponsible woman."

"Bethany has changed since high school. She's been employed with Allende for two years. She has her act together, at least most of the time. But I can't stop worrying about her; it's a hard habit to break."

"She's lucky you can't break that habit. You might be her best chance for surviving whatever has happened." He gave her another warm smile. "And for the record, you don't seem very risk averse to me. Not many women would come alone to Colombia to look for their friend."

"So far, that decision hasn't played out too well."

"Maybe not, but your heart is certainly in the right place."

"I've made it sound like it's a one-way street with Bethany, that she takes and I give, but she has also stood up for me, and I can't forget that."

"What did she do for you?" he asked curiously.

"It was nothing earthshaking."

"What was it then?"

"It happened in high school. She found out that the guy I liked was spreading rumors about me, really bad stuff. I was humiliated. Bethany got him to stop."

"How did she do that?"

"She got some dirt on him and blackmailed him. He was in the running for a college scholarship, and he was afraid he'd lose it if the truth came out."

"Bethany likes to fight fire with fire?"

"She does. It probably wasn't the best way to handle the situation, and she could have gotten herself into trouble, but it did work, and I was very grateful." She paused, seeing something play through Diego's eyes. "What are you thinking?"

"I'm wondering if Bethany stumbled into something and tried to get out of it by using the same tactics. If she tried to turn the tables on the wrong someone..."

"Then she could be in big trouble," she finished, her heart sinking once more.

"But I'm speculating, and that's not helpful."

"It's helpful to me just to have someone to talk to about all this. Someone who believes me."

"I asked you to trust me, so I need to trust you. We'll get a lot further if we're on the same page."

"I agree. But I have to ask, Diego—what's next? You made your call, and your contact came up with nothing. Are you done? This isn't your problem, and I know you need to find your brother, so..."

He met her gaze head-on. "I'm not done. Tomorrow, we'll go to the apartment where Bethany was staying. Then I want to speak to the tour company myself. After that, we'll see..."

"And your brother?"

"Another friend of mine is checking on his whereabouts. If I can get a location, then I will want to see him, but let's take it one step at a time."

"All right." She was relieved he was still willing to help her. "I saw the local news report on Father Manuel's shooting, but they didn't give out any other names."

"Lucas told me that a teenage girl with the last name of Salazar was injured as well as one of their security people. An elderly couple and an altar boy were the other victims."

"If one of the Salazar children was injured, that would imply that the shooting was conducted by the rival gang, wouldn't it?"

"I would think so, but there was a lot of crossfire. Who knows which bullet hit that girl?"

"Well, if she was hurt by someone of her own blood, that

could be even worse."

"But not unusual. These big crime families often spill their own blood."

"Is this what you do, Diego? Do you work on bringing drug cartels down?"

"No. I've been working on counterterrorism the last few years, which sometimes does involve drugs, but I've been more focused on intelligence gathering and weapons transactions."

"You speak so pragmatically about terrible things."

"Sorry. Compartmentalizing is part of the job."

"I don't know how you do it, Diego."

"Yes, you do. You're doing it right now, Tara."

"Am I? I honestly don't know what I'm doing," she said candidly. "I am way out of my depth. This is not how I normally spend my days. I've never been caught up in a violent attack like the one at the church. I've had to think about it, of course, because I'm a high school teacher, and active shooter drills have become part of what we do. But there's still a huge difference between thinking about something you don't believe will ever happen and getting caught in the middle of it. When the bullets started flying, I froze. I'm glad you grabbed my hand and dragged me out of there."

"I'm glad, too," he said simply. "And you've handled yourself really well—through everything. I'm impressed."

She was surprised and touched by the admiration in his eyes. "Thanks. I'm trying."

"That's all you can do." He pushed his empty plate aside. "That was good."

"I feel much better, too. Do you think I could make a call on the phone you got me?"

"Who do you want to call?" he asked quickly, his gaze sharpening.

"My parents. I try to check in with them every few days, and they might start to worry if my phone is off."

"You can call them. Just don't tell them where you are. The less they know, the better."

"I agree."

She felt a little awkward making the call with Diego sitting right there, so she took the phone and sat down on the bed. It rang a couple of times and then her mom answered.

"Hi, Mom. It's me."

"Tara? Where are you calling from? I don't recognize the number."

"My phone broke. That's why I wanted to call you—in case you were trying to reach me."

"Your dad tried earlier and said he thought your phone was off. Is this your new number?"

"No, it's only temporary. I'm going to try to get my old number back, but for now, you can reach me on this number."

"I don't recognize the area codes. Where are you?"

"I'm still in Mexico," she lied.

"But I thought you were coming back days ago."

"I'm having too much fun," she said, forcing a happy note into her voice. "You and Dad always tell me I should have more fun, right?"

"Well, that's true. But isn't spring break over?"

"I took a few extra days."

"Honey, I have something to tell you."

She stiffened at the tone in her mom's voice. "What? It's not Dad's heart, is it?"

"No. No. Nothing like that. Brian called us yesterday. He wanted to get in touch with you. I told him I would give you his number and let you know that he wished to speak to you, but that was all."

"Brian?" she echoed. "I haven't heard from him in five years."

"I know he broke your heart. And I would caution you not to go down that road again."

"I have no intention of getting involved with Brian again."

"Well, good. I didn't want to tell you, because I know how much pain you were in after the breakup, but we've never lied to each other."

Guilt ran through her at that comment. She'd done nothing but lie to her parents since Bethany had disappeared. "I'm glad you told me. I should go. I'll call you when I get a chance. I'm going to be traveling in some areas that don't have great reception, so don't worry if you can't get a hold of me."

"It sounds like you're having an adventure."

"You could say that. I love you, Mom. Tell Dad I love him, too."

"I will. Have fun. You deserve it, Tara. You so rarely let loose. I'm glad you decided to give yourself a break."

"Me, too. Bye."

As she disconnected the call, she felt a wave of homesickness and another rush of fear that her choice to come here could hurt a lot of people, especially her parents. If something happened to her, they'd be devastated. It was one reason she'd always been so careful—the stress of being the only child.

Diego got up from the table and came around the bed, taking a seat on the mattress facing her. "Don't think about it."

"You don't know what I'm thinking about."

"You're thinking that you could have died today and instead of you calling your parents, someone else might have contacted them, might have had to tell them you were injured or dead."

She blew out a breath. "Okay, you do know what I'm thinking about. I lied to them, Diego. I feel badly about it. I want to protect them, but maybe I'm not being fair to them."

"You can go home tomorrow, Tara."

"But then no one would look for Bethany."

"I would."

"For how long?" she challenged. "I know you'd try to

find Bethany. But once you hit a wall, would it end there? You have your own job, your own problems to get to. I wouldn't blame you for wanting to get back to your life. I have to stay—at least for a while longer."

"Okay. Then I have to ask you one more question."

"What's that?"

"Who is Brian?"

Six

———⟫⟪⟪—

Tara flushed at his question, and she gave a nervous swipe of her lips, before she answered. She didn't really want to talk to Diego about her past. On the other hand, he'd been forthcoming with her about his family. Besides that, the interested look in his eyes told her he wasn't going to drop the question until he got an answer.

"Brian was a man I dated in college—actually the relationship lasted from age twenty to twenty-three. We broke up five years ago."

"Why?"

"He had a job offer in London. He wanted me to go with him, but I had a teaching position in LA, and I wanted to stay in California. Neither of us was willing to compromise."

"Then you didn't love each other enough."

"That's probably true. It wasn't just the jobs that separated us. Brian didn't like how unadventurous I was."

"You?" he asked in surprise.

"I told you—this isn't the real me. I'm a very boring person. I've always been afraid to take chances. I think it started when I was a little girl. My parents got pregnant after me, but my mom lost the baby at six months. I remember her sitting in the baby's room crying and crying for days on end. I was seven at the time. I guess they had tried a long time to get pregnant, and the loss was terrible."

She paused, as the vivid memories played through her mind. "I remember telling her not to cry because she had me, and I was never going to leave. And she hugged me so tight, I almost couldn't breathe. She said she loved me and that she never wanted me to leave, either. I know it sounds silly, but that conversation kind of formed my life. When other kids were rock climbing, I was reading. I lived my adventures in books. I didn't want to take any chances that might take me away from the people I loved and who loved me. Anyway, Brian decided that he wanted someone who was more willing to take risks, so he left."

"Why is he calling you now?"

"I don't know."

"Maybe he realized there's a lot more to you than whether or not you want to jump off a cliff."

"I definitely don't want to jump off a cliff," she said lightly. "That sounds terrifying."

"Running from bullets and escaping a kidnapper is terrifying, too, but you handled yourself well. I don't think you give yourself enough credit, Tara. Real strength comes in the face of adversity. When your friend's life is on the line, you step up. You took a huge risk coming here."

"And I'm so out of my depth, I'd be drowning if it wasn't for you."

"That's not true. I know what survival instinct looks like, and I saw it in you when you fought for your life."

She was more than a little flattered by the admiration in his eyes. She'd gotten so used to thinking of herself in a certain way that it was difficult to change. It hadn't been only Brian who'd thought she was too safe. Her friends, Bethany in particular, had often teased her about the choices she made.

But this man, who barely knew her, saw something in her that no one else did. She didn't really have any words, so she settled for one. "Thanks."

"You're welcome."

Their gazes held together for a beat too long, and some other emotion passed between them. She felt a shiver run down her spine, and it had nothing to do with fear, but everything to do with attraction.

Why now? Why at this worst possible time did she meet a man whose words filled her with emotion and whose smile made her palms sweat?

Diego cleared his throat, as if he also needed to break the tension. "I'm going to brush my teeth."

"Sure," she said, not sure how to feel about his abrupt movement from the bed to the bathroom.

Relieved, she told herself; *you should feel relieved!*

The last thing she needed to do was add another complication to this already impossible situation.

She climbed under the covers and turned on the television. She needed something to take her mind off Diego and the fact that they were going to spend the night together. She was definitely not the kind of woman who jumped into bed with a man she barely knew...

⸺⟫⟪⸺

Diego stared at himself in the mirror, frowning at his swollen eye, but it wasn't really his bruised face that was bothering him—it was Tara. They'd gotten very close very fast. He'd told her more about the night his father had taken him away from his mother than he'd ever told anyone. And in that telling, he'd had to relive some of it, which had also been difficult.

And now she'd told him about herself in a way that had made him want to strangle her last boyfriend and tell her parents and Bethany that they needed to see Tara for who she really was.

And who was that?

A stubborn, determined woman willing to risk everything for her friend. And she was jaw-droppingly pretty, too. Her eyes changed with her feelings from deep, dark, shadowy blue to a lighter, sparkling, fiery blue. And it wasn't just her eyes that captivated him: it was her beautiful features, her feminine curves, the way she licked her lips and pulled at her necklace when she was nervous.

Man, he was in trouble. He'd noticed way too much about her. And she'd given him a look a few minutes ago…a look that had taken him out of mission mindset and into the idea of personal fun and games. But that would be reckless and impulsive and complicate things.

They needed to stay focused.

There were people after them, and they would strike again, because whatever they wanted, they didn't have. The attack outside the bar had definitely not been about killing Tara or himself. It had been about taking them somewhere, perhaps using them as leverage.

But leverage for what? What the hell had Bethany gotten herself into?

They needed a better strategy going forward. Tara had made all her decisions based on emotion and fear. That had to change. They had to be smarter.

Finding Bethany, dealing with her situation, was going to take him away from his search for Mateo, and that bothered him. But Bethany was in immediate danger, as was Tara. He might be in danger as well because he was with Tara. So, he'd deal with this problem first. Mateo had been missing for a long time. *What was a few more days?*

He changed out of his jeans into a pair of sweats, brushed his teeth and took a minute to get his head together.

When he returned to the bedroom, Tara had settled into her bed and was watching a rerun of *Friends* in Spanish. He pulled back the comforter and stretched out on the other bed.

When the show ended, the news came on. They both watched for some mention of the shooting in Cascada, but there was nothing. The show was mostly focused on what was happening in Medellin.

"Do you want me to keep the TV on?" Tara asked.

"You can turn it off, if you want."

She did so, plunging the room into darkness.

He closed his eyes, trying to sleep, knowing he needed to rest, because who knew what was coming tomorrow? But he still felt wired.

He heard Tara shift in her bed, back and forth, obviously also having difficulty sleeping. Her mind was probably racing with fear for Bethany and also for herself.

"Do you want to talk?" he asked. "It doesn't sound like you're sleeping."

"Sorry. These bedsprings creak a lot."

"You're not bothering me, but if you have something to say, go for it."

"I feel wound up," she replied. "I don't know how to let all my worry go. And I'm afraid to fall asleep. What if someone tracks us here? What if they come after us? What if they burst through that door with guns firing?"

She was working herself up, caught on a loop of terrifying *what-ifs*.

"I think we're safe tonight," he told her. "Tomorrow, I'm going to get a weapon, so we won't be so vulnerable."

"How are you going to do that?"

"Lucas said he could hook me up in the morning. He'll text me where to go."

"I've never liked guns, but I find myself feeling pretty happy that you're going to get one."

"Me, too."

"I can't imagine pulling the trigger, shooting someone dead. The gunshots earlier are still ringing through my head. I wonder how long it will take to forget them."

"Probably longer than you would like."

"You always tell the truth, don't you?"

"Not always. Lying can be a necessary part of my job."

"Do you work undercover?"

"Often, yes."

"So you can be whoever you need to be? Isn't that difficult? Do you ever forget who you really are?"

"Sometimes my real life starts to feel very far away," he admitted. "But I've never gone so deep for so long that I've lost my way. Most of my assignments end within a few weeks or months at the most."

"It sounds like an exciting job, traveling the world, pretending to be someone you're not."

He smiled to himself. "It has its moments, but you'd be surprised how much time is spent waiting and watching. It can be lonely, too. You don't have any support when you're under. You can't let people get close, because it could blow your cover."

"That's true. I've missed talking to my parents this week, and we only went a few days between calls."

"I can't imagine that kind of closeness with a parent."

"Like I said earlier, we're a tight unit. We've always been crazy about each other. When I went to college in San Diego, it was the first time we hadn't lived in the same city. I think the break was good for all of us, though. They ended up moving to Santa Barbara, and I wound up teaching in San Clemente. We're both in beach cities but about three hours apart, depending on LA traffic. Still, we manage to get together at least twice a month for a Sunday barbecue, and we talk all the time, especially since my dad has had some heart problems. It made me realize how precious time is."

He could hear the longing in her voice, and wished he felt even a hundredth of that kind of love for his father, but he didn't feel anything.

He turned over onto his side. His eyes had adjusted to the light, and he could see her in the shadowy glow from the split in the curtains at the window. She had also rolled onto her side and was now facing him.

"I'm sure I'm boring you," she said.

"Not at all. I'm happy to talk about your family. It's a nice change from the dysfunctional people who make up my bloodline."

"Do you ever speak to your father?"

"Not in the last couple of years and before that, only very rarely."

"Was your mother from Colombia?"

"No. She was born in Lima, Peru. But her parents immigrated to the US when she was about six. After she married my dad, her parents returned to Lima to take care of her grandparents, so they weren't around when I was growing up. I knew next to nothing about that side of the family, but when I started searching for my mom, I began in Peru."

"Were your grandparents still alive?"

"No, the older generation had passed on by then, but I met some second cousins. They said when my mother came back with her son, she stayed with her father for several weeks, but she was unhappy with his lack of support. He kept telling her go back to America, that he couldn't take care of her, and she should make things up with her husband. Eventually she left Peru. The family thought she had returned to the States, but, clearly, she did not. I don't know how she got to Colombia. I'm hoping Mateo will be able to tell me when I find him."

"I'm sorry my situation is delaying your search."

"It's only been a few hours since I found out my mom died and that she married into the Salazar family. It's probably just as well I have some time to wrap my head around things. Right now, I want to focus on keeping us safe and finding Bethany first and then Mateo."

"I'm very happy with that plan. Let's talk about something else. How did you get into the FBI? Were you recruited?"

"I was. I worked in Army intelligence after graduating

from West Point. When my tour was up, the FBI suggested I might want to work for them, and I agreed. I thought I would have more opportunity there. I've been an agent almost five years now."

"And you like it?"

"I do. I've had the opportunity to work in different parts of the world, especially South America, which also gave me a chance to look for my mother and brother—unsuccessfully, of course."

"Your last name is Rivera. Is your dad also from South America?"

"No. His family came from Spain three generations ago, so aside from the Hispanic last name and Latin looks, he's American in every way. He doesn't even speak Spanish."

"What does your father do for work?"

"He runs a hedge fund in New York now. He's very wealthy and lives a comfortable life. He has never remarried, but he's been living with a woman the last six years. She's a divorced socialite. Her family made a fortune in organic cereals. They travel a great deal." He paused. "I don't think you told me what your parents do."

"My dad is a college professor at UC Santa Barbara. He taught at Loyola for a long time when I was growing up, and then they decided to get out of the crowded LA area and move farther north. My mom teaches kindergarten and works in the school library. She's very big on reading and books."

"Teaching is in your blood."

"It is. Or as Bethany would say, I just did what my parents expected me to do."

"Sounds like Bethany could be a little judgmental."

"We could definitely criticize each other's choices, but there was always love behind the words."

"What made you decide to teach Spanish?"

"I love the language. I went to a Spanish Immersion elementary school. I did a summer study in Mexico in college, but I always wanted to see South America. That's why I decided I would try out for the tour guide job when Bethany told me I could just do it in the summers. I thought I could have the best of both worlds. But now…I don't think I'll be taking that job. Actually, I don't know if I'll be able to keep my teaching job if I take too much time off. My principal is not the most supportive person. But I can't worry about any of that now."

"I'm sure you could get another job if you had to."

"I'm sure, too." Her words ended on a yawn.

He smiled. "You're getting tired."

"I'm not feeling so stressed now. Sorry if I've been talking your ear off. I don't usually ramble on like this, especially to a stranger."

"We're sharing a hotel room; I'd hardly call us strangers."

"That's true. I feel like I could sleep now. What about you?"

"I think so," he muttered, although his answer was closer to a lie than the truth. He wasn't thinking about Mateo and his mother anymore, or the danger that had almost gotten them killed, but he was thinking a lot about Tara, about how close she was, how dark it was in the room, how intimate their conversation had become.

He couldn't remember the last time he'd spent hours just talking to a woman. And with Tara, conversation flowed surprisingly easily. Maybe because the normal barriers of a first meet had been shattered by bullets. Fighting off danger had also brought them closer together faster than normal.

Forcing himself to roll onto his other side, he faced the wall, thinking that might help him to stop thinking about her. But instead he found himself waiting to hear the next catch of her breath. Eventually, her breathing was slow and steady.

She was asleep. And he was wide awake.

Diego woke up to a phone call from Wyatt just before

eight o'clock on Friday morning. He didn't know when he'd eventually fallen asleep, but it felt like five minutes ago.

Tara's eyes were still closed, so he took the phone into the bathroom and quietly shut the door.

"Hope it's not too early to call," Wyatt said.

"It's never too early for information. What do you have?"

"I talked to my CI in New York. He was not familiar with a Mateo Salazar. He only worked with Juan Felipe and his son Rico, who's in his late twenties. He said there are branches of the family in New York and Los Angeles. They have an extensive distribution and money laundering pipeline. I've gone through our files on the family, and I'm texting you a family tree."

"Is there any mention of a Camilla Lopez Salazar on that tree?"

"Yes," Wyatt said.

His pulse jumped. "Who did she marry?"

"Tomas Salazar. He's a cousin to the three brothers who run the organization, and he was a lawyer in Medellin. They married sixteen years ago. Your mother died two years after they tied the knot, and then Tomas passed away of a heart attack two years after that." Wyatt paused. "I also found the death certificate for your mother and a few details on what happened. Apparently, she fell during a hike in the mountains near Cascada."

His stomach twisted with that horrifying piece of news. He sat down on the edge of the tub. "She died while hiking?"

"That's what it said on the police report. It had rained the day before. She slipped on some wet rocks and fell."

"My mother hated to hike. She didn't even like to walk with her friends."

"Maybe she changed," Wyatt suggested. "Sorry to be the bearer of bad news."

"I'm grateful you have any news." As he thought about what Wyatt had told him, he made mental calculations in his head. "Mateo would have been ten when my mother died and twelve when Tomas died. What the hell happened to him after that?"

"I don't know. I found no reference to a Mateo anywhere. Tomas was married to a woman named Lucinda Veracruz before he married your mother, but that union produced no children."

"No indication of that. Or that he raised a child after your mother passed away."

He thought about that for a moment. *Had his mother left Mateo at some point? Could she have sent Mateo to live with his biological father before she married Salazar?*

"How can there be no record of my brother?" he muttered in frustration.

"I don't know, but I can't find anything on anyone named Mateo with the last name Rivera, Lopez, or Salazar, who's within ten years of your brother's age. He has to be living under another name. You said your father left your mother because she cheated. What about that man?"

"No idea who he is or what his name is. I'm not sure my father knows, either, but if he does, he's determined to take it to the grave."

"Maybe you should ask him again."

"I don't have much hope he'll suddenly decide to cooperate since he's refused me every other time. I'm going to have to figure this out on my own."

"Well, the information I pulled together is sketchy on Salazar family members beyond those who are clearly running the organization. Tomas may have been involved in the cartel as a lawyer or may not have been," Wyatt continued. "I'll text you the list I've put together. Maybe something else will jump out at you."

"Thanks."

"What else do you need from me? Do you want me to dig more into this missing woman?"

"I asked Lucas to do that since he has contacts here in Colombia. There is one question you might be able to answer.

Do you know where Tomas practiced law in Medellin? Because I'm in the city now. Maybe I could find something out at his former practice."

"I looked into that. He worked with a partner—Hector Pilacio. Their office was located at 1220 Appian Boulevard, if you want to see if anyone there remembers Tomas and your mother. I was going to call this morning. I was waiting for the offices to be open."

"No problem. I'll take it from here."

As he disconnected from Wyatt, he opened his text messages and skimmed through the list of names that Wyatt had sent him.

Wyatt's information lined up with what he'd heard from Lucas. Caleb Salazar was the patriarch in charge of the organization. He was sixty-five years old, married three times. First wife Sophia had borne two girls: Catherine and Juanita. Second wife, Julia, had given him a daughter, Elizabeth, and third wife Lila had given him another daughter named Sonya.

Caleb's brothers, Juan Felipe and Santoro, were also married with children. Juan Felipe had two sons: Rico and William. Santoro had a son Pablo and a daughter Vanessa. In addition, Caleb's cousins were mostly married, and there were a bunch of kids in that generation.

It was strange that while Wyatt had found mention of his mother's death and her marriage to Tomas, there was nothing about Mateo.

Maybe his mother had handed him off to someone else to raise.

Hopefully, someone at Tomas's former law firm would remember his mother and possibly Mateo.

Standing up, he set his phone on the counter and then took a quick shower.

When he returned to the bedroom fifteen minutes later, he saw Tara standing at the window. She'd thrown open the curtains and her blonde hair sparkled in the sunshine. She wasn't wearing anything particularly sexy, but when she turned and gave him a nervous smile, her natural beauty made his gut clench.

He'd been so caught up in the call from Wyatt, and thoughts about his brother, that he'd almost forgotten her mission to find Bethany.

But they could do both. They *had* to do both. Because neither one of them was leaving without the information they'd come to get.

"I heard you on the phone," she said. "Is there any news?"

"Not about Bethany. My friend Wyatt sent me a list of Salazar names, the ones most obviously involved in the cartel."

"I thought you were talking to someone named Lucas," she interrupted.

"Wyatt is a fellow FBI agent, a good friend of mine. He's in California. He's helping me out, too."

"Okay. What did he tell you?"

"He hasn't found a Mateo Salazar anywhere in the family, but he did find my mother. She apparently married a lawyer, Tomas Salazar, about two years after she was kicked out of the States by my father. She died two years into that marriage, and Tomas died two years after that. But he worked here in Medellin until his death. I have an address for the firm where he worked. I'm hoping it's still in business and someone remembers him and my mother, and most importantly, my brother."

"That's great," she said, a gleam of excitement entering her gaze. "That's a solid clue."

"We'll see if it plays out."

"We can go there first if you want. I'm not really expecting us to find anything at the apartment where Bethany was staying, although I still want to go."

"All right," he said, happy that she'd made the offer. "I would like to check this law office out. I also need to make a stop on the way to pick up a weapon."

"And maybe we could grab a coffee and pastry somewhere," she said. "I'm hungry."

"You've got it."

"I'll get dressed."

As she moved past him and into the shower, his thoughts went with her, imagining her stripping off the black leggings and the oversized sweatshirt. Shaking his head at that errant thought, he shoved his sweats into a suitcase and rezipped his bag. Then he went on the internet and put in Tomas Salazar's name.

A dozen listings sprang up, the most recent being an obituary. He read through the one- paragraph tribute, but there was no personal information beyond the fact that Tomas was survived by his family and was a well-respected attorney.

He looked up the law firm next. It seemed to still be in business, with Hector Pilacio at the helm. His heart beat a little faster. Hector had worked with Tomas when he was married to his mother. He had to have known her and also Mateo.

This might be the break he'd been looking for...

Seven

After leaving the hotel, they made a quick stop at an auto shop. Tara waited in the lobby while Diego walked into the back room with a mechanic. He'd told her that one of his contacts had arranged for him to pick up a weapon. She'd thought they might be going to the police station or some other law enforcement office, but apparently this was some kind of a side deal.

She tapped her feet impatiently as she waited, feeling on edge now that they were back out in public. She'd put on low-heeled boots for this trip along with jeans and a cream-colored sweater under a short tan jacket. It might be spring, but the temperature in Medellin was only supposed to get up to the low sixties today. At least if she had to run somewhere, she was better prepared than she'd been the day before.

A woman came into the lobby, and she started, her nerves tightening once more, but the woman was only interested in getting a can of soda out of the vending machine.

Finally, Diego returned. He didn't say a word, just tipped his head toward the door.

"Did you get it?" she asked when they got into the car.

"All set." He pulled back his black leather jacket to show her the gun.

A week ago, she would have hated being so close to a man with a weapon, but after yesterday, she felt relieved they had a way to defend themselves.

As Diego drove across town, she couldn't help noticing his positive energy. He had a big lead, and she hoped he wasn't about to hit a brick wall at the law offices. She knew how it felt to be on the brink of something, only to be disappointed. She'd felt that way after she'd first spoken to Father Manuel, when he'd told her to come back on Thursday, and he would help her find Bethany. He'd been forthcoming in their first conversation, kind, eager to be of assistance, but the next day he'd shut down. She'd seen something in his eyes, a despair, a sadness, perhaps even an anger, but whoever had told him not to talk to her had had power over him.

She still wondered if he'd been targeted because of her, if someone hadn't trusted that he would remain silent. But why would other Salazars have been injured if that was the case? Unless, they truly had just been caught in the crossfire.

None of that mattered anymore. Father Manuel was dead and whatever information he'd had on Bethany had died with him. Now, she was back to square one.

She didn't know if they would find any more clues in Medellin, but hopefully one of Diego's FBI contacts would be able to come up with some trail they could follow.

In the meantime, she'd go with Diego to the law office where his mother's husband had worked. It would feel good to accomplish anything at this point, and she was grateful to Diego for not only saving her life more than once but for also getting his associates involved in Bethany's case. He was her best chance at finding her friend.

She didn't know if she was his best chance at finding his brother, but she could be supportive. She liked Diego, probably far more than she should. Besides being incredibly attractive, he was smart, protective, and caring. He was also a surprisingly good listener. She couldn't remember pouring out so much about herself to a man. She'd told him about her parents, about Brian, about Bethany. She'd confessed her inability to take chances, her unwillingness to put herself out there, and he'd made her realize that whatever mental and emotional restraints she'd put on herself in the past, they were long gone now.

She had no idea what she was doing, but she was doing it. She was pushing the envelope, pressing forward, taking risks. She might not have made the best decisions up to this point, but she was still alive, still fighting for Bethany. And she wasn't going to quit or let any lingering insecurities derail her.

As Diego took a sharp turn, she put a hand on the door to brace herself. "Are we being followed?"

"No. We're good," he said, glancing into the rearview mirror.

"Have you ever had to outrun a tail?"

"Many times. I'm a good driver. You don't have to worry."

"Worrying about your driving does not even make the top ten of my what to worry about list."

He flashed her that quick smile that lit up his dark eyes and made her heart tumble every time it happened.

"Do I want to know what the top ten worries are?" he asked.

"You really don't." She cleared her throat. "But this morning's mission is about your brother. What is Mateo like?"

"I haven't seen him since he was eight years old, so at twenty-six, I have no idea."

"As a child then...what was his personality?"

"He was a happy kid. He loved the Ninja Turtles and *Toy Story*. He liked making up games and acting them out. He could be kind of a brat, too. I'd have my friends over, and he'd keep coming into the room, interrupting us."

"That's what little brothers are supposed to do," she said with a smile.

"He did like my attention, and most of the time I enjoyed playing with him, but I was hitting my teenage years and starting to feel the age gap between us. I regret that I ever wished he'd just go away for a few minutes."

"You were being a normal kid. You didn't know it was going to end."

"I didn't know. I couldn't have imagined how our lives would change. My parents fought quite a bit, but my dad worked a lot, so he wasn't home that much, and when it was the three of us, we were good. We'd cook together, watch movies, do puzzles and homework. When my mom worked, I'd watch Mateo. We were tight."

"I didn't realize your mom worked. What did she do?"

"She was a nurse. She didn't work for a long time, and then she went back part time the last two years that she was in my life. I know my dad didn't like it. She didn't always have dinner ready for him when he came home, and he had come to expect his wife to be there when he wanted her to be there."

"Sounds like a traditional man."

"Yes. He was also demanding and arrogant. It was his way or the highway—literally."

"I wonder why your mother and brother had to disappear so completely, though. They could have just moved into a nearby apartment. Was it deliberate? Was your mom afraid of your father, that he might come after her, or that he might hurt her or Mateo?"

"He wasn't physically abusive that I ever saw. But he could certainly rip someone to shreds with his words. And he did do that quite a bit. I'm sure she was intimidated by him. But I can't imagine why she would have been scared he would come after her. Because he never wanted to see her again."

"Then why did she take such lengths to cover her trail? Clearly, she did, if you haven't been able to find her with all the resources you have at the bureau."

"I've asked myself that question a lot. A part of me wonders if my dad is the one who made her disappear. If he set her up somewhere so that I could never find her. Taking me away from her was her punishment for what she'd done to him. I was the pawn."

"It must drive you nuts that he won't help you find her. You know he has information, but you can't get it out of him."

"It makes me insane," he admitted. "I've wanted to put my hands on his throat and squeeze the words out of him."

"But you don't, because you're not crazy."

"I've been tempted. But there's also a part of me that isn't sure my dad knows where my mom is. Maybe the man she was with, Mateo's father, is the one who helped her disappear. Perhaps he didn't want my father to come after her. I'm hoping that Hector Pilacio can tell me how she met Tomas Salazar and whether Tomas was Mateo's real father. And, of course, I'd like him to tell me where I can find my brother. But, at this point, I'll settle for anything."

Several minutes later, they reached the two-story building that housed the law firm. The structure was modest and a bit rundown. Inside was no better. The paint on the walls was faded and stained in places, and the hallway carpet should have been replaced. But there was still a sign for Hector Pilacio, attorney, so they walked up the stairs and into the office.

There was an older woman sitting at a desk. She was painting her fingernails. There was a strong scent of acetone in the air. She gave them a somewhat surprised look, as if she hadn't expected anyone to come through the door. There was a private office off to her right, and the door was closed.

"*Buenos dias*," Diego said. "*Estoy buscando a Hector*

Pilacio."

"*Cuál es su nombre?*"

"Diego Rivera," he said, giving the receptionist his name.

"*Un momento.*" She got up from her desk, gave a short knock on the adjacent door, and then disappeared inside.

"He's here," Diego muttered.

"That's a good thing."

"If he's willing to see me."

"Do you care if he's willing?" she challenged.

"No. We're not leaving until I speak to him."

"That's what I thought," she said, giving him a smile.

The door opened, and the woman stepped out of the office, motioning them inside.

Hector Pilacio was a short, squat, balding man in his late fifties, early sixties. He stood up as they entered. "*Buenos dias.*"

"Senor Pilacio. *Habla Ingles?*" Diego asked.

"Yes. How can I help you?"

"My name is Diego Rivera. This is Tara Powell."

"*Hola,*" she said, as Hector gave her a nod.

"I'm hoping you might answer a few questions about your former partner, Tomas Salazar," Diego continued.

Hector's warm, welcoming gaze instantly clouded. "Tomas died many years ago."

"I know, but you were partners then, yes?"

"*Sí.*"

"Did you know his wife Camilla and her son Mateo?"

"Why are you asking?" Hector returned.

"Because Camilla is—was—my mother," Diego said, stumbling over the tenses. "And Mateo is my brother. I've been looking for them for a very long time."

"Camilla was your mother?" Hector echoed, looking a bit shocked by Diego's words. "I did not know she had another son."

"But you did know her and Mateo?"

"Mateo? Her son's name was Michael."

"How old was he?" Diego asked, uncertainty entering his voice.

"He was about ten, I think. I'm not that good with kids' ages."

Ten was about the right age, Tara thought, remembering the timeline Diego had given her.

"All right," Diego said slowly. "Tell me about Tomas's relationship with my mother."

"He was so happy to marry Camilla. He couldn't stop smiling. But the good times did not last. Your mother died a few years into the marriage."

Diego nodded. "I discovered that fact yesterday. Do you know how she died?"

"She took a fall in the mountains near Cascada. They would go there on the weekends. Tomas had family there. She was on a hike, and she lost her footing. It was tragic."

Tara moved closer to Diego, drawn to the sad turmoil she could feel going on inside him. He wasn't looking for her comfort, but she couldn't stop herself from putting her hand on his back.

"Did she die instantly?" he asked, a harsh note in his tight voice.

"I believe so. I'm sorry. Did you not know?"

"Actually, I heard about her fall this morning, but not from someone who knew her or knew Tomas."

"Tomas was beside himself. He was angry that he hadn't gone with her on the hike. He'd been busy working, and she'd gone on her own," Hector said.

"She was alone when she fell?"

"That's what I understand. The family went out to look for her, when she didn't come home before dark. They didn't find her body until the next morning. It was too late by then." Hector paused, giving them a pained look. "Tomas felt so guilty that he hadn't gone with her. He was completely devastated. He started drinking, and I think he was drunk for the next four months. Finally, he started to pull himself out of the depression, but I don't think he was ever really happy again. He died of a heart attack less than two years later. I sometimes think it was a broken heart."

"Or maybe the guilt was eating away at him," Diego said harshly.

"Perhaps," Hector replied in a neutral tone. "Does that answer your question?"

"Not completely. What happened to Camilla's son? Did he stay with Tomas until his death?"

"No. Tomas was in no condition to raise a child. His sister Irina came and got Michael. That's the last I ever saw of him. I don't even know if Tomas kept in touch with him or not."

Tara's heart went out for the little boy who had lost so many people. First Diego's father sent him away, then his mother died, and he was sent to live with a woman he probably didn't even know.

Diego moved over to the window, staring at the view for a long moment.

Hector gave her a compassionate smile. "I'm sorry to have to deliver bad news."

"We appreciate your time." As Diego seemed lost in thought, she pressed on. "Do you know where Irina lives? Is she here in Medellin?"

"No, she lives in Cartagena. I think I might still have her in my book," Hector said, reaching into a drawer. "She used to send me cards at Christmas, and I always reciprocated." He pulled out a black book and flipped through it. "Yes, here it is."

Diego quickly returned to her side as Hector handed her the address book. There was an address for an Irina Salazar Garcia.

Diego picked up a notepad and pen from the top of Hector's desk and jotted down the address.

"I don't know if she still lives there," Hector continued. "I don't believe I've heard from her in a few years."

"What about her husband? Is he alive? Was he taking care of my brother?"

"No, her husband died about three years before Tomas. She was a widow when she took Michael in."

"One more question," Diego said. "Was Tomas involved in the family business? With the cartel, to be more specific?"

Hector frowned. "He did some work for them out of loyalty to his cousin Caleb. I believe Caleb's father actually paid for Tomas's law degree."

"So, he was indebted to the family," she murmured.

"Yes. He went to Cascada twice a month to work on family matters," Hector said. "I know Camilla did not like going there. I think she wanted him to separate himself, but the ties were too strong. I would suggest you not ask the Salazars about your mother's accident. They don't take well to questions, and in that part of the country, they are the law."

Diego nodded. "What about Irina? Is she in the cartel, too?"

"No, she's a teacher, or at least she was." Hector paused. "I didn't know Camilla well, but she was very sweet when we got together. She was a bit shy but kind and caring."

"And Michael—what was he like?"

"I don't think he said much."

"Really? He used to be incredibly talkative."

"Well, he didn't know me, and when I saw him there were no other children around. He was probably bored. I hope my information has helped."

"It has, thanks," Diego said.

"Good luck with your search."

She gave Hector a grateful smile and then followed Diego to the door and down to the car. As she fastened her seat belt, she noted that Diego was not in a hurry to start the vehicle. She shifted sideways in her seat, so she could look at him. There were tension lines around his eyes, a bleakness to his gaze, a hard line to his mouth. "Are you all right?" she asked, almost afraid to intrude on his thoughts.

He turned his head to look at her. "Sorry. What?"

"I asked how you were doing. That had to have been rough, hearing about your mom's death."

"It doesn't make sense, Tara. My mother did not like to hike. Why would she go into the mountains alone?"

"You don't think it was an accident?"

"I'm not sure, but something is off."

"Maybe it was a beautiful day. Perhaps she wanted to see the waterfall, or she simply needed a break."

"But she wasn't with Mateo. Or should I say Michael? Why the hell would she have changed his name?"

"Was Michael his middle name?"

"No, it was Mateo Joseph Rivera. Joseph was my grandfather's name on my dad's side. I can see why she might have wanted to get rid of Rivera, even Joseph, both ties to my dad, but Mateo was the name she picked for my brother. She used to tell me that the one thing my father hadn't cared about was our names, so he'd let her choose, and she'd liked the rhythm of Diego and Mateo. I know that's a crazy conversation to remember, but I can still hear the laugh in her voice as she told the story while she made us empanadas."

"I don't know what to say," she murmured. "It's weird. Unless, it was a way to keep Mateo away from your dad. But she didn't change her own name. Maybe she thought your dad would want Mateo back, that he would decide he was just an innocent child. He had raised him for—what—eight years? He must have loved him."

"That love died when he found out Mateo wasn't his."

"Maybe that's it. Your mom wanted him to have his real father's name?"

"Well, we're not going to figure it out sitting here," he said, starting the engine. "We need to go to Cartagena, to talk to Irina."

"Do you want to do that now?" she asked slowly, not sure how she felt about leaving Medellin.

"We'll talk about it after we go to the tour apartment. I

haven't forgotten about Bethany." He took out his phone. "In the meantime, I'm going to text Lucas and see if he can get a phone number for Irina or any other information on her."

"At least we have someone else to talk to. Someone who was with Mateo for at least a part of his life. If Mateo went to live with Irina, and she doesn't participate in the cartel, then your brother might not have gotten caught up in that."

"I'm really hoping that's the case. Now let's go check out the apartment."

Eight

—➤➤❰❰◄—

The tour apartment was located on the third floor of an upscale apartment building. Tara unlocked the coded door and allowed Diego to enter first while she lingered in the doorway.

He took out his gun as he moved inside, making his way across the living room and into the bedroom. From her vantage point, the apartment looked empty and exactly as she'd last seen it. When Diego returned and put away his gun, she stepped all the way inside and locked the door behind her. Then she followed him into the kitchen.

As he opened cupboards, she couldn't help asking, "What are you looking for?"

"I don't know yet." He opened a narrow drawer by the sink and pulled out an array of shot glasses. Two of them were from the same nightclub—El Toro, the logo of a red bull on the glass. "Have you ever heard of this place?" He handed Tara one of the glasses.

"Yes. It's a bar in Cartagena. It's one of Bethany's favorite clubs. She always takes her tour groups there. In fact, she's friends with one of the waitresses. She introduced her to me when we went there on my trial tour." She frowned, wondering why she hadn't thought about talking to Rosa. "I can't believe I forgot about her. I was so focused on this city, this apartment and the bus station that I completely forgot about the other stops on the tour, the other places Bethany might have gone."

"Tell me more about the tour. Where does it start? Where does it end?"

"The company runs two tours in Colombia. One is seven days and one is ten. The shorter one starts in Bogota for three nights, then goes to the Coffee Triangle for two nights, and Medellin for two nights. The longer one adds a third night in Medellin and then moves to Cartagena for three nights."

"Is there an apartment in Cartagena like this?"

"Yes. There's one in Bogota, too. Occasionally guides will stay there before the beginning of the tour."

"I assume Bethany's last tour was the shorter version, ending here in Medellin."

"Yes."

"So, why are there shot glasses from Cartagena in this apartment?"

"I have no idea. Bethany, or one of the other guides, might have had a party here. They could have picked up the shot glasses at any time. I took one home with me after I went to the bar at Christmas. Why are you fixating on the glasses? We don't even know if they belong to Bethany."

"I'm trying to find something personal in this apartment." He opened the refrigerator.

She could see a dozen bottles of water, two bottles of white wine, a six-pack of beer, and some condiments.

"This is pretty clean," he commented.

"A housekeeping service comes in three times a week to check on the place, whether anyone is here or not."

"A service, huh? Do you have a name and number for that? They might have seen Bethany when she was last here."

"I did actually think about them, but when I contacted Tony at Allende Tours to ask for the name, he told me he wouldn't give me the information, that he didn't need me getting anyone else upset over Bethany when she was clearly on vacation. He was upset that I'd gone to the police. He told me my questions could ruin their business."

"You didn't tell me this Tony threatened you."

"Well, it wasn't a threat. He was just really annoyed with me."

Diego's phone buzzed, and he pulled it out of his pocket. "It's Wyatt."

"Would you mind putting it on speaker, so I can hear?"

"All right." He answered the phone. "Wyatt, what's up?"

"I was able to access Bethany Cooper's phone records," Wyatt replied. "Four days after she was seen at the bus station, which was a Wednesday, she made three calls to the Palumbo Airfield on Saturday. It's twenty minutes outside of Medellin. It's a small private airfield servicing prop planes and light jets."

Tara's heart skipped a beat at Wyatt's words.

"Any record of her getting on a flight?" Diego asked.

"No. I made a call to the airfield office, but the girl who answered the phone said she couldn't tell me anything about their customers. You might want to check it out in person."

"I will. Was there anything else of note on Bethany's phone log?"

"That same day, she also made two calls to a burner phone that I tracked to a Los Angeles electronic store, but when I called the number it was dead. And there was also a call to a bar in Cartagena called El Toro."

"Interesting," Diego muttered.

"Those were the only calls made since her disappearance. I can get one of our analysts to go through the calls prior, but that will take a little time."

"I'd appreciate if you'd set that up."

"No problem. Did you check out the lawyer?"

"I did. He remembered my mother. He confirmed what you told me previously about her death during a solo hike in the mountains of Cascada. It sounded like a very shady story. He also said that the little boy he met with my mother went by the name of Michael. I have no idea why my mom would have changed my brother's name, but if you come across a Michael Salazar, I'd like to know."

"What's next?"

"After my brother's stepfather died, he apparently went to live with a cousin by the name of Irina Salazar Garcia. I have an address for her in Cartagena. I texted Lucas to see if he can get me a phone number. That will be our next stop after we check out the airfield."

"You've got your hands full chasing down these two ghosts."

"We certainly do," Diego said. "Keep in touch."

"You, too."

He put his phone away and said, "Do you have any idea why Bethany would have been calling a small, private airfield?"

"She once took a private plane from Medellin to Cartagena. Maybe she did it again."

"Well, one thing we know for sure is that she was on her phone four days after she got on the bus to Cascada. That narrows the timeline once more."

"And if she flew to Cartagena on her own, maybe she's just hiding." Tara really wanted to believe in that theory, but one other thing Wyatt had said bothered her. "What about the burner phone calls to the LA electronics store?"

He stared back at her. "Whoever she was talking to didn't want anyone to be able to trace the call."

She drew in a worried breath. "Which is not good."

"No. But I think we're done here. Let's check out the airfield."

--->➤◄---

They arrived at the airfield a little before noon. It was located off a two-lane road in a rural area and consisted of a one-story terminal building, a hangar, and three small airplanes parked on the tarmac. A sign that was falling off its hinges touted flight lessons, sightseeing trips, and private charters.

After parking next to a dusty old Chevy and a newer sedan, they got out of the car and entered the building, finding themselves in a small waiting room, with two vending machines, a couple of chairs and a small table that was covered in newspapers.

There was no one behind that counter, but there was a small bell, which Diego hit somewhat impatiently.

A young female Hispanic woman came out of a back room. She was probably no more than twenty, and she had a mug of coffee in her hands. "Hola," she said cheerfully.

"I hope you can help me," Diego replied in English.

"Ah, you are American," she said. "You want to book a ride?"

"Possibly. Do you answer the phones here?"

"Sí. That's an odd question," the woman replied, giving them a curious look.

"I'm looking for my friend," Tara said, taking over the conversation. This young woman might be able to relate to her situation. "She disappeared a few weeks ago, and I'm desperate to find her. She made several calls to this airfield and we're wondering if she got on a plane. Her name is Bethany Cooper."

A wary spark flickered in the woman's eyes. "Someone else was asking about her. You said she disappeared?"

"Yes. And I think she might be in trouble. I'm really hoping you might know why she called here or who she spoke to?"

"I'm not supposed to talk about the customers." The woman cast a quick look over her shoulder.

"Please. It could be a matter of life and death," she said.

"Sí. I understand. All right. I spoke to her. She wanted to see if we had any open seats on a flight to Cartagena."

"Did she find a seat?"

"I think so." The woman got on the computer.

Tara's pulse sped up as several minutes ticked by. She really, really wanted a new lead on Bethany.

The woman looked up. "Yes. She got on a flight on March 26."

Her breath caught in her throat. "Are you sure?"

The woman checked the computer again. "Yes, the one o'clock flight last Saturday. Captain Ray Volero flew her there, along with two other passengers."

"Who were the others?" Diego asked.

"I probably shouldn't tell you that," she said hesitantly.

"Were they part of the Salazar family?" Tara asked.

"The Salazars? No. No," the woman said quickly. "It was an older couple, a bank executive and his wife. They fly back and forth between Cartagena and Medellin every two months to visit their grandchildren."

Relief swept through her at that information. She looked over at Diego, not sure what to do next.

"We need to get to Cartagena," he told the clerk. "Do you have any flights today?"

"Today? There is a flight in thirty minutes, but it's booked."

"When's the next flight?"

"Tomorrow. There are two seats available. The flight leaves at two p.m."

"That's not soon enough," Tara said, looking at Diego. "We can't wait until then."

"I agree," he said.

"You can check the Medellin airport. They might have an open flight," the clerk suggested.

"Before we do that, is there any chance we could speak to Captain Volero?" Diego asked.

"He's on the tarmac getting the plane ready for flight,"

she said. "You can go through there." She waved her hand toward a nearby door.

Tara was surprised at the lack of security, but she wasn't going to question it, as she followed Diego through the door.

A pickup truck was parked near a small plane about fifty yards away. The two stairs leading into the plane were down, and a man was standing near the bottom of those steps with a clipboard in his hands. He appeared to be in his thirties, with dark hair and a thick moustache.

"Captain Volero?" Diego asked, as they drew near. "May we speak to you for a moment?"

The captain looked up, giving them an inquiring look. "If you're on the next flight, we're not leaving for a half hour."

"We actually wanted to talk to you about a flight to Cartagena last Saturday," Diego said. "There was a woman on it, Bethany Cooper. She's an American, an attractive brunette with green eyes and a big smile—twenty-six years old."

The captain nodded. "I remember Bethany. She's flown with me a few times. Is there a problem?"

"She's missing," Tara put in. "She's a good friend of mine, and no one has heard from her in weeks. Can you tell us why she was going to Cartagena? Did she share her plans?"

"She said she was meeting friends. She was excited we'd had a last-minute cancellation."

"Have you seen or spoken to her since?"

"No, sorry," he said. "If you'll excuse me, I need to make a call before my flight."

As the captain headed toward the terminal, she blew out a frustrated breath. "What now? Should we wait until he comes back and press him some more?"

"I'm not sure what we'd get out of him. She was a passenger. They might not have spoken beyond a few words before takeoff or after landing. But this is still good, Tara. We know that Bethany flew to Cartagena last Saturday. That turns the search in an entirely different direction."

He was right, but she wanted more. She wanted to see Bethany. She wanted to know that she was all right, and that still hadn't happened.

A roar of engines drew her gaze toward the road leading up to the airport where a black SUV was speeding down the highway.

"Shit!" Diego swore.

"Who is that?"

"No one good," he said grimly. "I have a feeling I know who the captain went to call."

"Seriously?" she asked in shock.

"There's no way we're getting past them."

"There has to be something we can do." Terror ran through her as a truck roared down the road behind the SUV.

"Get in the plane." Diego grabbed her by the arm and shoved her toward the steps.

She scrambled into the plane, noting four empty seats behind the small cockpit where the pilot and copilot sat.

"We can't fly this without the pilot, and he's not here," she said, as Diego climbed on board and pulled the door closed.

"I can fly it." Diego moved quickly into the pilot's seat. He hit several buttons and the engine started, the propellers beginning to twist.

"Sit up here." He urged her toward the seat where the copilot would sit.

"Are you serious?"

"Sit," he ordered.

Looking out the window, she saw two men come through the terminal door with guns drawn.

She instinctively ducked as shots were fired at the plane. "Is this thing bulletproof?" she yelled, as Diego worked on the controls, and she tried to fasten her seat belt with shaky hands.

"Not even close," he said. "Hang on."

Nine

—➤➤◄◄◄—

Fear ripped through Tara, as the plane rolled down the runway. They were moving too slowly. A bullet cracked the window behind her, and she ducked down in her seat. "Are we going to make it?"

Diego didn't answer, as he focused on getting the plane into the air. As they neared the end of the runway, she felt more panic. There was nothing but dirt and rocks and trees in front of them.

And then suddenly they were airborne. She couldn't breathe for at least a minute. Her heart was pounding against her chest. Her eyes were half-closed. She was both afraid to look and afraid not to look. Finally, she managed to squeeze her lids open. She looked out the window as they climbed high above the trees.

"Oh, my God," she said. "We're flying."

"Did you have any doubt?" Diego asked with a triumphant grin.

"I had a million doubts. But we're okay." She paused. "We are okay, aren't we?"

"We're great. Thank God, this plane is just like the one my grandpa used when he taught me how to fly. What are the odds?"

"Pretty long." She drew in a deep breath and held it, then slowly exhaled.

"You okay?" he asked.

"Barely. I can't believe we stole a plane. Is someone coming after us? What's going to happen when we land? Will we be arrested?"

"Not if I can help it."

"Are we going to Cartagena?"

"No. We need to find somewhere less populated to put this plane down."

"Wait, somewhere less populated? You're still talking about an airport, right?"

"Maybe not. This baby can land on a road if needed."

"Are you crazy, Diego? We can't land on a road."

"Don't worry about it."

"I can't stop worrying."

He flashed her a reassuring smile. "Don't be scared, Tara. I've got this."

As they drew closer to a range of small mountains, she had another worry. "Shouldn't we go higher?"

"I'm trying to stay under the radar."

She shook her head in bemusement, feeling completely overwhelmed by the situation. "I can't believe this is happening. I do not understand how I ended up here."

"You went looking for Bethany. That's how you ended up here."

"Those men who came after us—they had to be Salazars, right?"

"Or hired by the family."

"How did they know we were at the airfield?"

Diego's jaw tightened. "The pilot or the receptionist might have called someone."

"But they would have had to be close by."

"I'm sure there are Salazars or members of their organization operating in Medellin. Hell, that airfield could have been owned and operated by the family. They fly private jets all over the country. Or we might have been followed from the apartment. I didn't see a tail, but it could have happened."

As the plane hit a patch of bumpy air, she hung on to the arm of her seat, feeling nauseous. "This might not be the best time to tell you this, but I don't really like to fly. Sometimes I get airsick."

"Well, try not to throw up on me."

"I'm trying not to throw up at all." She swallowed back another wave of queasiness. She needed a distraction. "You said your grandfather taught you to fly? Was that your dad's father?"

"Actually, my dad's stepfather. He was a Navy pilot and after the service, he taught flying at a small airport and did crop dusting in Virginia. When I was a sad, angry teenager, he got me up in a plane, and it helped me to breathe. Being up in the sky was the only thing that made me feel better. He let me rant about my dad, who he didn't particularly like, either, and it saved my sanity. Unfortunately, he died when I was sixteen, and the lessons stopped."

"I'm surprised you didn't become a pilot when you went into the service."

"I thought about going into the Air Force, but I wanted to be more immersed in the action. I didn't want to fly above it. I needed to be so focused on staying alive, I couldn't think about anything else."

His words revealed the depth of his teenage despair. She was really glad he'd had an outlet, especially since those flying lessons had probably saved their lives—at least for the moment.

Her momentary peace was interrupted by a flashing light and a beeping sound coming from the control panel. She'd been trying not to look at the panel, which was in front of her as well as in front of Diego.

"What's that?" she asked.

"The fuel is leaking. A bullet must have hit the tank."

"We're running out of gas? What are we going to do now?"

"We have a little time. We'll get as far away from Medellin as we can and then set the plane down."

"How can you sound so calm?"

"I'm working the problem. It's easier to focus if I don't get carried away with all the possible scenarios."

"Like crashing and dying?" she asked in a voice pitched high from fear.

"Like that," he said. "Breathe, Tara."

"Did I tell you how much I don't like risk?"

"Yes, and I told you how strong you really are. You can do this."

"What? Hang on? Because right now, I have no control over anything."

"I'm sure that's scary. But you have to try to trust me. Why don't you look out the window and see if you can locate any potential landing spots?"

She forced air into her lungs and then looked out the window. All she could see in front of her were mountains and trees and Colombian jungle. "I don't see any roads down there."

"We'll find something."

"Will we?" She racked her brain, trying to remember what she knew about Colombian geography. "I know it's an hour flight from Medellin to Cartagena, maybe longer in a plane like this. But are we even going in that direction?"

"We are," he confirmed, checking the panel in front of him.

She glanced down at her watch. "We've been flying about fifteen minutes. Although, it feels like fifteen hours."

"Hey, I'm not that bad of a pilot," he said lightly.

"I'll make that judgment when we're safely on the

ground. How are we going to get to Cartagena if we land in the middle of nowhere?"

"That's the next problem. Let's deal with this one first. I know you're scared, Tara. But we're going to make it."

"I like your confidence. I don't know if I believe it, but I want to."

"Then go with that feeling. We may not be in the best situation, but we're better than we were back at the airfield."

"They're going to follow us to Cartagena. The pilot will tell them what he told us. They'll know where we're headed."

"Again—that's a problem for later."

She knew it made sense not to think too far ahead, but she couldn't help it. "Last week I was teaching Spanish to a bunch of bored high school kids, and now I'm about to crash-land in the Colombian jungle."

"Let's leave the word crash out of the conversation." He paused. "Do you like being a teacher?"

"I—I can't talk about that right now."

"Yes, you can. Tell me."

She licked her lips. "Okay, I like teaching. I love the kids. They're at that crazy age between childhood and adulthood, and every day is filled with drama." She knew Diego was trying to distract her, and since she wanted to think about something else besides burning wreckage, she went along with it. "For all the kids' sarcasm and bravado, there's also innocence, joy and wonder. I like being around that. I like opening up their world even more by teaching them a new language, a different culture. Not that all, or even most, of them appreciate it. They have to take a foreign language if they want to get into college. Sometimes, they do the bare minimum. But for those few who really want to learn, it's fun."

"I'll bet they're missing you right now."

"And I am really missing them. I was hesitant to take leave, because I didn't want to let the kids down, especially the juniors and seniors, who are applying for college or getting ready to graduate this year. But I had to put Bethany first."

"Yes, you did." He cleared his throat. "We're going to need to set this plane down soon, Tara."

She stiffened. "We're almost out of gas?"

"Let's just say we really need to find somewhere to land. I'm going to take us down a little lower. Tell me what you see."

"Nothing but trees, lots and lots of trees. There might be a road to the right." She strained to see if the winding path was really a road or simply an illusion.

"I see it. It's not too far away."

"It looks like there's a town beyond it—maybe."

The engine started to splutter, and her heart stopped. "We don't have enough gas to make it to the road, do we?"

"No, but that canopy of trees will work."

"How is landing in the trees going to work?" she shouted.

"Trust me. My step-grandpa told me he did this once in Vietnam."

"I don't want to die, Diego."

"We're not going to die. But if you want to say a prayer, I won't stop you."

She was hanging on to the arms of her seat as tightly as she could, praying to God to save their lives.

Diego slowed the plane down as he went lower and lower.

And then they were skimming across trees, bumping along the branches.

She squeezed her eyes shut as the plane bounced and spun. It was so loud. Everything was breaking around her.

An enormous force flung her body forward. Her head hit something. Pain rocketed through her, and then she felt nothing at all...

—➤➤◄◄—

Diego's eyes flew open. He felt dazed, disoriented, and everything looked green. It took a second for him to realize that he was in a plane, that those were tree branches covering the window. The plane was at a slant, tilted slightly upward. But it was in one piece, and so was he. He did a mental check. There was blood on his hands and glass all around him, but there was no particular pain.

Turning his head, his momentary relief faded as he saw Tara slumped to one side. She was unconscious and there was blood on her face. He ripped off his seat belt and reached for her. "Tara!" He pressed his fingers against her neck. He could feel her pulse. She was still alive. Thank God! "Tara," he repeated, running his hand down her arm. "Wake up."

She didn't respond, and fear shot through him. The longer she was unconscious, the more serious her injuries could be, and he had no idea where they were or how far away help was. But he wasn't going to let her die. He couldn't. He'd promised.

He looked around the smashed-up cockpit. There had to be a first-aid kit somewhere. But even if he could find it, what could he do for her? She was breathing. She just wasn't waking up.

"Tara," he said again, taking her hand in his, squeezing her fingers, silently willing her to open her eyes.

She was a fighter. He knew that. He'd seen her in action. She might not have any training or any skills, but when it came to love, to loyalty, she didn't quit. And he wasn't going to quit on her.

"I need you to wake up. I need your help getting us out of here," he said. "We still have to find Bethany, and I can't do that without you. Bethany needs you." He paused, drawing in a breath. "I need you, too." He was shocked to realize how true the words felt, how much he didn't want to lose this beautiful, determined, passionate woman. He didn't want to be the reason she was dead.

Taking the plane had been the right move. They wouldn't

have been able to protect themselves at the airfield. He could have only held off the shooters for a short time. If they hadn't taken the plane, they would certainly be dead. But having made the right move didn't make this moment any easier.

"Tara," he said again. "It's time to open your big blue eyes, to ask me what the hell I was thinking stealing a plane and landing in the middle of the jungle. Then we'll figure out what we're going to do next. We'll do that together. We'll survive this. We'll get to Cartagena. We'll follow Bethany's trail. And we'll look for Mateo. We both have people we love that we need to find. You have to wake up."

Tara's lips parted as she started to stir. Her eyelids flickered opened, then closed, then open again. She gave him a bemused look, as if she didn't know who he was.

There was a slash of blood across her forehead where some glass had cut through her skin, but he prayed there was no real damage to her head.

"Tara. It's good to see you."

"Diego," she said slowly.

"It's me." He smiled with relief that she knew his name.

"We crashed."

"It was a hard landing," he joked.

"There are branches coming through the window," she said, her gaze moving toward the broken glass. "Are we in a tree?"

"I'm not sure exactly, but we're alive. That's all that matters."

She blinked a few more times, then put a shaky hand to her face, bringing away blood on her fingers.

"You cut your head," he told her. "How do you feel?"

"I have a headache."

"Do you have pain anywhere else?"

"I—I don't know. I don't think so. Are you all right, Diego?"

"I'm okay. Now that you're awake, I'm going to look for a first-aid kid. Your cut doesn't look too deep, but I don't want it to get infected."

"You have blood on your hand."

" It's a scratch. I'm going to take a look in the back of the plane."

"I'll help," she said, wincing a little as she shifted position.

"Stay put for now."

He moved behind their seats and found the first-aid kit. It was fully stocked with exactly what he needed. Pulling out antibiotic ointment, bandages, ibuprofen, and two bottles of water, he moved back toward Tara.

As he tended to her cut, he could smell the sweet scent of her shampoo, feel the silky strands of her hair brushing his face, and he had to force himself to concentrate on her wound, not on his attraction to her.

Using the light on his phone, he checked her cut for any sign of glass, but he didn't see anything. There was some swelling, but it didn't look too bad. When he applied the ointment, she jerked a little, biting back a gasp.

"Sorry," he said. "I know it stings."

"It's fine," she said tightly.

When he was done, he placed a bandage over her cut, then took out the ibuprofen and handed her a bottle of water. "You might want to take this."

She gulped down two capsules. "I'll do you now."

"I don't need anything."

"Let me see your hand," she ordered.

He extended his left hand. She put her hand under his, as she took a good look, then she reached for the same ointment.

"Your turn," she said.

She cleaned the cut, and he had to bite back his own gasp of pain. "That hurt," he said.

"I know. But that probably means it's doing its job. Do you want the ibuprofen, too?"

"No, I'm good."

"Tough guy."

"I didn't hit my head. I wasn't unconscious for several minutes. You scared me, Tara."

"I'm sorry. I'm all right. And now I have a big bump on my head to match your fading black eye. We're quite a pair."

"We are."

As their gazes clung together, he felt a jolt of desire. It wasn't the time or the place, but it was there.

Something shifted in her gaze. She licked her lips. "Diego."

"Yes?" he asked, feeling an incredible pull in her direction.

She put her hand on his face. His gut tightened.

"I don't know what's outside of this plane," she said.

"I don't, either."

"But I'm…"

"Grateful?" he offered.

She shook her head. "I am grateful to be alive, but that's not what I was going to say. I want to kiss you."

"What's stopping you?" He wrapped his arms around her back and pulled her into his arms, because the anticipation was killing him. But he still wanted her to make the move. And she did.

She put her mouth against his with a sexy shyness that was incredibly hot. But that shyness quickly evaporated with the heat of their kiss, with the sudden release of passion and adrenaline and joy at being alive. He kissed her again and again, wanting to lose himself in her, wanting to feel her mouth all over his body, wanting to taste her in every possible way.

Her hands ran up under his shirt, her fingers pressing against his hard abs. As they came up for a breath of air, he buried his face in her neck, inhaling her scent, letting his tongue trail around the curve of her ear and down to her collarbone.

At her gasp of pleasure, he raised his head and looked at her.

Her blue eyes were glittering with passion and need.

But there was something else in her gaze that tugged at him. It was vulnerability. It was trust.

He was taking advantage. He had to stop.

He abruptly pulled away.

Her eyes widened. "What's wrong?"

"We need to get out of this plane."

"But..." She licked her lips again.

"You need to stop doing that," he said, feeling a deep ache of desire that he didn't think was going away any time soon. It had been simmering just under the surface since he'd first seen her, but now it was a full-blown fire.

"Doing what?"

"Never mind. We need to figure out where we are and what to do next. Someone on the ground could have seen or heard the crash. We can't sit here. We have to make a move."

"Is that really why you stopped?"

He gave her a hard look. "It's partly why. That kiss was a result of what we went through. Whatever we're feeling right now isn't real."

"It feels pretty real. And to be honest, what I'm feeling right now started last night."

He cleared his throat. "We need to be smart."

"I'm usually the one who thinks that first," she muttered.

"Well, I didn't hit my head. I don't want to take advantage of the situation."

"The bump on my head isn't affecting my decisions, Diego."

"Good to know, but let's get out of here." He moved away before he gave in to temptation. Crossing to the door, it took him several attempts to get it open, but he finally got it ajar enough for him to put his head out.

"What do you see?" she asked.

"A lot of trees. But we're only about four feet off the ground." He came back into the plane. "Let's see what supplies we can find to take with us."

"There doesn't seem to be much. At least we have two bottles of water."

"And blankets," he said, pulling out four plastic-wrapped blankets. He stuffed them into the first-aid bag. "We're good to go. You, first."

She grabbed her tote bag, then moved to the door. She sat down on the edge and then jumped to the ground. He quickly followed.

"It's so dark. I can't believe it's one o'clock in the afternoon," she said, checking her watch.

"Once we get out from under the trees, we should have sunlight." He glanced down at his own smart watch, happy to have a compass app. "We'll head northwest. That should put us in the right direction to get to Cartagena."

"Do you really think someone saw the crash?"

"I don't know, but I don't want to stay too long in one place. We saw a road from the plane as well as buildings in the distance, maybe a small town. Hopefully, it's not too far."

"Hopefully," she echoed. "Because if we die here in the jungle, I'm going to be really mad that we didn't have sex first."

He was surprised at her words, at the glint of humor in her eyes.

"I appreciate you not wanting to take advantage of me, Diego," she continued. "But I can make my own decisions. I don't need you to make them for me."

"Understood."

"Good. Let's go."

"You want to lead? Call the shots?"

"Not even for a second. You're in charge of this trek back to civilization. But when it comes to more personal matters, we negotiate."

He met her smile with one of his own. "Deal."

Ten

$\twoheadrightarrow\!\!\!\gg\!\!\ll\!\!\leftarrow$

As Tara followed Diego through the trees, she couldn't help thinking about what had almost happened between them. Now that her brain was less fuzzy, she could appreciate Diego for stopping things before they got completely carried away. But she still felt an intense hollow ache of desire.

Maybe it was a mix of relief at being alive and the adrenaline rush of surviving what she had thought was probably certain death. But it was also more than that, because she'd been feeling an attraction to Diego since he'd first taken her hand in the church, and that attraction had intensified after their long chat the night before.

The danger had definitely amped up her feelings, and Diego had probably made the right decision in calling a halt to things. But she wasn't going to tell him that.

He liked to be in charge. And while she liked him to be in charge of a lot of things, when it came to whether or not they were going to sleep together, she wanted equal input.

As she watched him plow through the trees, she knew his mind was already back on the mission. Diego was very good at staying in the moment, addressing one problem at a time. She needed to be more like that, to stop thinking so far ahead.

Diego paused, holding back a heavy branch so that it wouldn't hit her in the face, and she couldn't help but appreciate him once more.

He was more protective than anyone she'd ever dated before. And yet he also encouraged her to be strong. It was an interesting combination.

Brian hadn't really been either—not protective nor encouraging. He'd been more of a disappointed critic. She had spent way too much time trying to pretend to be the girl he wanted her to be. It was good that they'd broken up when they had, even though it had been painful at the time. But she'd had a lot of time to grow up since then, and in the last few days, she'd really come into her own. She was starting to feel like she was becoming the person she was meant to be, which was an odd result of her search for Bethany.

Bethany would fall over in shock if she were to tell her everything that had happened. But she'd also be proud. Bethany would say: *This is just the beginning, Tara. You can be whoever you want to be.*

She actually didn't know exactly who she wanted to be. She liked her job, her students, her life in San Clemente. It was easy, quiet, maybe a bit boring, but it wasn't bad. And what would she do if she didn't do that? Travel the world? It sounded exciting, but would it really be the life she wanted? And then there was Diego…if something happened between them, would it just be a one-nighter? That seemed most likely. He was an adventurous, independent guy, who probably took off on jobs for weeks at a time. How could he possibly fit into her life, even if he wanted to, which he probably didn't?

She smiled at her foolish thoughts as she once again got caught up in worries of a future that was very far away at the moment. She didn't need to be worrying about what she would do when she got back. First, she needed to get back.

They weren't out of the woods yet—figuratively or literally. She had no idea if they were going the right way to find the road, the town they'd seen, or if they were heading farther into the wilderness. They didn't have food, and the water wouldn't last long, but for now she would simply put one foot in front of the other and keep going.

For the next two hours, she and Diego walked, pausing only occasionally to take a carefully rationed sip of water. They didn't say much during those brief breaks. As the afternoon shadows grew longer, they were both very aware that the night would only make their trek more dangerous.

Finally, the trees began to thin, and they stumbled onto a dirt path that looked like someone might have used it before them. Up until now, she'd felt like they were the only two people in the world.

Fifteen minutes later, the path widened, leading into a grassy field, and beyond that was a road. She felt giddy at the sight.

Diego paused, flashing her a smile that she hadn't seen in the past few hours. "We're getting closer to somewhere."

"I hope somewhere is a safe place and not a Salazar-owned town."

"Let's think positive. We haven't heard a helicopter searching for us, and the plane is buried beneath the trees."

"So, what now?"

"Follow the road into town and then look for a place to crash tonight."

"Please don't use the word crash."

His grin broadened. "Sorry. But like I said, we didn't crash. We had a hard landing."

"The wings fell off, Diego."

"My grandfather would have been impressed with that landing."

"Well, I'm impressed, too. You did a good job, Diego."

"How's your head?" he asked, as they fell into step alongside each other, now that they weren't dodging branches and squeezing through twisting tree trunks.

"It's down to a dull ache. The ibuprofen helped."

"I'm glad."

"At least I'm getting my steps in today."

"You're one of those people?"

"I am," she admitted. "I track my steps on my watch. I don't want to look yet. I'm afraid it will make me tired, and it's not time to rest yet."

"You're doing well. A lot of people would be complaining by now."

"I can't see how that would help."

He gave her a thoughtful look. "It never helps, but that doesn't usually stop people."

She shrugged. "I don't want to waste energy on a pointless rant right now. I'm trying to keep my feet moving."

"We're almost to the road."

"I feel both relieved and worried about that. I know we probably need to flag someone down, but who can we trust? It feels stupid to trust anyone."

"There are good people in Colombia."

"And bad people. I don't know how to tell the difference."

"I don't, either. We'll have to trust our instincts."

They turned onto the side of the road and began walking. It was another ten minutes before she heard an engine coming down the road behind them. They stopped and whirled around. It was a bus. She almost wept at the sight.

They started waving their arms. Thankfully, the bus pulled over. Diego moved on to the bus first, explaining in Spanish that their car had run off the road, and they'd pay for a ride to the next town. The driver told them the amount, which was ridiculously cheap. Apparently, civilization was not too far away.

Diego paid the driver, and then they made their way down the aisle. There was room for probably twenty people on the bus, but there were only seven.

They sat down behind two older women and in front of a mother and her young son.

There was an old man across from them and another old man in the back of the bus. No one looked at all dangerous, and as the minutes ticked by, she started to breathe more easily.

As she rested her hands on her thighs, Diego covered her hand with his, and gave her a smile. "I think our luck has turned," he said softly.

"I could say I don't think it could get any worse, but I don't want to jinx us."

"Good idea."

Diego kept his hand over hers as the bus lumbered down the lonely highway, and she leaned back and closed her eyes for a moment. She was aching and tired, but she knew she couldn't let down her guard completely. They still had to find a place to spend the night and then figure out how they were going to get to Cartagena.

—➤➤◄◄—

The bus pulled into a small station in the village of Tasco. It didn't look like the best place to spend the night. They felt like they would stand out too much. So after using the restrooms, they checked the map and the bus schedule and found a bus leaving for Cartagena in thirty minutes. They bought two tickets and had just enough time to grab some snacks and drinks from a small café next to the station before boarding a larger bus for the three-hour trip to Cartagena.

The bus was about half-full, with a couple of families and couples traveling to the coast. They took seats about midway back, with Tara sliding in next to the window, and Diego grabbing the aisle seat.

After eating the food they'd brought on board, exhaustion began to catch up to Tara. She found herself fighting to keep her eyes open.

"Go to sleep," Diego told her.

"I'm afraid to close my eyes."

"I've got this."

"You must be tired, too."

"I'm used to working off no sleep. It's fine."

"I'd argue, but I don't think I have the energy," she mumbled, dozing off before the words had fallen out of her mouth.

She woke up to a jolt. "What happened?" she asked wildly. "Why are we stopped?"

"It's okay. We're in Cartagena," Diego told her.

"I can't believe I slept the whole way." She tucked her hair back behind her ears.

"And you only snored a little."

"I do not snore."

"How would you know?" he asked, with a teasing glint in his eyes.

"I've never had any complaints."

"Men rarely complain about snoring when it comes to sleeping with a beautiful woman."

"We should go," she said, ignoring his flirty comment. "And how are you so awake after everything we've been through?"

"I told you. I'm used to no sleep."

She grabbed her bag from the floor by her seat and followed him off the bus. Even at almost eleven p.m., the Cartagena station was much busier than the one in Tasco, which made her feel a little less conspicuous. "Where should we go first?"

"A hotel. We need to regroup, and I wouldn't mind a shower."

"The last time I was here, I stayed in Centro, near Iglesia de San Pedro Claver. It's a beautiful five-hundred-year-old church. There were several hotels nearby. There are a lot of tourists in the area. We'll fit right in."

"That's perfect."

They grabbed a taxi to the church, and as they traveled through the streets, she marveled again at the beauty of the beachside Caribbean city that mixed colorful Colonial architecture with modern resorts. As they got out of the cab, she heard Latin music playing at an open-air bar, and laughter coming from a bunch of teenagers having ice cream in the plaza.

"This is such a pretty, vibrant city," she murmured. "It's true what Enrique said in the bar. Colombia is beautiful, but it can break your heart."

"Let's focus on the beauty tonight and leave the heartbreak for another day."

"I'd like to do that. I just feel on edge. Bethany came here, and whoever has her or is after her knows we talked to the pilot. They'll send someone to look for us, if they're not here already. But let's find a hotel. I don't think I can walk too much farther today."

They moved away from the church, heading down a side street. Three blocks later, they found a large, expensive hotel. She thought Diego would opt for something cheaper, but he told her if they were going to hide, they might as well be comfortable. He checked in under whatever name matched the credit card he had, assuring her that no one would be able to find them through that credit card. They were given a room on the fourth floor. Before heading up, they stopped in the gift shop and picked up some T-shirts, toothbrushes, cold drinks, and a couple of sandwiches to go. They'd left their suitcases at the hotel in Medellin, so they were traveling much lighter now.

Their room was larger than the one they'd shared the night before, with two full beds, a dresser, TV, a desk and a love seat with coffee table.

"Well, we don't have to unpack," she said, setting her bag on the dresser. "I guess I'll never see my suitcase again."

"Was there anything of value in it?"

"Not really. Just clothes. Nothing irreplaceable. What

about you?"

"Same. We can pick up more clothes tomorrow when the shops are open."

She nodded, flopping down on the bed. She pulled off her boots with a relieved breath. While she'd worn socks, her blisters were a little deeper after their long trek.

"Do you need our first-aid kit for those?" Diego asked, having brought the bag from the plane along with them.

"No. I'm fine. Is there a bath, though? Soaking my feet sounds like heaven."

"There is a tub."

"Do you want to shower first?"

"I'm happy to wait. Go take a long soak. I want to get on my phone and see what I can find out about Irina Salazar Garcia. I think we should see her tomorrow during the day and then do El Toro tomorrow night."

She got to her feet, then hesitated. "Did you want to do El Toro tonight?"

"I know you're dead on your feet, and I'm not leaving you alone."

"I can muster the energy if you think we should go now."

He shook his head. "No. It's probably better if we lay low tonight. Plus, we need to pick up more appropriate nightclub clothes."

She was happy with his answer. She wanted to keep going, but despite her long nap on the bus, her body and head were aching. "Then I will be in the bath."

"Don't lock the door. In case you fall asleep in there, I might have to come and pull you out."

"I think I can stay awake that long. But I will leave the door unlocked."

--->>*<---

As Tara took her bath, he kicked off his shoes, took off his jacket and stretched out against the pillows on his bed.

Then he searched the internet on his phone for Irina Salazar Garcia. He'd wanted to do it earlier, but on their many bus trips, he hadn't been able to get a signal good enough for search and social media. He was a little surprised that Lucas hadn't gotten back to him about her, as he'd texted that request hours ago. Hopefully he hadn't gotten Lucas into any hot water by asking for so many favors. He knew that Lucas had to protect his job and his relationship with the Colombian government.

Putting that worry aside, he entered Irina's name into the search engine. It quickly became clear that Irina did not participate in any social media. However, there was a listing for her at a primary school website where she was named as the art teacher. He also found her mentioned in an obituary for her husband Carl Garcia, who had apparently died of cancer.

There were no images for the fifty-seven-year-old widow, but he hoped to see her in person tomorrow.

He entered Michael Salazar into the search engine, and more than a dozen listings popped up. But skimming through them, he realized that both Michael and Salazar were very common names. He tried adding in other filters like Colombia and cartel as well as Tomas and Irina and Camilla, but there was nothing.

Why was his brother so difficult to find?

He was missing something.

His phone buzzed, and a text from Lucas popped up.

Sorry for the delay. Couldn't get a phone number for Irina Salazar Garcia, but your address matches her government records. Let me know what you find out.

He typed in a thank-you and said he'd check in tomorrow after he spoke to Irina.

Setting down his phone, he stared up at the ceiling, feeling his own exhaustion beginning to catch up to him. The day had been brutal, but they'd made it to Cartagena, and hopefully tomorrow would bring more answers and fewer questions.

Tara padded back into the room with her clothes in her arms. She was barefoot, clad only in the extra-large T-shirt she'd bought downstairs that skimmed the top of her knees. Her hair was damp, and she smelled like oranges.

Her scent brought his energy level immediately back, and he couldn't help thinking about the kiss they'd shared in the plane. But she was tired and so was he, and the last thing they should do was kiss again, no matter how much he wanted to.

She dropped her clothes on the table and crawled into the bed next to him.

"That was fast," he said.

"I was actually afraid I would fall asleep and drown in the bathtub, and after everything we've been through, that is not how I want to go."

He smiled, appreciating her humor. "That would be tragically ironic."

"Did you find anything on the internet about Irina?"

"No. And Lucas texted that he couldn't come up with a phone number, but her address looked good. We'll find out tomorrow."

"Hopefully it's a better day than today."

"Any day we survive is a good day."

"I do like your positive attitude, Diego. Anyway, the shower or tub is all yours. I might not be awake when you get back."

"Don't even try." He forced himself to swing his legs off the bed and stand up. As his gaze swept her pretty form, he told himself to be happy she was exhausted and that her eyes were already closing, because that drove all of his bad ideas out of his head. Although, as he headed into the bathroom, he decided to make it a cold shower instead of a warm bath.

Eleven

‒➡️➤⏴◀‒

After two cups of coffee and a big breakfast composed of huevos pericos, otherwise known as eggs with tomato and onion, arepo con quesito, corn cakes with cheese, as well as rice and beans, which seemed to appear with most meals in Colombia, Diego felt ready to take on the day and Tara had a spark in her blue eyes as well.

They took a cab to Irina's home around eleven, hoping she'd be home since it was Saturday. When Tara put her hand on his leg, he realized he was tapping his foot on the floor of the cab.

She gave him a smile. "Are you nervous? Because I think that might be a first."

"More like impatient. I hope Irina is home and can tell me what happened to Michael."

"I hope so, too."

"We'll get back to Bethany after this."

"I know. I'm not worried. Your brother is important, too."

The taxi pulled up in front of a one-story house in a modest neighborhood. There was a small, overgrown grassy area in front, and the building could have used another coat of paint, making Diego wonder what connection Irina had to her wealthy cousins. She certainly wasn't living a big life.

He paid the driver in cash and as they got out of the cab, he paused on the sidewalk, looking up and down the block.

"What's wrong?" Tara asked.

"I'm hoping we aren't walking into a trap. We don't know if Hector gave us this address to set us up."

"We don't. But why would he?"

"I don't know."

"We've come this far, Diego. Let's ring the bell."

He nodded and headed up to the porch to do just that.

A moment later, he heard footsteps. Then the door opened.

A short woman, barely five feet tall, with pepper-gray hair and a round face gazed back at Diego. She appeared to be in her late fifties. "Hola?" she said somewhat warily.

"Irina Garcia?" he asked

"Yes. Who are you?"

"Diego Rivera. This is Tara Powell. Hector Pilacio suggested we talk to you."

"Hector? I haven't spoken to Hector since my brother Tomas died. They were partners in a law firm. What's this about?"

"It's about Tomas's stepson, Michael. Hector said you took him in after Tomas died."

"What has Michael done?" she asked quickly.

"He hasn't done anything that I know of. I just want to find him."

"Why? Who is Michael to you?"

His pulse sped up. Irina knew something about Mateo. "He's my half brother. Camilla was my mother."

Irina's face paled as her eyes grew dark and wide. "No. That can't be true."

"It is true. My parents divorced when I was thirteen and Mateo was eight."

"Mateo?"

"I guess my mother changed his name to Michael after she and my brother disappeared. I never saw either one of them again. That was eighteen years ago."

Irina's eyes filled with shadows. "Your mother...you spoke to Hector, so you must know..."

"That she passed away. Yes, I do know that. But I'm eager to find Michael. Can you tell me where he is?"

She hesitated, her gaze darting around the neighborhood, as if she was afraid someone might be watching. "Perhaps you should come inside." She stepped back, waving them into a small living room with a couch, an armchair, and an old TV sitting on a weathered bookcase. Off the living room was a hallway leading to what appeared to be a bedroom with a kitchen beyond.

The only interesting and beautiful thing about the home was the art hanging on the walls, beautiful oil and watercolor paintings.

"Please, sit down," Irina said. "Do you want coffee?"

"I'm good," he said, as Tara also gave a negative shake of her head. They sat down together on the couch, while Irina perched on the edge of the armchair. "Did you take Michael in after Tomas passed away?"

"I did. He was a lost little boy. He was still hurting from his mother's death when Tomas had a heart attack. He was twelve years old, and he didn't feel like he belonged anywhere. I knew that Tomas had not wanted Michael to grow up with our family in Cascada, because Camilla had hated it up there. She'd disliked the fact that Tomas did work for our cousins."

"The Salazar cartel," he said.

"Yes."

"So, you raised Michael?"

"No. He only stayed here for six months. He was unhappy the whole time. He missed his friends in Medellin. He missed his cousins in Cascada. Even though his mother hadn't liked their trips to the compound, Michael had enjoyed them quite a bit. He'd made friends with the kids who lived there. Here, he had no one. He had trouble making friends at the new school. I had to work, so I wasn't home until late. Michael was lonely and bored. When summer came, he begged me to allow him to go to Cascada for a few weeks. He was close to one of Juan Felipe's sons, Rico, and he wanted to hike and fish and do boy things." Guilt flashed through Irina's eyes. "I knew it was wrong to let him go, but he was so eager to leave, and I was tired. I couldn't fight him. He never came back."

"He stayed in Cascada?"

"Mostly, yes. He went to a private boarding school in Medellin with the other Salazar children. But in the summers, he was in Cascada."

"Is he there now?"

"No. He went to a university in California. The family wanted him to go back to the States. He was an American citizen. And he was the perfect person to become embedded in the US."

"And embedded in the organization," he said grimly.

The truth was written all over Irina's face. "Sí. It was not what Camilla would have wanted for her son. I am sorry I let her down. She was a kind woman. She made Tomas happy. But Michael is strong-willed, and he was too much for me."

"Do you know where Michael lives now?"

"It's near Los Angeles. It's Santa...something. I can't remember. It's on the beach. Michael always liked the ocean. It was the only part of Cartagena he enjoyed."

"That's probably Santa Monica," Tara put in. "Did Michael go to UCLA?"

"I think the letters were different."

"USC?" Tara pressed.

"Yes, that sounds right," Irina answered.

"What is Michael doing now?" he asked. "Is he running drugs through the US?" It seemed unbelievable that he could be asking whether his innocent, goofy little brother, who liked PB&J sandwiches and riding his bike in the park was running drugs for the Salazar cartel.

"My sister told me recently that he's more involved in the money side of things, but I don't know. I try to keep my distance from that side of the family. My father didn't want anything to do with the business. He thought Caleb and his brothers were ruthless and immoral, which they are. I was able to stay out of things, because, frankly, they don't much care what the girls in the family do. It's another story for the boys. Tomas got roped into helping the family with legal problems. Our uncle had paid for Tomas's education, so he was obligated to pay him back." She paused. "I suspect this is not what you wanted to hear."

"Actually, I just wanted to hear something. My brother has been a ghost haunting my life. Did my mother talk about her divorce to my father? Did she tell you about the son she'd left behind?"

"She said that she cheated on your father and that Michael was born of her unfaithfulness. She told me that she deserved to be punished, but her greatest regret was that her oldest son had gotten caught up in her husband's desire for revenge."

"Did she say if he kept her away from me?"

"She told me that he forced her to leave the country and to cut off all contact with you, but I don't know how he did it." Irina paused. "She was working as a nurse in Medellin when she met Tomas. He had broken his finger, and she treated him at the medical center. They fell in love very fast. Tomas had never been so happy. And I think your mother was happy, too."

"I'm glad she went back to nursing. She loved it."

"She was such a caring person. I know her patients were very lucky."

"I just don't understand why she changed my brother's name to Michael?" he muttered.

"She never told me she had changed his name, and he never mentioned it."

"Did Michael ever talk about me, his brother in the US?"

"No, never. But, as I said, he didn't talk to me about much."

Maybe Mateo had forgotten all about him, but he still needed to see his brother face-to-face, to let him know that he'd been looking for him for a very long time. "So, he goes by Michael Salazar and you think he lives in Santa Monica. He went to USC. What else?"

"He doesn't use the name Salazar. He uses Winters. Michael Winters. It was the name your mother gave him."

"Michael Winters," he echoed, surprised once more. "His last name is Winters? Why?"

"I don't know. That was his name when he lived with Tomas."

"But his last name was Rivera."

"Diego," Tara said, drawing his attention to her. "Mateo's real father. His last name was probably Winters."

She made a good point. "That's possible," he murmured.

"Your mother also did not want Michael to be a Salazar," Irina said. "Tomas wanted to adopt Michael, but your mother refused because of the name."

"Well, now I know why I couldn't find Michael or Mateo Salazar in any database."

"You should be able to find him now," Tara said, excitement in her voice, a gleam in her eyes. "You have his name and a city."

"Yes. It's a lot more to go on than I had before."

"But perhaps you should not try to find him," Irina cautioned.

"Why not?" he asked.

"Because he's not the brother you remember. My cousins are criminals. Michael is one of them now."

"He has my blood, not theirs."

"I don't think Michael will see it that way," Irina said.

"He identified very strongly with the Salazars. He is part of the family. And he is part of the business. Anyone who threatens to expose the Salazar network will pay a heavy price. You should let him go, because he is already gone."

He understood what Irina was saying. If he was an objective third party, he'd say the same thing, but he wasn't a third party. He was Mateo's brother. And he would see him. He would talk to him. "Thank you for telling me everything. Do you have a photo of Michael?"

"Yes, I do. One moment." She got up from her chair and walked into the other room.

He glanced at Tara. There was a mix of emotion in her eyes, everything from relief to worry to fear. And all of those emotions were running through him, too.

"Michael Winters," he said. "I never would have guessed that was his name."

"Does the name Winters ring a bell? Do you know the man your mother had an affair with?"

"No, but he sounds American. She must have met him in DC where we were living. Maybe at the hospital where she worked part-time." He shook his head in bemusement. "The life Mateo has lived...is so different from mine. He had to bury our mother and then his stepfather. I can understand why he latched on to the Salazars."

"So can I, and I think Irina might be right. Michael may not be happy to see you, Diego."

"I don't care," he said flatly.

"You do care. I know you do."

"Fine, I care, but it doesn't matter. I have to play this out. I have to see him."

"And if he's a criminal, a drug dealer, a killer? What then? You're an FBI agent. You're his enemy."

"I'm his blood."

"Will that matter?"

"Only one way to find out."

Irina came back into the room with a large envelope in

her hand. "I found a dozen or so photos from when Michael was with Tomas and your mother. I'm sorry I don't have anything more recent."

He took the envelope but didn't open it. He needed to do that somewhere else. "Thank you."

"If you find Michael, I hope you'll tell him that I think of him often, and I wish him well."

"I'll do that. I'm going to call for a cab. Would you mind if we wait inside until it arrives?"

"Do the Salazars know you're looking for Michael?"

"Honestly, I'm not sure what they know. But I do hope we haven't put you in any danger."

"I will drive you where you need to go. That will be safer." She led them down the hallway and through the kitchen door into the attached garage. "I have errands to run anyway."

Tara squeezed into the backseat of a small coupe, while he took the front seat. As they left the garage and drove down the block, he looked for any sign of a tail, but the street was empty.

Hopefully they were still one step ahead of the Salazars or whoever was after them.

—❧—

Diego was very quiet, Tara thought, wondering why he wasn't peppering Irina with more questions but clearly, he was still thinking about what she'd told them so far. It had to be a blow finding out that his brother was a member of one of the most powerful cartels in South America and in the US. She couldn't imagine how difficult it would be to come to grips with that, and she questioned the wisdom of him meeting Michael face-to-face.

He needed to at least think about that for longer than five minutes. And while he didn't want to do that, practically speaking they were in Colombia and Michael was in the US, so he was going to have some time whether he wanted it or not.

Irina dropped them off at the side entrance to the hotel, and they slipped into the lobby without any problem, but then Diego paused.

"What's wrong?" she asked.

"I need to walk. I need to burn off some energy."

She smiled. She could solve one problem. "Okay. Let's walk."

"I don't know if it's safe."

"We're in a crowded area. We're probably as safe here as we are anywhere."

"I don't want to put you in danger, Tara."

"You've been thinking about me a lot. And I appreciate that. Let's do this for you. Besides, we need to go shopping for nightclub clothes, remember?"

"Good point."

"And if you want to talk, I'll listen. If you don't want to talk, I'm okay with silence."

He smiled. "You might be the perfect woman."

"I might be," she said lightly. "But I am serious."

"I don't know what I want to say right now."

"Then let's walk. But you're going to have to hold my hand."

"I think I can manage that," he replied, slipping his hand into hers.

They walked back out into the sunshine and strolled down the street. There were plenty of shops in the first block, but she knew Diego still needed to burn off energy and emotion, so they kept walking. They ended up at the harbor and stood at a rail watching the fishermen coming back from their morning runs.

"It is beautiful here," she murmured.

"It is," he agreed.

"Are you feeling any better?"

"Yes. Thanks for letting me process."

"No problem."

"I'm still going to find him, Tara."

She wasn't at all surprised. "I know. You have to see him."

"I do. I don't know what happens after that."

"Well, as a wise man has been telling me for the past few days, that's a problem to worry about later."

He smiled. "Very true. What have you been thinking about?"

"A lot of different things. Or people, I should say. You, your brother, Bethany, me...I'm happy you know where Michael is, and I think you'll be able to find him now that you have his last name and the state where he's living."

"I agree. I need to text Wyatt. I had to wrap my head around everything first."

"Completely understandable. Are you going to look at the photos Irina gave you?" she asked, tipping her head toward the envelope in his hand.

"When we get back. I'm not quite ready to see my brother and my mom with Tomas. It's still strange to think my mom had another family."

"Well, she had another husband, not really another family."

He shrugged. "It's just weird."

"I get it. It would be strange for me to think of my parents with anyone else."

"Enough about me. Let's get back to Bethany. We'll go to El Toro tonight and talk to Bethany's friend Rosa."

"If she's working."

"It's a Saturday night; I'm guessing most of the staff will be on duty."

"True. It's a very popular club—kind of dressy, too, at least for the women. I'll need to pick up a cocktail dress."

"No problem. Let's head back and we'll do some shopping. We can pick up some other clothes as well. My credit card has a very high limit."

"I can pay for myself."

"Not now. This card can't be traced, unlike your cards."

"Oh, well, then I saw some really expensive boutiques near the hotel that might have the perfect dress." She paused. "I am spending the bureau's money, not yours, right?"

He smiled. "We'll get it all sorted out. Let's go buy you something sexy."

She shivered at his words, at the promise in his eyes. It was a dangerous dance they were doing, but it was exciting, too. She was feeling very alive these days. Escaping death had made her appreciate the fact that she was still breathing and still had a life to lead. What kind of life that would be was up to her.

Twelve

———➤➤◄◄◄—

Diego had never really enjoyed shopping. He usually found it boring as hell, and when he did it for himself, he was in and out of stores as fast as possible. But with Tara, the experience was a lot more enjoyable, especially when he got her to try on different potential dresses and model them for him. And damn if she hadn't looked amazing in everything she put on. But he didn't think she had any idea how beautiful she really was.

Tara had an image of herself in her head that was not the image he saw. He didn't know why she didn't see herself for who she was, and he was probably too interested in showing her. That interest was another reason he kept the shopping excursion going. They had a bunch of hours to fill before they hit up the El Toro nightclub and filling those hours in their hotel room seemed like a bad idea.

When Tara finally decided on a slinky red dress that was sure to put his blood pressure through the roof, he focused on picking up a few items of clothing for himself to get through the next few days. Then they stopped in at a restaurant for a late lunch/early dinner.

For the first time since they'd met, their conversation was light, less personal, not intense or emotional. Tara told stories about some of her students, and it was clear she cared very deeply about the kids, even the ones who gave her a difficult time. He told her about one of his favorite teachers at West Point, a man who had inspired him to do better, reach higher, work harder.

And then they talked about books they'd read, movies they'd seen, places that they'd gone on vacation, all the little pieces of information that filled in the pictures of their lives. While Tara hadn't traveled at all really, she knew a lot about the world. Clearly, she'd been an armchair traveler all her life. And he found himself wanting to show her some of his favorite sights in the world like the glaciers in Patagonia and the Iguazú Falls in Brazil.

But the reality of them spending a lot of time together after all this was resolved seemed doubtful. His job required him to travel, sometimes for weeks or months at a time. He had to become another person. He couldn't communicate with people outside of his circle. The only way he could do it well was not to have emotional attachments. He had to be 100 percent into whatever he was doing. It was why he'd lost so many friendships outside his FBI circle. It was why the people he most counted on now were the friends he'd made at Quantico, who understood his life.

The one thing that had been easier for him was the fact that he had no family pulling him in different directions. There was no one waiting for him or worrying about him, which was both freeing and a little depressing. But he'd chosen this life, and it had worked for him for a long time. Whether it would work forever, who knew?

After their meal, they'd gone back to the hotel to shower and change for the evening. He'd spent a brief time looking through the photos that Irina had given him. Seeing his mother with Mateo and Tomas had been shockingly upsetting. It was one thing to know that his mother had moved on with her life and another thing to see it. He'd decided to leave a longer perusal of those pictures for another day.

He'd also checked in with Wyatt, sharing the information he'd received from Irina. If Michael Winters was in Santa Monica, then Wyatt should be able to find him easily. Hopefully he'd know more within a few hours.

At eight o'clock, they went downstairs and took a taxi to the popular bar known as El Toro. It was still early at the nightclub, so it wasn't as crowded as it would be later in the evening. But there were still plenty of people in the bar, with Latin music wafting down the stairs from a band playing on the rooftop deck.

There was a U-shaped bar on the main floor, with high and low tables scattered throughout the room. Artwork on the walls celebrated bulls and bullfighting. Apparently, El Toro's owner was a former bullfighter. There was even a display case with bullhorns from legendary fights.

"Have you ever seen a bullfight?" Tara asked, as they paused in the middle of the room, taking in the scene.

"I've seen the running of the bulls in Pamplona, where a bunch of idiots think they can outrun a herd of bulls," he said dryly.

"I can't imagine why anyone would want to do that."

"I've lost my ability to be surprised at the level of impulsive stupidity in the world."

"That's rather cynical, Diego. I thought you were an optimist."

"You think I'm an optimist?" he echoed with a surprised grin.

"I do. You generally focus on the positive like when the plane was going down. You were so excited to see a canopy of trees. All I could see was the ground about to shatter us into a million pieces."

"I try to focus on what will work in my favor."

"It's a good trait. I'm going to have to try that more often."

"Do you see Rosa?"

Her gaze swept the room. "No. She's not working at the bar. She might be upstairs. I think that's where she was the last time I came here."

"That was during your Christmas break?"

"Yes. Bethany and I came here after the tour. I was about to head home. She was going to stay a few more days before her next tour. We had a great time that night. It had been a long time since we laughed so much. I left here thinking how much fun I would have in the summer when we'd meet up in between tours or sometimes double up with a larger group. That's the last time I saw her in person. Of course, we exchanged texts after that, liked each other's posts online, but we weren't actually together, and we didn't talk on the phone. We couldn't seem to make our schedules line up for a long call. We both kept saying soon—we'd do it soon."

He heard the sadness in her voice and knew it was time to bring the optimism back out. "You'll do it again, and you'll have plenty of adventures to share with Bethany."

"That's true. She probably won't believe what I've been up to." Tara paused. "I really want to have that conversation with her, Diego."

"I know you do. Let's go upstairs and look for Rosa."

They made their way up to the roof where they found another bar, several grouping of tables and a dance floor in front of a stage where a band was performing.

"I see her," Tara said excitedly, taking his hand as they moved toward the bar and a tall, thin brunette with her hair pulled up in a ponytail.

Rosa was serving drinks at one end of the bar, moving with grace and efficiency, and giving her patrons a friendly smile as she poured cocktails.

"Rosa," Tara said, pushing her way up to the bar. "Do you remember me? Tara Powell?"

"Oh, sure," Rosa said, recognition in her eyes. "You're Bethany's friend. Is she back?"

"Back from where?"

"She was on her way to California last time I saw her."

"When was that?" Tara pressed.

"Uh, let's see. Last Saturday night—a week ago." Rosa's gaze narrowed. "Why? Is something wrong?"

"Can we talk to you for a minute?" Tara pleaded. "In private?"

Rosa hesitated. "It's pretty busy."

"It won't take long, but it's important. Bethany is in trouble."

"Seriously?"

"Life or death seriously," Tara said.

"All right. Hang on." Rosa said something to the other bartender, then stepped out from behind the bar and motioned them over to a quieter area near a low brick wall that looked out upon the city. "What's going on?"

"We're not sure," Tara replied. "This is my friend—Diego."

Rosa gave him a quick smile, then turned back to Tara. "So, does Bethany's trouble have to do with her boyfriend?"

"What boyfriend? Was she here with a man last Saturday night?" Tara asked.

"Not last Saturday, but about a month ago she brought him in. He was very hot. He had an edge to him, too, like he was some kind of dangerous. Maybe not the good kind," Rosa added with a frown. "Still, he was sexy as hell. He gave Bethany the kind of kiss that makes your toes curl."

"Her favorite kind," Tara murmured. "Did you catch his name?"

Rosa thought for a moment. "She called him Mitch or Michael. It started with an M."

His gut clenched. *Michael? As in Mateo who changed his name to Michael?*

But that was crazy. And Michael was a very common

name. Plus, Rosa didn't even remember if that was the guy's name.

"Did Bethany talk about her boyfriend when she was here last weekend?"

"She said she was going to Los Angeles to see him. She told me she might be in love, really in love, for the first time. But despite her words, she was sad, tense. Something was wrong; I didn't have a chance to find out what. But she was different than her normal happy self. She wasn't flirting with anyone, and she wanted to talk to my cousin, Reggie. He's a pilot. She needed to get to Panama City the next day, but she didn't want to go commercial. I gave her Reggie's number. I don't know if she spoke to him."

"We're going to need to talk to your cousin," Diego cut in.

"I don't want to get him into trouble," Rosa said somewhat hesitantly.

"Reggie is not in trouble," Tara said. "We just need to find out if he flew Bethany to Panama City or somewhere else and when that happened. Can you give me his number?"

"He's out of town until tomorrow. He flew a charter to Bogota. But I can give you his number if you want to try in the morning."

Diego didn't want to wait until the morning. He didn't know if they could trust Rosa to give them her cousin's real number or that she wouldn't warn him for some reason. "Why don't you text him now?" he suggested. "Ask him what happened with Bethany."

Rosa frowned. "I'm working."

"This won't take long. The sooner you help us, the sooner we'll be gone."

"Very well." She took out her phone and sent a text. "I don't know if he'll answer right away. He could be busy."

"We'll hang around here until he does." As he finished speaking, he saw her phone light up with an incoming text. "Is that him?"

"It's him." She opened her messages, then handed him the phone. "You can read it for yourself."

Tara huddled next to him as they read the message together: *Took her to Panama City Airport last Sunday morning. Didn't talk to her after that. Why? What's wrong?*

"I'm going to text him as if I'm you," Diego told Rosa as he typed out a text asking Reggie if Bethany said anything about being in trouble, because some people came into the bar looking for her.

Rosa didn't look happy about him commandeering her phone, but she didn't attempt to take it back.

Reggie answered: *She told me she needed to get out of Colombia fast and not to tell anyone I'd given her a ride to Panama City. I didn't ask questions. I didn't want to know. She paid me in cash. That was it. Did you tell someone you gave her my name?*

He wanted to protect Rosa, so he answered: *No, I didn't say anything. Don't worry.*

Good, I don't need any problems.

Diego handed Rosa her phone. "Thanks."

Rosa skimmed through the texts. "I appreciate you not telling him I told you about him."

"We're Bethany's friends. We're trying to help her. But anyone else who comes asking won't feel the same way, so please don't share the information."

"I won't. What kind of trouble is she in?"

"I really wish we knew," Tara said heavily. "But I think it's bad."

Rosa gave a quick look at the bar. "I need to get back to work."

As Rosa walked away, Tara turned to him with a light in her eyes that was both worried and hopeful. "Bethany isn't in Colombia anymore. Do you think that's a good sign?"

"I do. She left under her own steam."

"It also sounds like she's running from someone. What do we do now? Go to Panama City?"

"Yes. But before we do that, I'll see if I can get someone in Panama to check the airport security footage for Bethany. If we know what plane she got on, we'll know where she got off."

"It has been six days since she left Colombia. She could have gone anywhere."

"Yes, but we're one step closer to finding her."

"I'd like to think so."

He pulled out his phone and texted Wyatt.

"Who are you contacting this time?" Tara asked.

"Wyatt. While Lucas has more connections in South America, Wyatt has more powerful connections in the bureau. And we may need someone on a higher level to ask the Panama authorities for help."

"You have good friends willing to help you no questions asked. Is that how it is among agents?"

"Not always, but Wyatt is different. He's part of a group of six—five now—friends that I met at Quantico. We were put together early in our training, and we formed a tight bond that lasted beyond the academy. We know we can turn to each other for help, especially if we have to work off book, which is what I'm doing now."

"Why did you say six, then change it to five?" she asked curiously.

He leaned against the rail. "One of our group died a few weeks before graduation in a training exercise. His name was Jamie Rowland."

"I'm sorry. That's sad."

"His death ripped us apart. We all felt a little responsible, even though it was an accident. But I know I'm not the only one who went over every move I'd made, wondering if I'd done something differently if Jamie would still be alive."

"How did he die? If you don't mind talking about it."

"The training mission was to rescue a group of hostages who were being held on the top floor of an empty building. The structure was booby-trapped. The apartment door was wired with explosives. We had to disarm several devices, evade shooters, and rescue the group."

"But something went wrong."

"Tragically wrong. We were almost done, when explosions were set off. It felt like the building was coming down around us. But we had the hostages, and we were heading out the door. I gave the all clear to our team outside, but then Jamie thought he heard someone call out for help. He ran back inside. I tried to stop him, but he was gone. Later it was discovered that he fell out of one of the windows during a fiery blast." He swallowed a knot in his throat at the memory of that horrible night. He gave Tara a hard look. "He wasn't supposed to go back inside. The building we were in had been set for demolition. That's why we were able to use it. Once we were done, the building would go down and be rebuilt. It was planned out. No one was supposed to die."

Tara's face paled, her eyes filling with shadows as she faced him, putting her hands on his shoulders. Her warm touch was more than welcome.

"That's horrible, Diego. I'm so terribly sorry. I shouldn't have asked."

"You had no way of knowing."

"I had no idea training missions could be so dangerous."

"Like I said, it wasn't supposed to be, and it wouldn't have been if Jamie had not gone back inside. But that's who he was. If someone was in trouble, he was the first to act. We took his example to heart after that, telling each other we'd always be there if someone called. I think sometimes now we try to save each other, just because we couldn't save him. Not that I've been much help to the rest of the team. I've been in South America the last several years, and I haven't been very available. But Wyatt is still willing to help me. And I'm sure the others would, too, if I asked."

"Where is Wyatt located?"

"He's in Los Angeles, which should make finding my brother easier as well. I already sent him the details on

Michael Winters."

"And now he'll look for Bethany, too."

"He's caught up on the whole situation."

"What kind of work does he do in the bureau?"

"He's done a lot of undercover work. He's a chameleon. He can blend in anywhere. But recently he joined a task force run by another former classmate. It allows him to not be so covert, which is good, because he fell in love during an undercover assignment at an aerospace company last year. His girlfriend Avery is an astrophysicist, which blows me away, because Wyatt was never one looking to date smart girls, if you know what I mean."

She smiled. "I know what you mean. I've been a little too smart for quite a few of my dates. And I'm only a high school Spanish teacher."

"If you're too smart, then you don't want them."

"Probably true. Who else is in your group?"

"Bree Adams. She's also in Los Angeles. She was originally in New York, then worked a case in Chicago, where she hooked up with an old flame. They decided to move to the beach, which was fortunate for Wyatt, because Bree ended up helping him save Avery's life."

"So, it's not all guys on the team?"

"No. There's also Parisa Maxwell. She's a language expert, and she recently survived a kidnapping at an embassy in New York. She's apparently now seeing a CIA agent, who helped her stop a terrorist attack."

"That's a crazy way to fall in love."

"It is. Last but not least is Damon Wolfe, who works in New York. He has always been the leader of our group. He's focused, insightful, and fiercely loyal. He's been moving up in the bureau very quickly. I expect he'll one day be running his own field office."

"Sounds like a very talented group of people."

"Yes."

"What about you, Diego? Are you on vacation? Did you

take leave to search for your brother? Where would you be right now if you weren't here?"

"I had just finished an assignment when I got the lead from Tracy. I'm supposed to be in DC Wednesday. I told my boss I needed a few days off. I did not tell him I was going to Colombia. He would not be happy with this situation. He'd be afraid I'd do something to trigger an international incident."

"Like stealing a plane and crashing it in the jungle?"

"Exactly like that. But I still think it was the right move—the only move, in fact."

"I do, too, now that we're safely on the ground." She let out a breath. "Do you want to go back to the hotel and wait for Wyatt to get in touch?"

He wanted to go back to the hotel, but sharing the room with Tara tonight was going to be a lot different than the last two nights. There was no denying the attraction between them. He needed to make sure he was a lot more tired than he was now, before they entered that room. If he was exhausted, he could maybe stop thinking about kissing her again.

"Let's dance," he said.

Her eyebrows arched in surprise. "You want to dance?"

"There's nothing else we can do to find anyone tonight, Tara. I like the music. Don't you?"

"I do, but…are we safe? Will they look for us here? It's a bar that Bethany used to come to."

She was probably right to be cautious but at the moment, he couldn't bring himself to worry. "There are a lot of people here; I don't think we're in any danger, and I'm feeling restless. I'd like to burn off some energy. What about you?"

"I could dance."

"Good."

She smiled. "Let's see what you've got."

Thirteen

➤➤◄◄◄

What Diego had…was a smooth, sexy style of dancing. Tara shouldn't have been surprised he was good at dancing, because he was good at so many things. But she should have thought a little harder before moving into his arms, because the pulsating beat of the music, the sultry voice of the female singer, the crowded dance floor, and the sparkling stars overhead completely transported her into a world that was only her and Diego, their bodies moving together, the heated desire flowing between them.

Diego didn't try to kiss her, but every move, every touch sent her blood pressure skyrocketing. He'd said he wanted to work off some restless energy, but the dancing wasn't doing that for her. Instead, it was making her feel vibrant and alive, reckless and impulsive. She was in Colombia, far from her normal life. She was in the arms of an incredibly attractive man, one she wasn't just physically attracted to, but one she liked very, very much.

They probably had no future, but they had tonight.

Did she really have the courage to live in the moment?

Or would she choose to retreat the way she normally did?

The music moved into a slower beat, and Diego pulled her even closer. His hard body and her soft curves seemed made for each other.

She told herself to stop thinking and just enjoy, let the music take her away, but it was really Diego who was sweeping her off her feet. His hands moved up and down her back as they spun around and around until she was dizzy with delight, and one song blended into the next. She thought she might never want to leave this dance floor. She hadn't felt this happy in…maybe ever?

But then the band ended their set, announcing that the next group would be starting shortly.

"Do you want a drink, or shall we leave?" Diego asked, his arms still around her.

She looked into his handsome face, his dark, compelling eyes, and knew exactly what she wanted. "Let's go back to the hotel."

"Good idea." He took her hand. "I don't want to lose you in this crowd."

She didn't want to lose him, either, and she wasn't just talking about in the crowd.

After leaving the club, they flagged down a taxi, and within a few minutes were walking back into the hotel. Their room was exactly as they'd left it, a good sign that no one had found them in Cartagena.

Diego took off his coat and tossed it on the nearest bed. Then they exchanged a long, hot stare.

"Nothing has to happen," he said.

"I know. But what if I want something to happen? Would you turn me down again? Like you did in the plane?"

"I don't think I have it in me to say no twice, so you need to be sure, Tara. Adrenaline and danger can color your thinking."

"My thinking is perfectly clear." She took a few

purposeful steps forward. "I know this is not my real life, Diego. You and I would probably have never met in my real life or in yours. But we're here now. Neither of us knows what tomorrow will bring, or if we'll even have tomorrow." She licked her lips, and his gaze immediately followed her action. She liked his response, liked the power she seemed to have over him, even though he had as much power over her. Every time he smiled, her stomach clenched, and tingles jangled her nerves. She drew in a deep breath and let it out. "I want you, Diego. I want us to be together tonight."

He breached the distance between them, resting his hands on her hips. "I want that, too. You've been driving me crazy all night. Actually, you've been driving me crazy since we met. It wasn't an accident that I stood behind you in the church. After I saw you talking to the priest, I was more than a little intrigued. And it wasn't just that you were upset, that I was curious about you. I thought you were stunning. I was drawn to you. I looked for you when I went into the church. I was going to talk to you after the service. But you know what happened."

"Do you think we were fated to meet in our mutual quests?"

"Do you?"

"Sometimes I think so. You've saved my life four times already."

A grin parted his lips. "You're giving me credit for the hard landing?"

"Yes, because I'm alive."

"I'm really glad you're alive." He pulled her into his arms, his breath a warm whisper on her cheeks. "By the way, you're an incredible dancer."

"It's the only place I've ever felt comfortable letting go. I'm a bit of a control freak in the rest of my life. But when the music starts, something comes over me."

"I like it when you let go. Think you can do that now— without any music?"

She smiled at the question. "I haven't been able to control anything since I got on a plane for Colombia. And I don't want to control you. I like the way you move, the way you touch me, the way you kiss." She caught her breath as his mouth covered hers.

A delicious warmth spread through her, and she closed her eyes, sinking into the kiss, savoring the taste of Diego's mouth, loving the way he was taking charge.

He was wrong about there being no music. She was hearing their song—the beat of their hearts, the swoosh of their breath between kisses, the rustle of their clothes as they got closer and closer.

Diego ran his hands through her hair, trapping her face for another kiss, and then he reached around her back and pulled down the zip of her dress. As the cool air hit her back, she had one sudden thought.

"Protection," she said shortly. "I—I don't have anything. Do you?"

"Yes. I got condoms earlier when you were trying on sexy dresses."

"Thinking ahead," she teased.

He gave her a sexy grin. "Hoping. Now let's get rid of some clothes."

She shimmied out of her dress, letting it fall to the floor. She'd picked up some new lingerie, too—silky black lace. She felt a momentary shyness under Diego's intense, appreciative gaze, but then she got busy working on the buttons of his shirt. She wanted to see him, too. And when she got his shirt off, she was more than a little turned on by the flat abs and rippling muscles. She'd seen evidence of Diego's physicality before, but this was even better.

"Nice," she said approvingly. "I was wondering what you were hiding."

"All you had to do was ask me to take off my shirt. I would have been happy to do so."

She liked how easy everything felt. It wasn't awkward at

all. It was right...perfectly right.

She threw her arms around his neck and gave him a kiss. And then they stripped off the rest of their clothes in happy abandon.

"I want to explore every inch of you," Diego said, pushing her onto the soft mattress.

"I feel the same way. I want to go slow and fast...at the same time."

"Or we could make love twice—three times." He slid his mouth down her neck as his hands teased her sensitive breasts and his hard body bore down on hers. Passion, desire, reckless need ran through her. She wanted to be wild. She wanted to be free. Every touch felt like Diego was releasing a weight that had been holding her down. *Why had she ever been so afraid of being herself?*

Heat ran through her as he tasted her breasts, as he slipped his fingers between her legs. She gasped with pleasure at his touch, his kiss, his...everything.

And that was the last clear thought she had for a very long time.

— ❯❯❮❮ —

Diego woke up to the buzz of his phone and the sunlight streaming through the part in the curtains. He had to slide out from under Tara, who was snuggled up against him, in order to grab his phone off the bedside table.

"Who's calling?" she asked, blinking her sleepy but beautiful blue eyes.

"It's a text from Wyatt. He's working on getting the security video from the Panama City Airport. He'll get back to us as soon as he has anything. He's also going to see what he can find on Michael Winters."

She sat up in bed, drawing the sheet over her breasts with a shyness that made him grin.

"I did see everything, you know," he told her.

"Oh, I know, believe me." She smiled back at him, as their remembered intimacy flowed between them. "Last night was...spectacular."

"That sounds right." His phone buzzed again, and he looked back at the screen, surprised to see another text from Wyatt.

"What does he say now?" Tara asked.

"Tracy got in touch with him last night. She's been trying to reach me. She has some information, and she wanted to know if I'd been in contact with him. He said he hadn't heard from me but wanted to let me know in case I decide I need whatever info Tracy might have."

"Do you want to call her back?"

"Not from this phone."

"You really don't trust her?"

"I'm not sure why, but I don't."

"What if she does have important information?"

He considered that possibility. "I can check in with her when we get back to the States. Right now, I'm more focused on Bethany's trail and what Wyatt can find out. I'll let him know to keep my whereabouts a secret for the time being."

"While you're doing all that, I'm going to take a shower."

As Tara left the room, he turned his attention back to his phone. He texted Wyatt his concerns about Tracy, and Wyatt agreed that keeping her out of the loop for the time being was a good decision. They exchanged a few more texts and then signed off.

Putting his phone down, he considered joining Tara in the shower.

Then he thought about giving her some privacy, some space.

Then he decided to get up and knock on the bathroom door.

"What took you so long?" she called out.

He opened the door and moved under the hot steamy spray of water, planting his hands on her gorgeous curves. "I wasn't sure if I was pressing my luck," he said. "The night is over. It's back to reality."

"Not quite yet." She put her palms against his chest as she took her time with a long, sweet kiss that made his gut ache with desire for her.

He didn't know how Tara had gotten under his skin so fast, but she was there. And he didn't know what he was going to do about it long term, but short term...that was another story.

An hour later, the blood was finally getting back into Diego's brain. After sharing an incredible shower with Tara, they'd dressed and gone downstairs to eat breakfast. As they were finishing up their meal, he got another text from Wyatt.

"What is it?" Tara asked.

"Bethany got on a nonstop flight out of Panama City to Los Angeles last Sunday at one p.m. She arrived at LAX at ten p.m. but that's where the trail ends. They need to check additional cameras around the airport to see if they can determine whether she left in a private car, a taxi, a ride share, or a bus."

"I can't believe she's in Los Angeles. And she got there last Sunday. I didn't leave for Colombia until Monday. We were in the same city, and I was calling her nonstop. Why didn't she text me or call me back or reach out on social media? She could have come by my apartment or gone to the school where I teach. I went to her apartment on Sunday. I have a key. Her mail was piled up on the floor. She definitely hadn't been there. Unless, I missed her by a few hours or something. You said she didn't get in until ten. I was there around five."

He waited until she ran out of breath. "The good news is she's not in Colombia anymore, and LA has to be safer than here."

"Maybe not, since she's still missing. Or maybe she's not missing." Tara blew out a breath. "What is going on?"

"I don't know. Perhaps, she's hiding. She didn't contact you because she didn't want to put you in danger."

"Was she alone at the airport?"

He glanced back at his phone. "Wyatt said she was carrying a duffel-sized bag and did appear to be on her own. He hopes to have more later."

"We need to get to Los Angeles."

"I agree." He paused as another long text came in. "He also has info on Michael. Apparently, my brother went to the University of Southern California and got a degree in economics. After graduation, he went to work for a wine distributor. Two years later, he opened his own wine bar in Beverly Hills, servicing a wealthy, celebrity clientele. It was so successful that he opened a second location in Newport Beach six months ago. He owns a condo in a luxury building in Century City."

"He's very successful for being how old?"

"Twenty-six," he muttered. "He had to have come up with a lot of cash to open two businesses." He paused, reading the next text. "Wyatt is digging into the financials. On first glance, everything looks legit, but it's doubtful that it really is."

"But it could be," she said.

"Now who's the optimistic one?" he asked, a bad feeling in his gut. He wanted to believe his brother was an honest businessman and not in league with the Salazars, but that would be stupid. "Where would a twenty-six-year-old get the money to do what he's done?"

"He could have a business partner."

"Well, we'll find out."

"It doesn't sound like he's hiding."

"No, it doesn't. He's living a very public life, according to Wyatt." He looked back at her. "All roads lead to LA."

"Is there any evidence of Michael and Bethany possibly

being involved with each other?"

"I forgot to ask." He sent another quick text. "I'm sure he would have let me know if he'd seen a link."

"Shall we go to the airport?"

He frowned at her question. "I think we need to be as careful getting out of here as Bethany was."

"You want to call Rosa's cousin again?"

"I don't think he'd want to help us, but I will try Lucas. He might be able to find a pilot who can take us to Panama City." He saw the uncertainty in her eyes. "It won't be like the last time."

"I'm still not thrilled about getting onto another small plane or even going to a small airfield."

"I know, but we do what must be done, right?"

She made a little face at him. "Yes, we do."

He smiled. "It's all forward progress, Tara."

"I agree. We know both Bethany and Michael are in Los Angeles. And Michael should be particularly easy to find. But what if..." Her voice fell away. "Never mind." She tucked her hair behind her ear, not looking him straight in the eye. "We should get our check."

"I know what you were going to say, Tara."

She gazed back at him. "No, you don't."

"I do. You were going to say what if he sees me, and he wants to kill me."

"Well, I wasn't going to put it exactly like that, but if he is working for the Salazars, and you end up on opposite sides of the law, what happens then? You will be his enemy, and he will be yours. Do you really want to face him, face that moment where each of you might have to make a terrible choice?"

"I'm still hoping for a different outcome than brother against brother." He paused, searching for the right words. "I need Mateo to know that I didn't forget about him, that I missed him, loved him, searched for him. I need him to know that there's a difference between my father and me. I didn't abandon him."

"Don't you think he knows that already?"

"I'm not sure. I was thirteen. He was eight. He looked up to me. I was his protector, but I didn't protect him that night. I didn't stay with him. I'd always promised him that I'd be there if he ever needed me. I didn't keep that promise."

"You were a kid yourself."

"It's not an excuse."

"No, it's not an excuse; it's a fact."

"I hear you, Tara. I don't even think you're wrong. I just have to play this out." He texted Lucas, requesting what he hoped would be his last favor, and then he called the waitress over and asked for their check.

While they were waiting for a reply, they went back to their room and packed the one suitcase they'd bought the day before to hold their new clothes.

Lucas got back to them a half hour later with the details. They needed to travel by bus to a small airfield near the village of Monteria. It would take approximately one hour. A pilot would be waiting to fly them to Panama City. They would be booked on a commercial flight from there.

Diego put his phone back in his pocket and looked at Tara. She'd put on new jeans and a knit top under her tan jacket, her hair swept up in a ponytail. "Ready to get out of Colombia?"

She got to her feet. "More than ready. But I must admit I'm going to miss this hotel room."

"There are other rooms," he told her, knowing exactly what she was going to miss. "We may be done with this country, but we're not done with each other."

"Not yet anyway," she murmured, an odd look in her eyes.

Fourteen

Tara felt incredibly tense as they took a long bus ride to an airfield near Monteria. They had to walk the last half mile, and every step in the open air made her feel like a target in a shooting range. But they made it to the tarmac without any bullets whizzing past her ear. Their pilot, Freddie De Salvo, had an easygoing smile and didn't ask them any questions, just ushered them into a small plane, much like the one they'd crashed in.

As she took a seat by the window and buckled her seat belt, memories of those last few moments before they'd hit the trees ran through her head. She could feel the plane shaking, feel the force of the trees as they hit, feel the thundering blow against her head.

"What are the odds?" Diego asked, drawing her attention to him, as he sat down next to her.

"Of what?" she asked distractedly.

"Running out of fuel, having to make a hard landing? What are the odds it would happen again?"

"You have the uncanny ability to read my mind."

"We'll be fine. The hard part is over. We made it to the plane without any gunshots."

"We still have to get off the ground and then get back down safely." She grabbed Diego's hand as the plane rolled down the runway, catching her breath as they took flight.

"Piece of cake," Diego said with a smile.

"I'd like some cake. I think it would make me feel better. A triple-layer chocolate cake with chocolate icing."

"That's rather specific."

"It's my favorite. My mom always made me that cake for my birthday. I miss her. I miss my dad, my life, Bethany. I miss being normal."

"I thought you said your normal life was boring."

"True, but I don't panic every other minute."

"You'll get back to your life. You'll see your parents again. Hopefully, Bethany, too."

"Hopefully," she echoed. "I'm okay now." She attempted to pull her hand away from his, but he hung on tight.

"I know you're okay, but I still like holding your hand. I like holding you. We hit the ground running this morning, and we're looking ahead, but before we get too far down the next road, I want to say that last night...it was something else."

She flushed at the intimate look in his eyes. "It was definitely something else. I don't know if it was the smartest idea."

"It was the best idea either of us have had in the last few days."

She couldn't help but smile at his words. "I had fun."

"Me, too."

She took a breath. "It's weird how connected we are, isn't it? Talk about odds. We both go to the same church to talk to the same priest at the same time. We're looking for different people, but now it appears those people are together—and so are we. It does feel fateful."

"It does. I might have to rethink my position on destiny.

While I'm doing that." He took her hand and raised it to his lips, pressing a kiss on her palm. "I'll need to hold your hand."

"I can live with that." She scooted closer to him and rested her head on his shoulder. "Can you live with being my pillow for an hour?"

"Absolutely. Why don't you get some rest?"

"You should sleep, too. Who knows what's going to be waiting for us when this plane lands?"

"Whatever it is, we'll face it together."

She closed her eyes, feeling completely safe for the moment. She just didn't think it would last.

They made it to Panama City without incident and an hour later, boarded a plane for Los Angeles. At some point during the seven-hour flight, she fell asleep again, her head on Diego's shoulder. When they landed at LAX, she let out a breath as she stepped off the plane. It felt good to be back on American soil.

"Where should we go now?" she asked, as they cleared customs and headed toward the exit. "Another hotel? Or we could go to my apartment, but it's about forty-five minutes from here, maybe an hour depending on traffic, and there's usually traffic."

"I don't think your apartment is a good option. I've made other arrangements."

She was surprised by his answer. "When did you do that?"

"I texted Wyatt from the plane. I bought internet while you were asleep. He's going to pick us up and take us to an FBI safe house."

"Do you still think we're in danger?"

"I'm not sure. We managed to stay out of trouble in Cartagena. It's possible we left the bad guys behind, but the fact that Bethany and Mateo are here makes me cautious. I would like to check out Bethany's apartment some time tomorrow."

"We can do that. I'm sure Michael is going to be at the top of your list, though."

"He is, but so is Bethany." Diego waved as a gray SUV approached. "There's Wyatt. Do you want the front?"

"No, I'll take the back."

As she got into the car, Wyatt gave her a smile. He was attractive, with wavy brown hair that was lighter than Diego's, brown eyes, and a stubble of beard on his jaw.

"You must be the beautiful, determined Tara," Wyatt said.

"I am determined," she said, liking how Diego had described her to his friend. "It's nice to meet you. I really appreciate all your help."

"No problem," Wyatt said. "I have to say I'm intrigued and curious as to whether the paths of your friend and Diego's brother are going to intersect."

"We've been wondering that, too," she murmured.

As Wyatt pulled away from the curb, he turned to Diego. "How was the flight?"

"Uneventful, which was appreciated," Diego replied.

"Good. I have some information for both of you. I thought the trail for Bethany had gone cold at the airport. But Bree did more digging, expanded the search area, and we have video of Bethany getting into a car." Wyatt handed Diego his phone. "Recognize this guy?"

Tara unbuckled her seat belt and scooted forward so she could watch the video over Diego's shoulder. Bethany stood at the curb, a duffel bag at her feet. Then a dark van pulled up. She looked both ways then picked up her bag, opened the door and got in. As the van moved forward under the light, she could see a dark-haired man at the wheel. "Who's driving?" she asked.

"His name is Pablo Salazar," Wyatt returned. "He's

twenty-four years old. He was born in Colombia to Santoro Salazar. He came to the US six years ago to go to school at Long Beach State. He dropped out after two years. He worked part time at a liquor store for a while and then was a driver for a catering company. Fourteen months ago, he was arrested for assault after a bar fight, but the case was dismissed when the victim chose not to pursue charges."

Everything Wyatt said made her nauseous. *Bethany had jumped into the car with one of the Salazars? What on earth was going on?* "Can I see the video again?" she asked.

Diego handed her the phone. "Bethany doesn't appear to be scared of Pablo. She gets in the car of her own volition," he said.

"I know, but I don't understand," she muttered, as she watched the video play once more. "Why would she go with this guy? We've been under the assumption that she's running from the Salazars."

"Maybe the wrong assumption." Diego took the phone back, so he could watch the video again. "She clearly knows Pablo. Maybe he's the man she's in love with."

"Rosa thought the guy's name started with M."

"Rosa didn't really remember," Diego said. "Is there anything else, Wyatt?"

"Pablo's last known address is an electronics store. It was obviously not his real address. But we can check at the store tomorrow and see if anyone knows him."

"An electronic store," she said. "The burner calls."

Diego met her gaze and nodded. "Another lead to check out." He turned back to Wyatt. "Anything more on my brother?"

"His wine bar is sponsoring a celebrity golf tournament tomorrow in Palos Verdes. Michael should be there. I think it would be a good place for you two to meet. It's a public venue—neutral ground."

"I'm not sure I want our reunion to be in public," Diego said.

"It's safer," Wyatt returned. "There's no telling how your brother will react when he sees you. You might not have been able to find him all these years, but it's possible he looked you up. He could know you're an FBI agent."

"If he'd looked me up, he would have come to see me," Diego began, then stopped abruptly. "No. He wouldn't have done that, not if he found out I was with the bureau, not if he's tied up with the Salazars."

"Exactly. You need to tread carefully," Wyatt said. "I think the golf tournament is a good option."

"You're right."

"As always," Wyatt said with a laugh.

As they got on the freeway, Tara sat back and refastened her seat belt, thinking about Bethany getting into the van with Pablo Salazar. *Was he her lover?* He was a couple of years younger, not that that mattered. But he was a criminal. He didn't seem to have a job, or one that was paying taxes. And he'd gotten arrested for assault, which meant he could be violent.

Her stomach continued to churn, and more questions ran around in her head. *Had she been wrong all this time? Was Bethany in trouble or was Bethany the trouble? Was her best friend, her little sister, a criminal, too?*

She really did not want to believe that.

Lost in thought, she barely heard what Diego and Wyatt were talking about, although it seemed like they were catching up rather than exchanging information.

She looked out at the window at the city lights. It was almost midnight. They'd started the day in Colombia and they were ending it in Los Angeles. What a crazy life she was now leading. And she had no idea where she'd be tomorrow.

A few minutes later, Wyatt turned in to a parking garage under what appeared to be a duplex. There were four spots in the garage; three of them were empty, a silver sporty SUV in the last spot.

"You can stay in this condo tonight and tomorrow—

longer if you need," Wyatt said. "There's no one in the second unit, so you'll have complete privacy. That's Bree's car. She's upstairs stocking your refrigerator. We went to the store on the way in."

"You called Bree in, too?" Diego asked.

"She was with me when you texted. All for one—one for all, right?"

"Right," Diego agreed, as Wyatt parked the car.

"I'm glad you're out of Colombia. It will make things easier."

"I hope so," Diego said. "But let's see what LA has in store for us."

Wyatt unlocked one of the two doors leading out of the garage and waved them inside.

She went up the stairs to the main floor, impressed with the thick carpeting under her feet and the beautiful white leather furniture in the living room. There was also a wall of windows that apparently overlooked the ocean.

"Wow," she said. "This is not what I expected."

"We use it as both a front and as a safe house," Wyatt explained.

"Hello," a woman said, as she came out of the kitchen. She was a pretty woman, with brown hair and sparkling green eyes. She gave Diego a big hug and then turned to her. "I'm Bree."

"Tara Powell."

Bree shook her hand. "It's great to meet you. I'm sorry about your friend, but we will do everything we can to help you find her."

"I am so grateful."

"It's what we do. I got you both some food. I thought you might be hungry and we all know airplane food is terrible." Bree smiled at Diego. "I can't believe we're finally in the same room, on the same continent, Diego. It's been too long."

"It has. I just wish the circumstances were different."

"Unfortunately, these are usually our kind of

circumstances," she said with a laugh.

"Good point."

"This place has a great security system," Wyatt added. "There's a door through the bedroom closet that leads into an enclosed room where you'll find security camera monitors for all entrances and exits to the building, including the garage. You'll also find some weapons there. The code for the door is 4362. You can use the SUV for transportation. Bree will give me a ride home." He tossed the keys to Diego. "I also brought you a laptop from the office." He tipped his head toward the computer on the dining room table.

"You've thought of everything," Diego replied.

"Do you want backup at the golf tournament tomorrow?" Bree asked. "I assume you are going there, right?"

"Yes, I'm going. No, I don't need backup."

"I'll be your backup," Tara interjected.

Diego frowned. "We'll talk about it."

"No, we won't talk about it, because that's what's happening. We're still working together, Diego. Don't think we're not."

He put up a hand in retreat. "All right. You're coming, too."

"You bet I am."

Bree smiled at their exchange. "Come by the office afterward," Bree said. "I'll text you the address. By the way, Parisa and Damon will be in town tomorrow with their significant others, so you'll get to see them, too."

"Really?" Diego asked in surprise. "Why?"

"It's for the dedication," Bree answered. "For Jamie. I know you were invited, Diego."

"I vaguely remember an email about that."

"Jamie's father is funding a new wing at the children's hospital in Jamie's name. They're breaking ground on Wednesday, and he'd like us all to be at the ceremony and at a party later in the evening."

"It's all coming back to me. I meant to answer the email.

I've been on the road a lot the last few weeks."

"Well, you're in town, so maybe you can go. It wouldn't be bad for you to talk to Vincent again," Bree added. "We can get your take on whether you think he's playing us."

"I can't think about that now."

"You should think about it. Because it feels like it's your turn, Diego, like someone is pulling the strings, and you're dancing on hot coals, running for your life, like I did, and Wyatt did—Parisa and Damon, too. You're the only one who hadn't had a secret from his past come back to haunt him—until now."

Tara didn't know if Diego was swayed by Bree's words, but she certainly was. Maybe Diego needed to pay more attention to what Bree was trying to tell him.

"I hear you," Diego said somberly. "I will think about it."

"Good. Once this is all resolved, we can talk further. In the meantime, I really hope things go well with your reunion with your brother. I remember the first time you told us the story back at Quantico. It was when I realized how much scar tissue you carry around."

"We all have our wounds," Diego said quietly.

"We'll see you tomorrow," Wyatt said.

"Oh, Diego," Bree said. "There's a special dessert in the kitchen." She gave him a wink.

"Thank you," Diego said.

After they left, he bolted the door and said, "I'm hungry. Shall we see what's in the kitchen?"

"I could eat." She followed him down the hall into a gourmet kitchen. Bree had definitely bought out the store, with plenty of bread, crackers, chips, and cereal on the counter as well as a bowl of fresh fruit, and… "Oh, my God." She gave him an amazed and delighted smile as she held up a plastic container holding a triple-layer chocolate cake. "This is the special dessert? Did you do this?"

"Maybe."

"I can't believe you asked them to pick up the cake."

"I know it's not your birthday—actually, I don't know if it's not your birthday."

"It's not. I was born in September."

"Okay then. Anyway, you've had a rough couple of days and I thought you deserved some cake, and it's big enough to share."

She was amazed by his caring gesture. In the midst of everything that was happening, he'd thought about her. She walked over to him, threw her arms around his neck and gave him a long, hot kiss. "We'll eat the cake later. Let's go into the bedroom."

"Really?" he asked with surprise. "It just took some chocolate cake—"

"No, it just took you being you." She gazed into his eyes. "You're a good man, Diego Rivera."

"I feel the same way about you—well, not the man part," he said with a laugh.

She smiled back at him, then leaned in to take another kiss.

* * *

Tara woke up hungry at eight fifteen in the morning. She rolled over onto her side and saw that Diego was still asleep. She smiled, allowing herself to savor the handsome features of the man next to her. His thick brown hair was completely tousled from where she'd run her fingers through it. There was a shadow of beard on his jaw that made him even sexier, if that was possible. His face was so perfectly formed: wide-set eyes, long nose, and strong jaw. The hint of the bruise from the shiner he'd gotten a few days earlier only made him more ruggedly appealing.

This man could not only make her scream with pleasure, he could protect her; he could make her laugh; he could inspire her. No matter what happened next, she would never regret what they'd had together.

As her gaze drifted down to his broad shoulders and powerful arms, her heart beat a little faster. She couldn't help but remember their night of lovemaking, how perfectly they'd fit together, how they'd moved as if they were one person. She'd never experienced such explosive chemistry with anyone.

She'd always been a little restrained when it came to sex—too shy, not adventurous enough, sometimes a little awkward—but with Diego that had certainly changed. And what was weird was that she actually felt more like her real self with him than with anyone else.

They'd been through a lot together and she'd not only come to respect him and trust him, she also really liked him. And the fact that he'd had Bree pick up a chocolate cake for her made her heart melt.

That thought also made her stomach rumble.

Sliding out of bed so as not to wake Diego, she used the bathroom and grabbed a terry cloth bathrobe off a hook on the door. Then she went into the kitchen and opened the plastic container.

Cake for breakfast actually sounded perfect. But she also needed coffee. She started the coffeemaker, then cut herself a slice of cake and took it to the small table by the window. They had a beautiful view of the Pacific Ocean and there were already surfers in the sea taking advantage of the sunny morning.

It felt good to be back in the States, although she was nervous about what the day would bring. She was more than a little curious to meet Diego's brother. However, she still had a sinking feeling in the pit of her stomach that the reunion between brothers might not be as joyful as Diego wanted it to be.

But there was no turning back. The truth would be whatever it was, and Diego would have to face it and deal with it.

He wasn't a man who backed down from a challenge, but

she suspected this might be the biggest personal challenge he'd ever faced.

"Cake for breakfast?" Diego asked, coming into the kitchen, wearing a matching robe. He walked over and gave her a kiss.

"You taste like toothpaste," she said with a smile.

"And you taste like chocolate. Maybe that's the way I should eat my piece, off your lips."

A shiver ran down her spine at that sexy thought. "You didn't get enough of me last night?"

"Not even close."

"Well, still, this piece is mine. You need to get your own."

"Ah, territorial when it comes to cake. Good to know." He straightened. "I think I'll start with coffee. Thanks for getting it going. Do you want some?"

"Yes, please."

He filled a mug and brought it over to her. "I'll check for some creamer."

"This is fine. I like it black. I'm using up my calories on the cake."

He opened the fridge. "How about some eggs to go with that? Maybe an omelet? Bree stocked up on vegetables: mushrooms, onions, tomatoes."

"That all sounds delicious. Do you want me to make it?"

"I can do it."

"You can cook?"

"Of course. I've been on my own a long time."

"So have I, but I'm still not much of a cook. Did your mom teach you?"

"She did. Cooking was one of her passions. I remember her soups the most," he said, as he placed ingredients for the omelets on the kitchen island. He paused, a fond look in his eyes. "She made a great chicken tortilla soup and her chili was amazing. It would simmer in a pot all day. The house would smell of garlic and onions. I'd come home from baseball or basketball practice and inhale a couple of bowls."

It was nice to hear Diego share a happy memory. "My mom did not care much for cooking," she said. "But my dad loved to barbecue, so he would go out on the patio and throw whatever meat or fish he had on the grill and my mom would open a bagged salad or throw some potatoes in the oven. I eventually learned how to make some sides to go with my dad's proteins, and we all ate a lot better. But when I'm not with them, I don't cook much. I do a lot of takeout." She paused. "Where exactly is your home, Diego?"

"I have an apartment in DC, but I haven't been in it much the last few years."

"And that's where you'll go when you're done with all this?"

"That was the plan, but it might change. I took this particular job assignment because it allowed me to travel in South America, and I could look for my mother and brother at the same time. Now that my mom is dead, and Michael is here, well, I don't know that I need to be down there anymore, or if I even want to be down there anymore." He cracked a couple of eggs into a bowl, tossing the shells into the trash.

She got up and went over to him, putting her arm around his waist. "I know that whatever is coming next might be really hard for you. If there's anything I can do…"

He smiled down at her. "I'm good. And you've done a lot for me, Tara, more than you probably would believe."

"I haven't been the one saving your life, Diego."

"No, but you've been the one helping me sort through everything, letting me talk things out, and most importantly, just listening."

"I'm always happy to listen. We do make a pretty good team."

"I think so, too. So why don't you make yourself useful and cut up some tomatoes?"

"You've got it." As she went to work on the tomatoes, she once again felt a wave of contentedness. This kind of relationship was what she had always wanted. But she was very aware of the ticking clock in the background. They didn't have time to enjoy this moment for long. They had to find Michael and Bethany, and then who knew where they would end up?

Fifteen

—⟩⟩⟨⟨—

Two hours later, they headed down the Pacific Coast Highway to the golf tournament, which was being held at the Bella Vista Golf Course in Palos Verdes. Along the way, Tara rolled down the window and let the sea air blow through the car. The familiar sights made her feel a lot less terrified than she'd been the past few days. She still didn't know if danger had followed them or would catch up to them as soon as they started asking questions, but at least she was on her home turf. They also had backup, maybe not with them in the car, but Wyatt and Bree had made it clear that they were available for whatever was needed. Diego had made some really excellent friends at Quantico.

"It's a nice day," Diego murmured, tipping his head toward the ocean view.

"Beautiful. I wish we could take better advantage of it, like a walk along the beach."

"Maybe later."

"That's optimistic."

"Apparently, that's me," he said lightly.

"Yes," she agreed, exchanging a warm smile with him. "And clearly you are not looking too far ahead." She would have thought he'd be more nervous about possibly seeing his brother this morning.

"No, I'm not. I'll deal with whatever happens when it happens."

"I'm a little surprised you didn't want one of your friends to come with us this morning," she said, considering why he'd made that decision. "It's because you don't want them to be involved directly, isn't it? It's fine if they do the background stuff, but you want to keep them away from the Salazars."

He shot her a quick look. "I'm not afraid they can't handle themselves but bringing FBI agents into this situation makes it less personal, more professional, and I'm not prepared to go there yet."

"Because then your friends might be obligated to bring Michael in for whatever illegal actions he's involved in."

"Yes. And I don't want the first time I talk to my brother to be about what he does for a living."

"I can understand that, but as Wyatt pointed out earlier, Michael might already know you're an FBI agent. If you show up and surprise him, he could react negatively."

"He could, but we'll be at a celebrity golf tournament. I think he'll handle himself accordingly."

"Or pick up an iron and take a swing at you."

"I have quick reactions."

"I hope so."

"I don't think my brother is a danger to me or to you, Tara, but I'm not sure if that's my heart talking instead of my brain. He could be a cold-blooded killer for all I know."

She shivered at that thought. "I'm going to side with your heart for now. It makes me feel better."

—➤➤◄◄—

Despite his best attempt to stay in the moment, Diego felt

his muscles tighten with each mile. By the time they pulled into the parking lot at the golf course, his heart was beating a little too fast, which was unusual for him. He'd always been able to keep his calm in intense situations. It was that ability that made him a good agent. But this was different. This was personal.

He had no idea what he was going to say to his brother or what Mateo would say to him. *Would they even recognize each other?* It had been eighteen years. They were men now—very different men.

As they got out of the car and walked toward the main entrance, Tara slipped her hand into his and said, "Whatever you find out—at least you'll know. That will be better than the wondering."

"I keep telling myself that."

The country club was beautiful, and Tara murmured appreciation as they walked up stone steps into a castle-like building. They passed through the lobby with its dark-paneled walls, by a gourmet restaurant and a pro shop. On the back deck was a bar and grill with open-air seating as well as the check-in area for the tournament. A digital board showed the current score leaders and what hole they were playing.

It was almost noon, so some of the first groups were starting to come off the course. He searched for Michael Winters but didn't see him on the list of players. His gaze then swept the crowd. When he saw a man with dark hair and eyes similar to his own, his heart stopped. He grabbed Tara by the arm. "He's there," he said, tipping his head toward the edge of the deck where Michael was talking to two older, white-haired men, who had to be in their seventies.

Michael wore charcoal-gray slacks and a button-down shirt, a Rolex on his wrist. He looked every inch the young, wealthy entrepreneur that he claimed to be.

He struggled to take in a breath. *Was this really his brother? And was his brother really a criminal?* It was hard to correlate this confident, laughing young man with the

Salazar cartel.

"He's handsome," Tara said. "He looks a little like you."

"We both took after our mother." Michael was tall, but he thought he still had an inch or two on him. "Let's do this."

As they approached the group, his brother turned his head and locked eyes with him. Then his gaze widened, shock in his eyes.

Mateo recognized him.

"Hello," Tara said brightly, smiling at the two older men. "I hope you don't mind if we steal a few moments with Michael."

"Not at all," one of the men said. "We were heading into lunch anyway."

As they moved aside, he let go of Tara's hand and stepped forward. She hung back a little, giving him this moment. He swallowed a sudden knot in his throat, not sure he could even speak. He'd thought about this meeting a million times, but now it was here. Finally, he got out one word. "Mateo."

His brother paled. "It is you, isn't it?"

He nodded. "And it's you, too. I wasn't sure we'd recognize each other. But I knew you right away, and you knew me."

"My name is Michael now," his brother said, a harsh note in his voice.

"Michael Winters. I heard Mom changed your name."

"Who did you hear that from?"

"I've been looking for you and Mom for a long time. I know now why I couldn't find either of you. Your names were changed."

"What are you doing here, Diego?"

"I wanted to see you again. Can we talk?"

"I'm busy."

"And I'm not leaving until we have a conversation, Mateo."

"It's Michael, and I don't want to discuss the past."

He pushed past his brother's reluctance. "It wasn't my choice to go with Dad. He forced me."

"Stop talking," Mateo ordered.

"Not a chance. We can do this here, or we can do it in a more private setting. Your choice, but this discussion is happening."

His brother sent him a hard, stony look. "Fine. Let's take a walk. I can give you five minutes. That's it. And you can leave your shadow behind."

"Sorry. Tara comes with me. It's only a conversation. What are you afraid of?"

"Nothing. I'm afraid of nothing." Michael blew out a breath, then strode briskly toward a nearby flight of stairs.

They followed him down the steps, past a row of golf carts and along a tree-lined path that led away from the clubhouse. When there was no one in sight, his brother stopped, folding his arms across his chest, his gaze almost defiant.

It reminded him of the time he'd forced his brother to tell him who was bullying him in the third grade. Mateo had been reluctant to talk, to ask for help. He'd never wanted Diego to think he was weak.

"I saw Mom's grave in Cascada," he began. "I didn't even know she was dead until a few days ago."

Mateo gave what appeared to be an uncaring shrug. "She died a long time ago. I barely remember her."

"There were fresh flowers on her grave. Who put them there?"

"Probably someone in the family."

"Or maybe you pay someone to do that when you can't do it yourself. She loved flowers at Easter. I remember that. I think you do, too."

"What do you want, Diego? Do you want me to say I'm glad you found me after all these years?"

"That would be nice," he shot back. "We are brothers."

"We *were* brothers. We haven't been since the day your

father kicked me and my mother to the curb."

"She was my mother, too. I loved her. I loved you. But I couldn't get back to you. Dad wouldn't tell me where either of you had gone. It drove me crazy. I thought Mom would try to come back, but she didn't."

"She couldn't. Your father made sure of that," Mateo spat out.

"What did he do?"

"I don't know exactly, but she said we had to disappear forever. She insisted we start a new life. She got married again. And then she died."

"And you were alone."

"I wasn't alone. I had family—the family she married into. They're my family now."

"The Salazars."

Michael's gaze narrowed. "What do you know about them?"

"I know the Salazars raised you after Mom's second husband Tomas died. I know they run a very lucrative drug cartel with operations all over the world, including here in Los Angeles. I know you went to USC, and now you run two wine bars and live a very expensive life."

"I'm a smart guy."

"And well connected."

"Most rich people are; that's how they become wealthy. What do you do?"

He hesitated, not wanting to end this conversation just yet, and it certainly would end if he revealed his job. "Dad sent me to military school because I was causing him too many problems. I ended up in the Army."

"You're a soldier?"

"I'm out now, but, yeah I was a soldier."

"Probably an officer. You always liked to order people around."

"I can't deny that," he said, for a brief moment, seeing his brother's guard come down. "I missed you, Mateo."

"I told you to call me Michael."

"Sorry—Michael." He paused. "Your last name—Winters. Is that the name of your biological father?"

"That's what Mom told me when she changed my name. I asked her where he was, but she couldn't tell me. I said if he didn't want me, either, I didn't need his name—but I was eight, I had no choice. She insisted that if she changed my name, it would make it impossible for your father to ever find me and hurt me."

"It did make you difficult, almost impossible, to find. But I don't think my dad would have hurt you."

"Are you serious?" Mateo challenged, anger in his gaze. "Your father raised me for eight years. He called me his son. He told me he loved me. He said I was just like him. And then he found out I didn't have his blood, and he tossed me out, as if I were nothing. The family I'm with now is loyal. They don't throw people away."

His heart sank at his brother's words. Mateo definitely felt loyalty to the Salazars, which meant he was involved in the organization.

Tara put a hand on his back, and he knew she was reminding him not to forget about Bethany. "There's another reason I came to talk to you, Michael. Do you know Bethany Cooper?"

A light flickered in Michael's eyes. "Why do you ask?"

"Because she's missing," Tara interrupted, drawing Michael's gaze to her. "She's my friend, and I'm worried about her. She said she was in love with a guy named Michael. Is that you?"

"She's not in love with me," he said flatly. "She was supposed to come to LA last week, but she blew me off."

"You haven't seen her this week at all?" Tara challenged. "Because she landed in LA a week ago Sunday."

"Well, she hasn't been in touch with me. And I'm done talking."

"Wait." Tara jumped in front of Michael. "Please. You

have to help me. Bethany is like my younger sister. She moved in with me and my family after her mom died. I'm Tara—Tara Powell. Are you sure you didn't hear her talk about me?" She paused, then moved on. "It doesn't matter. Bethany is in trouble, and I'm pretty sure your family is involved, because I went to Colombia to find her, and someone tried to kill me several times."

Michael's gaze narrowed. "I don't know what you're talking about. I've been in LA the past month."

"But you know things are happening in Colombia," Diego put in, drawing his brother's attention back to him. "You must have heard about the shooting at the church, Father Manuel's murder. If you grew up there, you must have known him."

"Yes, I knew him, and that was tragic," Michael said somberly. "But that doesn't have anything to do with me, and I don't know where Bethany is."

"You can find out if someone in your family knows something," Tara put in.

"They don't."

"They do," Diego corrected. "Pablo Salazar picked Bethany up at LAX when she got off the plane from Colombia."

Michael stiffened. "You're mistaken."

"We're not." He opened up the video on his phone and played it for Michael. "That's Pablo, isn't it?"

"Where did you get this? Are you a cop?" he asked suspiciously.

"No, but we've talked to law enforcement, and they're looking for Bethany, too. I'm sure they'll be speaking to you soon."

"About what? It looks like Bethany jumped into the car with Pablo. They're probably hooking up," he said, an edge to his voice. "I knew I couldn't trust her. All women cheat and lie."

He wondered if that was a dig at their mother.

"They're not hooking up," Tara argued. "I would bet my life on it. In fact, I have bet my life on it."

Michael looked back at the video. "Why do you think she's in trouble?"

"Because of what's been happening ever since I started looking for her," Tara explained. "I went to Cascada and asked questions all over town and then someone shot at us."

"How do you two know each other?" Michael asked suspiciously.

"We met in Cascada," Diego said. "I had a lead on Mom. I went to talk to Father Manuel. Tara was looking for Bethany. When the shooting occurred, we ran for cover and ended up in the cemetery. I had just discovered Mom's grave when another shooter came after us. Later that day, we discovered that Tara's room at the hotel had been searched. We went to Ventana's and were jumped outside the bar. We barely escaped."

"And then we went to Medellin," Tara continued. "We went to an airfield, because we had heard Bethany was looking for a private flight to Cartagena. The pilot left for a moment, and more shooters arrived. Does any of this ring a bell?"

"Not one word," his brother said. "And, like I told you, I don't know where Bethany is."

"But you probably know where Pablo is," Tara said. "If you care for her at all, you'll help us find her before someone hurts her."

Michael's jaw tightened as he thought about what they'd told him. "Pablo wouldn't hurt her."

"Are you sure about that?" he challenged. "Did you know she was in Cascada without you?"

Michael stared back at him. "If I see or hear from Bethany, I'll let her know you're looking for her."

"What about Pablo?"

"I'll talk to him. But for now, I have to get back to the tournament."

"Mateo—Michael," he corrected again, as his brother shot him an angry look. "We still have a lot to talk about. You can't walk away."

"We have nothing to talk about, Diego. Whatever relationship we had ended a long time ago."

"Whatever relationship we had?" he murmured in bemusement. "We were brothers."

"But we aren't anymore."

"That's not true. We're blood. And that means something."

"You need to stay away from me. I'm not the brother you remember. That kid is gone. Mateo died a long time ago. I'm Michael Winters, and you mean nothing to me."

The words stabbed him in the heart. "I can't accept that."

"You don't have a choice. Stay clear."

"Is that a threat?"

"It's a warning. I have another family now. My loyalty is to them."

"Even if one of those family members kidnapped your girlfriend?"

Michael's eyes burned with anger. "That didn't happen."

"Find Pablo. Do it soon."

Michael brushed past them, striding down the path with quick, furious strides.

Tara gave him a desperate look. "Should we go after him? Press him harder?"

"We've planted the seed. I think he'll dig it up. He wants to know what's going on with Pablo and Bethany."

"Is that your heart or your brain talking?"

"Both. Michael was surprised that Bethany was missing, and even more confused that she and Pablo were together. I guarantee he's going to find out what that was all about."

"But what will he do about it?"

"That I don't know."

Sixteen

—⟩⟩⟨⟨—

When they walked through the lobby and out the main entrance, he saw Mateo heading toward the valet.

"Let's get to our car," he said, picking up the pace. "Michael is heading out, and I'm guessing he's going to talk to Pablo."

"Do you think so?" Tara asked a bit breathlessly, as he hustled her across the parking lot.

"I really do."

When they reached the car, he fired up the engine and drove back toward the front entrance. He was relieved to see Michael still waiting for his car, so he pulled over behind a golf cart to wait. Michael was on his phone now, and his body posture was angry.

Pulling out his own phone, he texted Wyatt, asking him to see if he could get access to Michael's phone records. They could at least find out who he'd called if all he did was drive home or back to his wine bar.

"Do you think he's talking to Pablo?" Tara asked.

"Or someone who can tell him why Pablo was with

Bethany."

"I wonder if Bethany thought Pablo was taking her to Michael."

"That's a possibility."

"Or were Bethany and Pablo hooking up as Michael suggested?" She blew out a breath in frustration. "I really want some answers to my questions."

"We're getting closer."

"I'm sorry, Diego."

"For what?" he asked in surprise.

"I'm making this all about Bethany when what happened back there was a big moment for you and your brother. How are you feeling?"

"Honestly, I'm not sure. He definitely wasn't happy to see me. Mateo made that clear." He thought back to their discussion. "But there was a moment…"

"When he mentioned that you liked to order people around."

He met her gaze. "Yes. It almost felt like we were brothers again. When he was a little kid, he used to tell me not to order him around. I said I was the big brother; it was my job. But he didn't like it. He still doesn't. Clearly, he doesn't want a relationship with me."

"He's probably scared to let you back into his life. He had to let everyone go—first you and your father, then his mom and stepfather. It's a lot of loss for one person. And even though you were a kid yourself and you weren't responsible for the family breaking apart, trusting you again might be difficult. It might hurt too much."

He thought about her words and wanted to believe that fear was the reason Michael didn't want to see him again. But it was possible it was just outright hatred.

"I don't know," he said.

"Think about it, Diego. You were the chosen one. He was the mistake, the baby who broke up the family. He was rejected by your father. It was different for you."

"Not that different. My mother rejected me and kept Mateo. She never looked for me. She never tried to get me back."

"I can't imagine why she didn't fight harder to see you. Frankly, the whole situation is tragic, and I blame both your parents for hurting you and your brother. They should have put both of you first. That's what good parents do."

"You're right. They really suck. All these years I put my mom on a different level than my dad. I had all kinds of reasons in my head for why she couldn't see me. But whatever my father did to make her stay away...she still could have chosen to come back. She got married again, and to a lawyer. Surely, Tomas would have helped her find me if she'd wanted to. Hell, she probably could have gotten the Salazars to back her up. Even my father would have been no match for them. But she didn't do any of that."

"Maybe she thought you would reject her because so much time had passed."

"Maybe." He pulled out from behind the golf cart as his brother got into his car and drove toward the exit. He kept a little distance between them, which wasn't difficult since his brother seemed to be in a hurry to get to wherever he was going.

"He's driving fast," Tara commented.

"Looks like he's heading for the freeway."

"Do you think he'll spot us?"

"Hopefully not."

He pressed his foot down on the gas as he followed his brother onto the 405. Mateo was heading south, toward the beaches of Manhattan, Hermosa, Redondo and Newport.

Was he going to his wine bar in Newport? Was this going to be a completely wasted trip?

That question was answered when Michael exited the freeway in Long Beach and drove away from the ocean into a lower-income neighborhood.

When Michael pulled over in front of an apartment

building, Diego slid into a parking spot a block away.

"What now?" Tara asked.

"We see where he's going, and then I follow him." He shot her a quick look. "I want you to stay here, Tara."

She immediately shook her head. "I don't want to stay here alone, and we're better together."

"I don't know who's in that apartment building. There could be multiple members of the Salazars present. It could be very dangerous."

"Bethany could be there, too."

He sighed. "I was thinking your stubbornness was a good trait until now."

"I'm going to follow you, Diego. So I can go with you or I can come in behind you."

"Or I could drive away."

"Then I'll find a car and come back. Look, you're not responsible for me. It's my decision." She opened her car door and stepped onto the sidewalk.

He jumped out of the car, thinking if he didn't act fast, she'd barge into that building without him. "Okay," he said, grabbing her arm. "But we still need to be smart."

"I'm fine with you taking charge. I'm not looking to get hurt or cause a bigger problem. Just don't leave me out of it."

He saw the determination in her gaze and couldn't help but admire her courage. "All right. We'll check out the building, but we'll go in quiet, see what we can hear before we make any moves."

"Deal."

He led the way, keeping Tara behind him. When they got to the two-story building, he saw that the lobby door was ajar. The building showed four mailboxes—four units. They had a twenty-five percent chance of finding the right one. He pulled out his gun, keeping it at the ready, and then walked into the lobby. Tara kept a hand on his back, staying close to him. The first floor showed two apartment doors, but it was very quiet. There appeared to be voices coming from the floor above.

He motioned for Tara to follow him up the stairs. When they got to the landing, he heard two male voices in the first apartment. They were arguing.

He stopped by the door to listen. Tara crowded in next to him.

"What the hell did you do?" Michael yelled. "Where is Bethany?"

Diego couldn't hear what the other man said, but he heard a body being shoved up against a wall, followed by a groan of pain.

"That must be Pablo," he murmured.

"It doesn't sound like Michael knows where Bethany is," she whispered back.

"She's definitely not here."

"Why didn't you tell me you picked her up at the airport?" Michael demanded. "What were you doing with her? Were you hooking up? Don't lie to me."

"No. No. It wasn't like that."

"Then what was it like?"

He heard a crash, as if someone had knocked over a chair.

"You broke my fucking nose!" the other man yelled.

"I'll break your arm if you don't start talking."

Diego's gut twisted at the menace in Michael's voice. It was difficult to believe this was the same younger brother who never wanted to step on a bee or a spider, preferring to get the insects to a safer place. Clearly, Michael had changed. And he could not underestimate what he might do.

"Stay here," he told Tara.

"What are you going to do?"

"I'm going in. Please, hang back. And if there are any shots, get the hell out of here and call the cops. If we're both dead, there's no one left to look for Bethany." As he said the words, he knew he probably should have started with that argument.

Indecision played through Tara's blue eyes, but then she

nodded.

Putting his hand on the doorknob, he realized it hadn't latched. Michael had probably been too pissed off to close it.

"Tell me where she is," Michael yelled again.

He pulled out his gun and kicked the door open. Michael jumped, taking out his own weapon, while the other man sank to the ground.

It was the man from the photo. Pablo had long brown hair and a thick beard that was dripping with blood from his nose.

"You followed me?" Michael demanded, fury in his dark eyes.

"Yes. You were in such a hurry to get here, you didn't notice. This must be Pablo. Where is Bethany?" He couldn't believe he was pointing a gun at his brother. But Michael wasn't backing down, and neither was he.

"I don't know," Michael said. "And this is not your business."

"It's my business," Tara put in, coming into the room behind him.

Apparently, she'd assessed the situation and thought he was in control, which wasn't even close to the truth.

"Stay back," he told her.

"Oh, my God," Tara said suddenly, ignoring his order, as she walked over to the table. She picked up a small clutch purse. "This is Bethany's purse. She was here. Where is she now?"

"We just want Bethany," he told his brother. "That's all we want. We don't care what else is going on here."

"Why do you have a gun?" Mateo asked suspiciously. "You said you weren't a cop."

"I'm not, but I thought I might need a weapon once I found out you were involved with the Salazars. I didn't know what kind of man you'd become. I'd like to believe you're not a man who hurts a woman, especially a woman he loves."

Michael paled, but he didn't lower the gun. "I'm my own

man. And I'm not involved with the Salazars; I am one of them. The Winters name allows me to move under the radar, to separate myself from the Salazars when it comes to law enforcement and other business parties. But make no mistake. They are my family."

"I get it." Disappointment ran through him. "Like I said, we only want Bethany. So why don't we lower our weapons and talk?"

Michael stared back at him. "You first."

For a split second, he wondered if his younger brother would actually shoot him, but it was a risk he had to take, not only for Bethany, but to prove to Mateo that he still trusted him in some small way. He put his gun back in the waistband of his jeans. And then Mateo lowered his weapon.

"What happened to Bethany?" he asked again.

"Pablo said she took off." Michael shot a dark look at his friend. "And as you can see, she's not here."

"She wouldn't leave without her purse," Tara said. "Her wallet is in here. Her credit cards. What did you do to her?"

"I didn't touch her," Pablo said, staggering to his feet. "The bitch stole from me."

"Stop talking," Michael told the younger man.

"First you want me to talk, then you don't," Pablo muttered, as he moved toward the kitchen to get a towel.

"Are you the one who searched my room in Cascada?" Tara asked Pablo. "Were you looking for what you say she stole?"

"Did she give it to you?" Pablo asked.

Tara didn't answer his question. "Where is she?"

"I don't know. She ran out of here," Pablo said, trying to stem the flood of blood from his nose.

"When was that?" she asked.

"Last Sunday."

"That's it. We're done," Michael said. "Get out—both of you."

"You're protecting him?" Tara asked in bewilderment.

"Bethany loves you, Michael. How can you choose him over her?"

"Because I'm his family," Pablo answered. "Right, Michael?"

"Right." Michael raised the gun once more. "I'm not going to ask you again. Leave now."

"No way," Tara argued. "I want Bethany back."

"Diego—get her out of here," Michael ordered.

He weighed his brother's words, sensing a hint of desperation in his tone. Michael couldn't go against Pablo, at least not in front of them. Pablo also probably didn't live in this apartment alone. There were at least two bedrooms that he could see. This situation could get worse. Right now, Michael had it under control. That could change.

"Tara, let's go," he said.

She gave him a look that suggested he was out of his mind. "No, not until we have more information."

"We'll keep looking for Bethany, but like Michael said, she's not here."

Tara looked like she wanted to argue, but she must have read something in his expression, because she finally nodded. Then she turned to his brother. "This isn't over. If either of you hurt her, you will pay."

He almost smiled at her crazy threat. *Did she even realize who she was threatening?* Probably not. She was too caught up in her determination to find Bethany. She stormed out of the apartment, and he quickly followed. She had a fire going on inside her, and they made it back to the car in seconds. Once inside, she slammed the door, and blew out an angry breath.

"You want to yell at me for leaving?" he asked her, as he started the car.

"I'm guessing you had a good reason," she said tightly. "And I told you I'd let you call the shots."

"Which you didn't do when you came into the apartment."

"You had your gun on Michael. I thought you could take him."

"I'm flattered by your confidence."

"So, what was your reason?"

"It was the tone in Michael's voice. He had control over Pablo. The guy didn't fight back, or if he did, he was terrible at it. But I don't think Pablo lives there alone. I got the sense Michael wanted us out of there before anyone else showed up."

"I thought it was something like that."

"You do realize you just threatened two members of the Salazar cartel?"

"So what?" she asked with a cynical shrug. "They're already trying to kill us."

"True."

"I know it wasn't smart," she admitted. "But when I saw Bethany's bag on the table, I wanted to explode. It confirmed that she's still in trouble. She wouldn't leave without her purse. Pablo threatened her, or he hurt her. God, he might have killed her, and he just didn't want to tell Michael."

"Let's not go that far. It's possible he told the truth. Maybe she did run away."

"But where did she go? That was a week ago Sunday. Where has she been since then?"

"I don't know, but she's in LA. She knows the area. She's probably hiding somewhere."

"I need to turn on my real phone. Maybe she left me a message."

"Go ahead," he said.

Tara dug into her bag and pulled out her phone. As it whirred to life, she said, "It didn't seem like Michael knew where she was, though."

"I agree. Pablo and Bethany are caught up in something, and Michael is in the dark. He's very angry about that."

"What do you think she stole from Pablo—money?"

He considered her question. "It had to be more than that.

They wouldn't have put so much effort into trying to find her, to see if you had something, if it was just cash."

"What I don't understand, though, is why Bethany got into Pablo's car. Wasn't she running from him?"

"That's an interesting question. Maybe she thought Pablo was a friend."

"But she stole something from him."

"I don't know. There's a piece we're missing."

"There's a lot we're missing. We take one step forward and three steps backward," she complained. "Where are we going now? What are we going to do next?"

"Pablo said Bethany ran from his apartment. She was on foot. We know what day that was. I noticed a gas station a hundred yards away from that apartment building. I also saw a market and a bank. All of those places will have security cameras. I'll get Wyatt and Bree to tap into all the cameras we can find. We'll see if we can pick her up again."

"You can do that?"

"Yes."

Hope returned to her gaze. "It's a good idea."

"You need to focus on what else is good—Bethany ran. She's alive."

"I really hope that's what happened." Tara looked at her phone. "My missed calls are from my parents and a couple of friends. There's nothing from Bethany. If she was in trouble here in LA, why wouldn't she call me?"

"She obviously doesn't want to involve you, Tara. I suspect it's because there's something criminal going on. And the police might not be an option, either, for that same reason." He paused. "You grew up here. You have a history with Bethany. You know how she thinks. Where would she go?"

"I don't know all her haunts anymore, and I doubt she's hanging out in public anywhere."

"Well, think about it. We'll meet up with Bree and Wyatt at their work and go from there. Frankly, I'm more optimistic now than I've been in days."

"I don't know why. Your brother just threatened to shoot you."

"But he didn't."

"He beat up Pablo," she pointed out.

"That was interesting. But not surprising, considering how he grew up. I'm sure there are power struggles within the family. Clearly, Michael has power over Pablo. He certainly was colder and harder than I remember. For a moment there, I thought he could pull the trigger. I thought he could shoot me."

"I didn't. I don't believe he's forgotten who you are to him. He just doesn't know what to do about it."

"I don't know about that, but I hope he hasn't forgotten the man my mother wanted him to be. She would hate what he's become."

"He didn't have much of a choice, Diego. He was orphaned at twelve. He had no one but the Salazars to care for him. It's not surprising he believes they're his family. But he spoke so deeply about family that I can't imagine he would be able to kill you. Me—he probably wouldn't have a problem with at all. I know I got a little crazed back there. I'm lucky that Michael had the gun and not Pablo. Do you think Pablo was behind what happened to us in Colombia?"

"He seems young and lacking in funds to have that much power in the organization. But he's part of it. We need more of the story."

"Maybe Michael is getting the story now. But will he use the information to find Bethany, or will he protect his family over her?"

"Let's hope we find her first, and then we won't have to answer that question."

Seventeen

➤➤◀◀◀

They didn't go back to the apartment. Instead, Diego took her to a two-story office building in Santa Monica. There was no signage on the structure, but there was a great deal of security at the entrance, including two security guards, a code required for the elevator, and another code required to enter an office suite. Inside the suite were eight desks holding the latest computer technology as well as a wall of monitors, most of which were currently off, but one was playing a cable TV news show.

Three people she didn't recognize were working at their desks: one female with dark-red hair and pale white skin, a young male who looked to be no more than early twenties wearing glasses and an intense look on his face, and a second male with longish black hair, wearing jeans and a brown leather jacket. No one gave them a passing glance, caught up in their own work.

Nearby, inside a glass-walled conference room were Wyatt, Bree, and a third man, who was dressed in jeans and a T-shirt and had dirty-blond hair and a ragged beard. When

Wyatt saw them, he opened the door and waved them inside.

"I was filling Flynn in on what happened with your brother," Wyatt told Diego.

"Diego. I haven't seen you since Quantico," Flynn said with a faint British accent, as he shook Diego's hand. "Wyatt and Bree have read me in on the weekend's activities."

"Thanks for helping me out," Diego replied. "This is Tara Powell."

Flynn gave her an interested smile, and his sharp blue eyes held curiosity. "I've been hearing a lot about you Ms. Powell. I'm Flynn MacKenzie."

"Nice to meet you."

"Since your text," Wyatt said, "we've started pulling in footage from cameras in the vicinity of Pablo Salazar's apartment. Flynn has given us the green light to get the rest of the team involved, which should allow us to get results more quickly."

"I'm also going to check with some private companies whose cameras we can't instantly access," Bree put in. "Hopefully, we can catch a glimpse of Bethany."

"I also did a little more research on Pablo Salazar," Wyatt said, motioning to a digital board on the wall that displayed several photos. "And I've put together some of the central figures in the Salazar organization. By the way, I haven't yet managed to get Michael's phone records, but one of our techs is working on that."

Tara moved closer to the board to get a better look. She recognized Pablo immediately, as well as Michael, but the other people were a mystery to her.

"Of course, you know Michael Winters," Wyatt said, moving over to the board. "Let's go over the rest of the family or at least the main players. This is Caleb Salazar." He tapped beneath the photo of a white-haired man. "He's the current head of the family. He hasn't left Colombia in years." He moved to the next photos. "This is his younger brother Juan Felipe, who was in LA over Thanksgiving. Juan comes to the

US several times a year to check on a chain of laundromats he owns in California, Nevada, Colorado, and Pittsburgh. The DEA has had Juan on their radar for a decade, but they have been unable to make a case against him." Wyatt pointed to the two photos next to Juan's. "Rico Salazar and William Salazar are Juan's sons. They're thirty and twenty-eight years old, respectively. Rico lives in Los Angeles with Pablo. He actually pays for the apartment where you went this morning. William resides in Medellin."

Wyatt took a breath, then moved on. "Moving on, we have Santoro Salazar, Caleb's youngest brother. Santoro also resides in Medellin and has not been to the US in more than a decade. His son Pablo went to school at Long Beach State, as you know. His daughter Vanessa is a fashion designer and travels between Colombia, Paris, and New York quite often. And there's one more player to discuss. This is Stefan Salazar. He's the son of one of the cousins—Franco Salazar. Stefan is a wine distributor in New York and has been in contact with Michael on numerous occasions. According to my sources, there is growing dissension in the Salazar ranks. Caleb's health has not been good, but he's unwilling to step down. Others are ready to take matters into their own hands. The younger generation is chomping at the bit to have more power."

"A family coup in the making," Diego murmured, crossing his arms as he stared at the photos with a hard look in his eyes.

She gave him a concerned look. It had to be difficult to see his brother surrounded by known criminals. And now that the FBI was getting more officially involved, there was a good chance Michael was going to go to jail for what he was doing. How would Diego handle that?

But once again, she was getting ahead of herself.

"There are rumblings that there is a war brewing, especially after the murder of Father Manuel, who was very close to Caleb," Wyatt continued. "Although there are suggestions the Pedrozas were involved, others maintain it was an inside job, that Caleb was very close to the priest, and that it was a message for Caleb to step aside or more people close to the family would die."

She hated to think that the kindly old priest had been a pawn in this criminal enterprise. On the other hand, maybe he'd been more involved with the Salazars than they'd thought. He'd certainly backed off his promise to help her after he'd probably talked to someone in the family about Bethany's disappearance.

"What does all this mean for Bethany?" she asked.

Bree gave her a compassionate look. "Diego said it didn't appear Michael knew about Bethany's interaction with Pablo, or her actions over the last few weeks. It's possible Michael is being kept on the outside of whatever Bethany and Pablo are involved in."

"You're suggesting that Bethany is doing something criminal?" she asked tightly.

"We don't know," Bree said. "But everything you've both told us leads us to believe she's either witnessed something or done something and the family is not happy about it."

"But why wouldn't they tell Michael? He was the one who was dating her. Why is he in the dark?" she asked.

"Maybe because he's not their blood," Wyatt suggested. "From what I've managed to pull up about him, he has a wealthy benefactor, possibly Caleb. If Michael is Caleb's favorite, he might be on the wrong side of this power grab."

"I'd like him to be on the wrong side," Diego said with a frown. "But Michael certainly had control over Pablo."

"We'll keep going," Wyatt said.

"Lucky for you, we just wrapped up a case, Diego," Flynn put in. "But is there a reason why you aren't bringing your boss into this?"

"Roman doesn't go off book. He would not appreciate anything I've been doing the last few days. I needed to bring in people I could trust."

"And the old Quantico group came to the rescue," Flynn drawled.

Tara couldn't quite figure out if Flynn was jealous of Diego's tight group or simply making a lighthearted comment. He was a little difficult to read.

"They did," Diego said simply.

"And we'll soon have Parisa and Damon to help, too," Bree put in. "I just spoke to Damon. He and Parisa will come by around two. Apparently, Sophie is guest lecturing at UCLA today and Parisa's new love Jared has a meeting downtown."

"It will be great to have everyone together," Diego murmured.

Tara thought it was great, too. The more people on the team, the better chance they had of finding Bethany as soon as possible.

"One more thing," Flynn said. "Wyatt told me you got your first lead from Tracy Cox."

"Yes," Diego said.

"Tracy called me this morning. She's working out of LA this week. She asked me to meet her later today."

"Why?" Diego asked sharply.

"She said she came to town for Jamie's dedication. And she wants to catch up."

"Did she mention me?"

"She asked if I'd heard from you. I said I hadn't, which was the truth. Apparently, she also contacted Wyatt. Any reason why you've cut off communication with her?"

"I don't trust her. She wouldn't tell me her source for the lead to Cascada, and considering I got shot at while I was there, I'm bothered by that."

"I thought the shooting was related to the missing Ms. Cooper," Flynn said.

"It might have been," Diego conceded. "But my gut tells me to be wary of Tracy, so I'd appreciate if you can keep her out of this."

Flynn nodded. "No problem. I know Tracy rubbed you all the wrong way back at Quantico, but haven't we gotten past all that?"

"I have. I'm not so sure about her," Diego replied.

"Tracy has been a thorn in my side, too," Bree put in. "She was not at all helpful when I was on the kidnapping case in Chicago. I understand why Diego has reservations about her. I think we should keep the operation within this task force."

"Got it. She'll get nothing from me," Flynn said. "I have to take off. I'll catch up with you later."

"Let's get back to work," Wyatt said. "Diego, do you want to help check cameras?"

"Sure," he said, glancing back at her. "You want to be my partner, Tara?"

She smiled. "You know I do."

While she was excited to be included, after an hour of looking at worthless security footage, she began to realize they were looking for a needle in a haystack. "I'm going to get some coffee," she told Diego. "Do you want anything?"

"Coffee would be good."

When she walked into the adjoining kitchen, she found Bree making a new pot of coffee. "Great minds think alike," she said lightly.

"This is almost done," Bree said.

"Great. I could use a shot of caffeine. And sugar," she added, grabbing a cookie out of a jar on the counter.

"There's other food in the fridge," Bree said. "Help yourself."

"I will." She leaned back against the counter as she ate her cookie. "I'll start with this."

"How are you holding up, Tara?"

"Honestly, I don't know. This has been quite the roller-coaster ride. One minute, I think we're on to something and that we are a second away from finding Bethany. Then it feels like we're right back where we started."

"For what it's worth, I think we're getting closer."

"I hope so. I keep reassuring myself that Bethany had the ability to run away and that she's probably hiding. She's definitely a resourceful girl, especially when it comes to getting herself out of trouble. I just wish she was better at not getting herself into trouble."

"I got myself into a lot of trouble when I was a teenager."

"But Bethany is twenty-six years old. She should be mature by now. Anyway, I really appreciate all the help. When I first started looking for Bethany, I couldn't get anyone to even believe she was actually missing. Now I have an entire FBI task force looking for her. It's a bit surreal."

"It's what we do."

"For the job or for each other?"

"Both."

She nodded in understanding. "Diego told me how you all met at Quantico, how you bonded after the tragic death of Jamie, how you're always there for each other now."

"It's nice to know there are four other people who always have your back."

"I've never felt that way about one person, except for my parents, of course, but that's different."

"Well, you have a lot of people supporting you now."

"Because of Diego. I met him at the unluckiest moment of my life, while being caught in a shooting. But our meeting changed everything for me. He has not only saved my life several times, he's helping me find Bethany."

"It was destiny that you met."

"I never used to think I believed in fate, but this experience makes it hard to dismiss so easily."

"You and Diego have gotten close," Bree commented, a curious gleam in her eyes. "He cares about you. I can see it in his eyes."

"I care about him, too." She gave Bree a helpless smile. "I honestly don't really know what we're doing, but we have a connection that is really strong. It probably won't last after this is all over, but for now, it's kind of amazing."

"You never know if it will last. Wyatt and Avery fell in love in a few days, and they're still going strong."

"What about you and Nathan?"

"We almost missed our second chance at love. I was stupid enough to let him go when I first met him as a teenager. Back then, I fell for the bad boy, and I mean really bad. But when Nathan and I reconnected last year, it was like we'd never been apart. Only it was better than it had been before. We were grown up. We were smarter—at least I was—and we knew what we wanted. Nathan is my rock. He's the best person I've ever known. I don't know if Diego told you, but we're getting married this summer."

She smiled, enjoying a moment of girl talk. Normal moments like this had been missing in her life the past few weeks. "I'm so happy for you."

"I'm happy for me, too. By the way, I want to give you my phone number," Bree said. "Do you have your phone with you?"

"Actually, I do," she said, pulling it out of her pocket.

"I'll put my number in," Bree said. "In case you need someone to talk to who isn't Diego."

"Thanks."

As Bree handed her back her phone, she let out a squeal of delight, her gaze moving past Tara to the man walking into the room. He was followed by three more people, and suddenly there were excited hugs and big smiles.

Tara would have left them alone, but they were blocking the door, so she smiled awkwardly and sipped her coffee.

"Tara, this is Nathan," Bree said, pulling a solidly built man over to her. "Nathan, this is Diego's friend, Tara."

"The one who has been keeping my fiancée busy all weekend," Nathan said with a grin.

"Guilty," she said.

"And I want you to meet these wonderful people as well," Bree continued. "This is Damon Wolfe and Parisa

Maxwell, the other two members of our fearless Quantico group."

"I've heard a lot about you," she said, shaking each of their hands. Damon was a handsome man with penetrating blue eyes, and Parisa was an exotic dark-haired beauty.

"And we've heard nothing about you," Parisa said speculatively.

"Diego and I only met a few days ago," she said, realizing again how fast she'd become entangled in Diego's life.

Bree pulled the last woman forward, another pretty brunette. "This is Avery Caldwell, Wyatt's girlfriend."

"Wyatt is the other person Diego and I have been keeping busy," she said. "Sorry, Avery."

"Don't worry about it," Avery said. "I'm used to Wyatt working long and erratic hours. Plus, I heard you're looking for your friend, and I know what it's like to search for answers about someone you love."

There were shadows in Avery's eyes now, and she would have liked to learn more, but Diego had entered the kitchen and was now engaged in hugs and hellos.

It was nice to see him with all his friends. She could see his tension disappear, surrounded by so much affection. He'd grown up very much alone after his mother and brother had left, but he'd built other families, including this one from Quantico.

Wyatt came into the kitchen, a somber note in his eyes. "We found Bethany on one of the cameras."

Everyone in the room suddenly fell quiet.

"Where?" Diego asked.

She moved across the room, needing to be close to Diego. Whatever Wyatt had seen wasn't good. She could tell from the expression on his face.

"We picked her up in the parking lot of a bank. She was moving quickly, looking over her shoulder. Then she disappeared around the building. Five minutes later, we found her again at an intersection." He paused. "There's no good way to say it, so I'll just say it—Bethany was hit by a car while she was crossing the street. It was a red-light runner."

She gasped, putting a hand to her mouth. Diego's arm came around her shoulders.

"Did she survive?" Diego asked.

"She was taken away by ambulance. Caitlyn is on the phone now with the ambulance company to determine where they took her."

"I want to see the footage," Diego said.

"So do I," she said.

Diego frowned. "Let me watch it first, Tara. There are some things you can't unsee."

"I have to see it. You've all seen her photo, but I'm her best friend. I have to know if it was really her."

She and Diego followed Wyatt back to the conference room. Bree came along as well, although the others stayed back in the kitchen.

They gathered around a large monitor and Wyatt hit play.

She held her breath as she saw Bethany standing at an intersection. She hit the walk button repeatedly and when the light changed, she dashed into the street. She had taken no more than ten steps when a car came out of nowhere. Bethany froze for one split second and then her body was flung into the air.

"Oh, God," she breathed, watching her friend crumple like a rag doll. "The car didn't even slow down."

"No, they didn't." Diego met her gaze, then looked back at Wyatt. "Could you get the license plate?"

"No. We'll check with the police, who are also investigating the accident." Wyatt paused as a red-haired woman entered the room. "Do you have the hospital, Caitlyn?"

"The woman in the accident was taken to St. Anne's," Caitlyn said. "But she was admitted under the name Laura Harper, which was the name listed on the passport she had in her possession."

"Laura Harper?" Tara asked in bewilderment. "Maybe it's not Bethany. But it looked like Bethany. I recognized the jacket she had on. Who is Laura Harper?"

"Maybe a fake name, fake passport," Diego told her. "Is this woman still alive?"

"Yes," Caitlyn replied. "She sustained a head injury, a broken wrist, and several cracked ribs. She was in a coma for three days, with swelling in the brain, but she appears to be out of danger now and is considered stable. She's in room 436."

"Let's go," she told Diego.

Diego nodded, as he grabbed his jacket off the back of a chair.

"I'll send a security guard to the hospital," Wyatt said. "If the hit-and-run wasn't an accident, Bethany could be in more danger. Text me when you get to the hospital and let me know her condition."

"Will do," Diego replied, as they left the room.

They hurried out of the building and into the car. As Diego fiddled with the GPS, she said, "I know where St. Anne's is. It's about ten minutes from here. Get back on the 405 going south."

"All right." He gave her a reassuring look. "You'll see her soon."

"It doesn't sound like she's in very good condition."

"She's alive, Tara. That's the most important thing."

"I know, but she might have brain damage. She might not be the same person. Hell, she might be this Laura Harper, whoever she is."

"One step at a time," he reminded her.

Eighteen

—➤➤❮❮❮—

Tara tried to take Diego's advice and not let her thoughts run away from her, but it was difficult, especially with the video of Bethany getting struck by a car played over and over again in her head. "I can't believe Bethany escaped Colombia and Pablo to get taken down by a red-light runner. Do you think she was terribly unlucky or was that driver connected to the cartel?"

"Hard to say. Since apparently no one has gone after her at the hospital, I'm leaning toward bad luck. If they had run her down, they would have followed up the way we did. They would have figured out what hospital the ambulance took her to, and they would have gone after her again."

"Not if she still has something they need. Maybe they need her to be well enough to tell them where it is. Maybe they're waiting for her to get better."

"Fair point." He flashed her an approving look. "You're getting good at this."

"I wish I wasn't having so much practice."

His smile faded. "I know. I'm sorry you had to see your

friend get hurt. That was brutal."

"It was, but I had to see it."

"You don't shy away from what's difficult, Tara. I like that about you."

"I have to admit, it's kind of a new attitude for me. I used to shy away from difficult things all the time, but I guess I've realized that some things in life are too important not to fight for, like my friends and my family."

"And yourself," he said. "That's the most important person."

"Yes, you're right. If this whole terrible situation has taught me anything it's that I have to be a participant in my life. I can't sit back and wait or watch." She drew in a breath and let it out. "Anyway, I hope it's not all for nothing. Bethany has to recover from this. She just has to."

"We'll do everything we can for her."

"If the Salazars weren't responsible for the accident, they still might be able to find Bethany the same way we did. I bet they have connections in the police department, maybe even the FBI. There are more than a few people working with Flynn. Are we sure they're all trustworthy?"

"I've learned you can never be sure about that," he said, for the first time sounding a little more cynical than he normally was. "But Flynn handpicked his people, and they operate off book all the time. They're set up to be agile, to move without a lot of red tape. According to Wyatt, Flynn runs a good team. Right now, I'm putting my trust in them. And for the moment, I'm thinking we might actually be one step ahead of the Salazars."

She wanted to cling to that thought. "I really hope so."

A few moments later, Diego turned into the parking garage at St. Anne's. As they got out of the car and walked toward the elevator, the sun slipped over the horizon and shadows filled the chilly early evening air. It was almost six o'clock, and the twilight felt a little foreboding, but she tried to shake off the bad feeling, concentrating on the most important fact that Bethany was alive.

Diego took her hand as they stepped into the elevator, giving her fingers a warm squeeze. "It's going to work out," he told her.

"I hope so."

When they entered the hospital, they bypassed the information desk and headed up to the fourth floor. Monday evening visiting hours weren't over until eight, so there were a lot of people walking the halls. That made her feel better, as if Bethany was less alone, even though that wasn't true at all. Bethany had been alone in this hospital for over a week. But even before that, Bethany had been alone since her mother died.

While she and her parents had tried to fill the void, she knew that Bethany still felt that gut ache of loneliness, of not really having anyone who was family, who was blood. It was why she loved being social, why she was always up for a party, why she always fell quickly into relationships; she was looking for that connection, that feeling of belonging, being a part of something.

She wondered if that was what had drawn her and Michael together. Michael had been both rejected and abandoned through divorce and death. He had to feel that deep core of loneliness, too.

She wondered what Michael had told Bethany about his life. *Had he hidden his criminal ties from her? Did she think he was just a hotshot wine bar owner, a young, handsome, rich guy?*

But the fact that she'd known Pablo, that she'd been to Cascada belied that possibility. Bethany had to know that Michael was in bed with the Salazars and their criminal organization.

Had she tried to walk away from him? Had she tried to set him up? Had she done something incredibly foolish, like steal money or drugs from the family?

But Bethany wasn't a drug addict. And she wasn't a thief.

Whatever she'd stolen had to be something else.

If she hadn't suffered a head injury, Tara had no doubt she could get Bethany to open up, but if there was some brain damage, it might be impossible.

Diego paused outside of the door to Bethany's room. "Are you ready?"

She nodded, mentally preparing herself for what might be coming. Then she opened the door and stepped into the room. Diego followed behind her.

Bethany looked small and fragile in the bed. Her brown hair was pulled into a messy knot on the top of her head. There was a bandage across her forehead, visible bruising on her face, and a cast on her wrist, but her eyes were open, and the TV was on, and somehow that made it all feel more normal.

"Bethany?" she said, as she moved toward the bed.

Bethany blinked a few times as she gazed in her direction. "Is that my name? They said my name was Laura— Laura Harper."

She frowned at Bethany's words. "Your name is Bethany, and I'm Tara." She gave her friend a warm, reassuring smile. "I've been looking all over for you. I've been so worried."

"Who's he?" Bethany asked, giving Diego a wary look.

"This is my friend, Diego. You've never met him before, but he's been helping me search for you. Do you know what happened?"

"I—I don't remember anything really. They tell me I have amnesia."

"You do?" Caitlyn had left that out of her medical briefing.

"Look at me," she said as Bethany's gaze shifted toward the television.

Bethany slowly turned her head.

"You're practically my sister," she told her. "You grew up next door to me. You spent a lot of time at my house, with me and my parents, Kathy and Bill Powell. I had a trundle bed. You used to sleep on the bottom mattress. We'd talk all night."

"Sorry," Bethany said.

"It's okay. You were hit by a car. It's understandable. You were running away from someone when you got hurt. It's possible you don't want to remember what happened, because you're afraid."

"I want to remember; I just can't. You should go."

"I'm not leaving. I am going to wait here until you know me."

Diego nudged her shoulder and murmured, "I think you're scaring her."

Bethany did look a little worried by her promise to never leave. "I'm not trying to scare you. I love you. I want to help you. I can tell you things about yourself. I can jog your memory." As she finished the statement, she realized what was playing on the television. It was a rerun of the sitcom *Sex and the City*, a show that had been Bethany's favorite. *Had her subconscious recognized that when she'd flipped the channels?* "You used to love this show," she said, tipping her head toward the screen.

"I don't even know what it is." Bethany picked up the remote and flipped the channel, directing her gaze toward the TV.

"You know what," Diego interrupted, "I'm going to step outside and see if I can talk to a doctor about Bethany's condition."

"Okay." She wondered if he really wanted to speak to a doctor or if he thought Bethany might react better if they were alone. When the door closed behind Diego, she turned back to Bethany and tried to infuse a cheerful note into her voice. "Let's see. What would you want to remember? Your favorite ice cream is mint chip. You love dogs, not cats. You had a golden retriever named Daisy when you were young. You used to sleep with her. And you and I—we were always best friends, from the first day we met. I had a playhouse in my backyard, and we'd make up all kinds of imaginary games. One day it would be a restaurant and another day a store. Even though you were a few years younger, I adored you. I felt like your big sister."

"Stop," Bethany said, her gaze filling with emotion, as she locked eyes with her. "I know you, Tara."

"What?" she asked in surprise. "You do? You just remembered?"

Bethany gave her a guilty look. "No. I've known who I am since I woke up, but they found the passport that I had in my pocket and everyone was calling me Laura, and I didn't want to correct them. I'm in trouble, and I figured if no one knew who I was, maybe no one could find me."

"If that's the case, why did you pretend that you didn't recognize me?" she asked in confusion.

"Because I didn't know the guy you were with, and he looks kind of familiar to someone I do know."

"Michael Winters?"

Bethany's eyes widened in surprise. "You know Michael? How is that possible?"

"So much has happened, Bethany. And, yes, I know Michael. I met him earlier today. He claims he doesn't know where you are. He didn't even know you were in LA."

"I was going to call him, but I didn't get a chance. But I don't understand. How did you meet him? Why were you looking for me?"

"Because you disappeared. You stopped answering my calls and my texts. I called Allende Tours. They said you were on vacation, but it didn't make sense that you'd completely drop out of sight. After a week, I went to Colombia, to Medellin. I asked the police to look for you."

Bethany's eyes widened. "Are you serious? You went to Colombia by yourself?"

"I did. I told you I was worried about you. The police weren't very helpful, but they did find an image of you getting on a bus headed to Cascada, so I went there, too."

Dangerous Choice 207

"Did you talk to people about me?"

"Everyone I could find."

"Oh, Tara. That wasn't a good idea."

"Yeah, I found that out. I got caught in a shooting at the church. The priest there was killed, and later several more attempts were made on my life. Luckily, Diego was there for most of them. We got tangled up together at the church, and we stayed together after that, because people kept shooting at us everywhere we went. And my room was searched, too. It seemed like whoever was after us thought I had something."

"God," Bethany breathed. "You're lucky you're still alive."

"Believe me, I know that. What kind of trouble are you in, Bethany? What did you do? Pablo said you stole something from him."

"You talked to Pablo, too?"

"Yes. Tell me what's going on." She decided to leave out the part about Diego being an FBI agent for now. She didn't want Bethany to decide not to tell her the truth because of that.

"If—if I tell you, it will put you in more danger, Tara. I didn't call you because I didn't want that to happen. I didn't want to lead anyone to you. I can't believe you got involved in this. I never imagined you would get on a plane and go to Colombia to look for me. Not in a million years would I have thought that would happen."

"Well, when the life of someone I love is at stake, I can do anything. I've learned that the past few weeks. And it's too late to protect me now. I'm in this. Both Michael and Pablo know that Diego and I are looking for you."

"Why is Diego helping you? Who is he?"

"He started out just being a nice guy, someone who got me out of the shooting at the church, who helped me get out of Cascada. But since then we've become really close. And we're connected in some very strange ways." She paused. "Michael is Diego's half brother. Diego went to Cascada looking for Michael and his mother."

Bethany's eyebrows shot up once more in both amazement and confusion. "His half brother? But I don't understand. Is Diego a Salazar? You said his name was something else."

"It's Rivera. He's not a Salazar and neither is Michael. Michael and Diego share the same mother. She later married into the Salazar family."

"I know that. Michael told me that after his mom died, his stepfather took him in, and then he went to live with his cousins." Bethany paused. "But Michael said something once about his brother, and then he immediately shut up. I didn't know who he was talking about. I didn't think he had an actual brother. When I started asking questions, he told me he wasn't going to talk about it."

"It's a long story, but Diego's father found out that Michael was not his real son, and he kicked Michael and his mother out of the house, separating the two half brothers. Diego didn't know where his mom and brother went. He didn't even find out until a few days ago that his mom was dead. Then he became determined to find Michael. Actually, he knew Michael as Mateo. His mom changed his brother's name. We've spent the last several days looking for both you and Michael. And here we are. Now it's your turn. What the hell is going on? What did you take from Pablo Salazar?"

"Pablo didn't tell you? Did he tell Michael?"

"I don't know what Pablo told Michael, but it appeared to me that Michael was confused about why you were in LA, why you left LAX in Pablo's car."

"How do you know that?"

"Enough with your questions. I want answers," she said forcefully.

Bethany blew out a breath. "Okay, I'll tell you everything."

"Good," Diego said, as he walked into the room. "I see you've recovered your memory, Bethany. I thought it might come back when I left the room."

"I'm talking to Tara," Bethany said, giving Diego a dark look.

"You're talking to both of us now," he said. "We're here to help you. There's also a security guard outside your room, to make sure you're safe."

Bethany appeared to have mixed feelings about that. "Does that mean everyone in the hospital knows my real name now?"

"No. I told hospital security that you're a witness to something and we need to keep you safe," Diego replied.

Bethany's gaze narrowed. "You talk like a cop."

"I'm an FBI agent."

Her jaw dropped. "Wow. I didn't expect you to say that. Why didn't you tell me, Tara?"

"I was getting to it."

Bethany looked back at Diego. "And you're Michael's brother? Does he know you're a federal agent?"

"He does not, and I'd like to keep it that way for now."

"Bethany, talk," Tara interrupted. "No more stalling. We need the whole story. We've risked our lives for you, and we deserve the truth."

Bethany slowly nodded. "Okay, I'll tell you. But I don't want to do it here. I don't want to stay here. I'm afraid they'll find me."

"There's a guard at the door."

"They can get to guards. They can get to everyone. The Salazars are really powerful. After I talked to Father Manuel, he ended up dead. I don't think that's a coincidence."

"So, you did talk to Father Manuel," Tara said. "I thought he knew something. He was helpful at first, but then he backed off, and then he was dead. Why did you speak to him?"

"I needed a ride out of Cascada. He set it up for me. I didn't know I was putting him in danger."

"Why did you need a ride? Did you steal something in

Cascada from the Salazars? What was it?"

Bethany drew in a breath. "Okay. Here's what happened. I finished my tour, and I was at loose ends for a few weeks. Michael had gone back to the States, but he was going to be traveling on business for a while, so we couldn't see each other until he got back. I had time to kill, and I was partying in Medellin when I ran into Pablo and Vanessa, Michael's cousins. I'd met them a few times before when I was with Michael. Vanessa told me she was having a birthday party a few days later in Cascada, and she invited me. I'd wanted to go to the compound for a while, but Michael kept putting me off. I was curious to meet more of his family."

"You'd never gone to the compound before?" Tara asked.

"No. I took the bus up there, and Pablo picked me up and took me to the compound. It's kind of an amazing place. There is one huge house and two other really big ones. They have a lake where people can boat. They have two pools, a basketball court, a tennis court. It's like the best resort you've ever been to, only it's private."

"Because it's paid for by drug money," Diego put in. "Did you know that?"

"I had my suspicions," Bethany admitted. "I'd been in Colombia enough times to know that the Salazars ran a cartel. But Michael told me about his wine bars, and he'd gone to school at USC. He didn't have their last name. I thought maybe he was not part of it. And he was such an amazing person, I didn't want to look too hard. Being with him was different than being with anyone else. I felt like we were soulmates."

"But eventually you figured out Michael was in with the cartel," Tara said, wanting to bring Bethany's attention back to what had brought them all to this point.

"Yes, it changed when I went to Cascada. I was there for a couple of days before the party and everyone was really nice. They were very curious about my relationship with Michael and why he hadn't brought me there himself. But they didn't ask too many questions. Vanessa and I went hiking and horseback riding; it was fun. I think in retrospect, Michael wanted to keep me away from the compound, because he knew I'd figure out what kind of business they were all in."

"What happened at the party?" Diego asked.

"It started out great. I met a lot of fun people. There was tequila being poured every time I turned around, and I was just having fun. But later in the night, I overheard some of the guys talking. They were wasted, and they were trashing Michael. I was shocked, and I stopped to listen."

"What did you hear?"

"They were bragging about a plan to take Michael out."

"Kill him?" Tara asked.

"I wasn't completely sure. But they were saying that Michael didn't deserve to be Caleb's favorite, that he wasn't even blood, that he shouldn't be getting all the money and the opportunity. They were the real Salazars. They should be in charge." She paused. "I moved a little closer, and I saw Pablo waving a flash drive in his hand. He said it was going to take Michael down, that once Caleb saw all the evidence they'd created, he'd realize that Michael was stealing from him, betraying the family, working with their competitors, and Caleb would destroy him for that." Bethany blew out a breath. "My heart was pounding so fast, I thought they might hear it. I crept away, trying to figure out what I should do. I knew I had to save Michael."

"What did you do?" she breathed.

"I started flirting with Pablo. He had the drive in his pocket. He was so drunk and stupid. I kept plying him with tequila and eventually he passed out. I stole the drive, and I replaced it with one I had in my purse. You know, Tara, the ones we give out on the tours for people to store their photos. It looked pretty similar. I figured Pablo might not notice the difference for a while, and then I left town."

Tara shook her head at her friend's deception. "Were you

out of your mind?"

"Crazy in love," Bethany answered. "I realized once I left Cascada that I needed to get out of Colombia fast. Father Manuel got me a ride to Medellin. Then I took a private plane to Cartagena and I got Rosa to hook me up with her cousin Reggie who flew me to Panama City. I thought I had covered my tracks. But when I got to the airport, Pablo was waiting for me."

"Why didn't you run? You had to know you were in trouble when you saw him," Tara asked. "But you got into his van."

"I had to. He had a gun. And I was hoping he wouldn't kill me until I handed over the drive, which I had stashed at the airport."

"I was just going to ask," Diego muttered. "Where in the airport?"

"In a locker. I put the key in my shoe. Pablo tried to search me when we got to his apartment, but I hit him over the head, and I ran. Unfortunately, I didn't get too far. I ended up getting hit by a car. I woke up here three days after the accident. The nurses called me Laura. I decided to go with it."

Tara shook her head, amazed and bemused by everything Bethany had done. "You did all this for Michael?"

Bethany met her gaze. "I'm in love with him. He's not like anyone else. I know I've said I was in love before, Tara, but this is different. This is real. I know he's not perfect."

"Not even close," she muttered.

"But he didn't have a lot of choices growing up. He lost everyone he loved, just like I did. We both know what it feels like to be alone."

"I understand."

"I have a question," Diego interrupted. "Why didn't you call Michael and tell him what was going on? Why didn't you ask him to help you?"

"I didn't think he would believe me. He always told me the Salazars were the only family he had, that they had raised him and supported him, and they knew what loyalty was all about. He would never have believed what Pablo and some of the others were trying to do to him. I felt like I had to show him proof."

"He told us you blew him off."

"I was supposed to meet him last Monday. I had texted him from the airport, but then, of course, I didn't show up. I've been going crazy here, wondering if they were able to put their plan into motion without the drive, but I didn't feel strong enough to call Michael."

"Or maybe you weren't certain he'd believe you and take your side," Diego said.

"That, too," she admitted. "I also didn't know what Pablo might have told him. I thought I needed to wait until I could leave here, get the drive, and meet Michael alone."

It all made sense in a crazy, impulsive, Bethany kind of way. She was a loyal person to those she loved, but she definitely made questionable choices.

"Where's the key now?" Diego asked.

"It's in the bag of personal items in the cupboard," Bethany said. "I finally got out of bed yesterday and I saw it. I put it in the toe of my sock."

Diego went over to the cupboard and brought the bag containing Bethany's clothes back to the bed. He pulled out a sock and slipped his hand inside, then removed a key. "Well, you weren't lying about this."

"I'm not lying about anything," Bethany said with annoyance. "And since you're both here, I need your help to get the drive and see Michael."

"I'll get the drive out of the locker," Diego said. "It will be less conspicuous for me to do it. Why don't you wait here with Bethany, Tara? There's a guard outside. You two can catch up. When I come back, we'll figure out our next move."

"No," Bethany said. "I have to be the one to get the drive. I don't know you. I don't trust you."

"I know him, and I trust him," Tara said. "Now you have

to trust me." While she didn't particularly want Diego to go on his own, she thought it would be safer than for all three of them to trek to the airport. Pablo might even suspect that Bethany had stashed the key at the airport and have someone watching for her to return.

"Well, I guess I don't have a choice," Bethany said.

"Did you actually see what was on the drive?" Diego asked.

"No, I didn't have a computer with me. But I heard what they said was on it."

"Well, let's find out for sure." Diego gave her a questioning look. "Are you okay with this, Tara?"

"Yes. We'll be fine here."

"It shouldn't take too long. The airport is only about ten minutes away. Where are the lockers, Bethany?"

"They are outside of United baggage claim, near the bus terminal. The number is on the key."

"Got it. Keep your phone on, Tara. If I can't find it, I'll call you."

"Okay."

As Diego left, she pulled up a chair next to Bethany's bed and sat down. "That's quite a story you told. Did you leave anything out because Diego was listening?"

Bethany gave her a guilty look. "You know me too well. I did look at the drive."

"And?"

"They made it look like Michael was skimming money off the top, and there were photos of him and Alan Pedroza. His drug cartel operates out of Cartagena. I'm sure Michael was not working with him. There were also inventory lists. I think the Salazars might be shipping drugs in the wine bottles that go through Michael's bar."

Tara blew out a breath at that piece of intel. "Well, that's damning for your boyfriend."

"He became an orphan when he was twelve. He had no choice but to live with the Salazars. They made him do bad things."

"He's a man now, Bethany. He can make his own choices."

"But they would kill him if he ever went against them. That's another reason why I took the drive. I was thinking that if I showed him what was on the drive, he'd agree to get out of the business. We could run away together. The world is a big place. We could live anywhere. We could change our names. We could make it. I don't want to lose him, Tara."

"Oh, Bethany," she said with a sigh. "Couldn't you pick a better man?"

"You can't pick who you love. And Michael is a good man at heart. I know I have a track record of falling for bad people, but Michael treats me so well. He's the only one who's ever filled the hole in my heart. I just..." Her voice drifted off.

"What were you going to say?" Tara asked.

"I just don't know if he'll hate me for bringing him the truth. I think that's why I've been stalling. I'm afraid he'll blame me as much as them for ruining his life, for destroying the love he has for his family." She paused. "You said you saw him earlier. What did he say about me?"

"Not much. He didn't want to talk to us. But he did break Pablo's nose trying to find out what happened to you."

Bethany's eyes lit up. "Really?"

"He also made us get out of the apartment, and Diego thought it was because someone else might be coming back, and he didn't want us there. Michael wants to figure out what's going on himself and take care of it."

"Rico lives with Pablo. I think he's far more dangerous than Pablo."

"I guess it's good we left when we did."

Bethany stared at her. "What's Diego going to do with the drive, Tara?"

"I don't know. We'll figure that out when he gets back."

"Will he want to help save Michael from the Salazars?"

"I'm sure he will. He still thinks of him as his little brother, Mateo. But Michael tried to give him the brush-off earlier, so I'm not sure if Michael would take his help."

"He's very independent and strong-willed."

"Like his brother," she muttered.

"And then there's the fact that Diego is an FBI agent. Can he walk away from Michael without trying to arrest him?"

She saw the worry in Bethany's eyes. "I want to reassure you, but I honestly don't know."

"Would he put his brother in jail?"

"Earlier today, Michael pulled a gun on Diego, and there was a moment there when I wondered if Michael would shoot his brother."

"But he didn't." Bethany paused, her eyes bright with new ideas. "If Michael and I disappeared, started over, and weren't part of any criminal activities, maybe Diego could let him go, look the other way."

"I'm sure Diego would like to find a way out of this," she said carefully. "But he's also a man with integrity, and he's a patriot. He was a soldier before he was an FBI agent. He has spent his entire adult life fighting for other people, working hard to take down criminals, to protect the innocent. I don't know what he'll do, but I do know he'll be incredibly conflicted. Because he still loves Michael."

"Maybe that love will win out."

"Maybe."

Bethany gave her a thoughtful look. "Let's talk about you for a minute."

"What about me?"

"You like Diego. He's not just helping you as an agent or a friend—you have feelings for him. Did you sleep with him, Tara?"

"That's kind of personal," she protested.

"Which I'll take as a yes," Bethany said with a surprised smile. "And you only met him a few days ago?"

"I know it's fast. The circumstances have been extreme.

We had to steal a plane and then we crashed it in the jungle."

"And then had sex?"

"Stop. I am not talking about that with you."

"Why not? We always used to talk about boys and sex."

"We're not teenagers anymore."

"I know. I'm really touched you went to Colombia to look for me, Tara. I had no idea you would do that. Do your parents know?"

"I didn't want to worry them. They think I went to Mexico for an extended spring break."

"What about your job?"

"I took a leave of absence."

Bethany shook her head in bemusement. "You did all that for me?"

"You're like my sister, Bethany. You know that."

"But still…"

"There is no *but*. I love you."

"I love you, too, Tara. So, do you think this thing with Diego will go the distance?"

"Probably not. He travels all over the world for his job. He's based out of DC. I don't see how it could work."

"You're talking about geography. You can't let that stop you."

"It's not the time to think about any of that."

Bethany winced as she shifted position.

"Are you in pain?" Tara asked.

"My ribs hurt, but I can tolerate it. My head is a lot better now." Bethany swung her legs off the side of the bed. "Before Diego gets back, help me into my clothes."

"I don't know if you should leave the hospital. You were in a coma."

"That was days ago. The doctors have been talking about discharging me soon anyway. I don't want to stay here any longer. I'd rather be with you and Diego. It will be safer."

Seeing the determined look on Bethany's face, she knew arguing would be a waste of breath. Fortunately, Bethany wasn't hooked up to any IVs so all she had to do was help her out of bed.

It actually took a good ten minutes to get Bethany into underwear, jeans, a bra, and a camisole top. While Bethany's jeans showed spots of blood, her sweater was completely stained, so Tara tossed it aside and took off her own jacket and handed it to Bethany. "Wear this. I'll be fine."

As Bethany put on the jacket, Diego entered the room, his brow arching in surprise when he saw them both on their feet.

"Did you get the drive?" she asked.

"I got it," he said. "What's going on here?"

"We're leaving," Tara told him. "Bethany will feel safer at the apartment. I know you went to a lot of trouble to set up the guard, but she doesn't want to spend another night here. Now that we've found her, she's afraid someone else will, too."

"All right. We can leave."

Relief ran through Bethany's eyes. "Thank you."

"Don't thank me until we get you out of here," Diego replied. "I'm going to talk to the guard. He can walk with us out to the parking structure. By the way, I haven't looked at the drive yet. I hope you're not lying about what's on there and using us to get you out of here."

"I wouldn't put Tara in danger," Bethany said.

"Everything you've done has put her in danger," Diego returned.

"Well, I'm not lying about the drive."

"I believe her," Tara put in.

Diego gave her a measured look. "I hope you're right."

"He doesn't trust me," Bethany said, as Diego stepped out of the room.

"He doesn't know you the way I do."

Bethany gave her a somewhat sad look. "Oh, Tara, I'm not sure you know me as well as you think you do."

Nineteen

———➤➤◄◄◄———

Bethany's foreboding words rang through Tara's head as they made their way down the stairs and into the parking garage. She hoped Bethany had told her the whole truth behind the flash drive, but Bethany did have a way of telling a story that put her in the best light.

At least Diego had found the drive. That was a good start. She was very curious to see what was on it.

The guard escorted them to the car, then waited nearby as Diego started the engine and pulled out of the lot.

Bethany was in the backseat, and as they drove away from the hospital, Tara glanced over her shoulder, seeing shadows in her friend's gaze. "Are you doing all right?"

"I feel so weak," Bethany said. "I didn't realize."

She frowned at the pallor of Bethany's skin, hoping they hadn't made a terrible mistake taking her out of the hospital. She looked at Diego. "Are we doing the right thing?"

"We'll make it right. If she needs medical care, we'll get her some."

"I'll be fine," Bethany piped up. "I'm just tired. It will be nice to sleep in a real bed. Where are we going anyway?"

"We're staying at an apartment not far from here," she told her, as Diego drove through the dark and somewhat empty city streets. It was after eight and the commute traffic was gone. She should have been glad that there weren't many cars on the road, but it also made her nervous. Every shadow seemed like a possible threat and when a car raced by them, she almost ducked, thinking someone was coming up next to them to take a shot.

"Easy," Diego told her, giving her a smile.

"I'll feel better when we're inside the apartment."

"Almost there."

"Are you sure no one followed you to the airport or back to the hospital? Or is following us now?" she asked, turning to look over her shoulder.

"I've been keeping a close eye on the traffic. I think we're in the clear."

Ten minutes later, they pulled into the garage under the apartment building. After the gate swung closed, Diego parked, and then got out of the vehicle first, his weapon drawn in case they ran into trouble. There were no other cars in the garage and nothing to hide behind, so she helped Bethany out of the car, and they took the elevator up to the apartment.

Once inside, Diego locked the doors, while Bethany flopped onto the couch.

"You need to get into bed," she told her.

"I want to see what's on the drive first. You have a computer, right?"

"We do." Diego grabbed the laptop off the table that Wyatt had left there the night before. He brought it over to the coffee table and plugged in the flash drive.

All three of them huddled on the couch together. She sat in the middle, with Bethany on one side and Diego on the other.

The first thing that came up was a list of files.

"We've got something," Diego muttered. He clicked on a folder labeled Photos.

The first picture showed Michael standing by a bar. Facing him was a dark-haired man with a moustache.

"That's Alan Pedroza," Bethany said.

"How do you know that?" Tara asked.

"I met him once at a party Allende Tours threw in Colombia. Alan and Tony are friends."

"Are you saying there's a connection between Allende Tours and the Pedroza organization?" Tara asked in astonishment.

"I didn't know at the time that Alan was anything more than a banker in Medellin. But since then I've learned a lot," Bethany said. "But that photo is a fake. I was with Michael at that bar, and we were not talking to Pedroza. We were talking to Pablo."

"It's pretty good work if that's true," Diego commented. "I can't see any blend on the picture."

"Amelia, one of the Salazar cousins, is a graphic artist. She's particularly close to Rico. I'm sure she did it," Bethany said.

Diego flipped through several more shots, all suggesting that Michael had had a series of meetings with Pedroza. He clicked out of that file and opened another. This one showed inventory and shipments of wine bottles.

That information didn't make any sense to Tara, but it was probably damning for Michael.

There were more files with financials, deposits, withdrawals, and then a copy of an alleged email between Pedroza and Michael about going into business together. Michael wrote that he had no allegiance to the Salazars. They were not his blood.

"Clearly, Michael didn't write that," Bethany said. "He very much thinks of the Salazars as his family. He's incredibly loyal."

"He seemed that way to me, too," Diego muttered.

"What else do you think?" Tara asked. He hadn't said much as they'd looked through the drive.

"It's going to take some skill and some additional knowledge about the Salazar operation to make sense of what we're looking at," he said, punching several keys. "I'm sending this to Wyatt."

"Who's Wyatt?" Bethany asked, concern in her voice. "I thought we were handling this on our own."

"Wyatt is a friend and a damn good FBI agent with a lot of connections in organized crime," Diego replied. "He's the one who helped us find you."

"But this information could put Michael in jail," Bethany said. "Do you want that for your brother?"

"We're not building a case against Michael; we're trying to figure out what this is," Diego retorted. "And it's happening, so get on board." After hitting Send, Diego got up from the couch and walked into the kitchen.

Tara sensed his patience was hanging by a thread, so she let him go without a word.

"I don't want Michael to go to jail," Bethany said, worry in her eyes. "I didn't steal the drive to give it to the FBI."

"Well, this is where we're at, Bethany, and I don't think Diego wants to send Michael to jail, either. But whatever happens is not the result of what Diego does or I do, or even what you've done. It's about Michael. If he's a criminal, he's going to have to pay for what he's done."

"But the Salazars forced him into his life."

"A life that seems to have provided Michael with money and opportunity, and I don't think he's an innocent, Bethany. He might not be conspiring against his family, but it looks to me like he's involved with drug distribution and/or laundering money. You need to start accepting the fact that while you might be able to save his life, you might not be able to save him from jail."

"There has to be a way," Bethany said, undaunted by her words.

"I can't see one."

"That doesn't mean there isn't one. And Diego is Michael's half-brother. Doesn't that count for something?"

"I'm not sure. But we're going to have to play this out."

"I want to show Michael what I found," Bethany said, pulling the drive out of the computer. "I'm going to call him. Give me your phone."

She was astonished at Bethany's request. "You can't do that. I'm sorry, but we need to play this through Diego."

"We don't need Diego to call the shots. We can decide what we want to do. Come on, Tara. It's you and me—just like the old days. Are you with me?"

She wanted to be with Bethany, but she also wanted to be with Diego. "No."

Bethany's gaze filled with shock. "No?"

"No. Diego almost lost his life looking for you. I will not go against him. We three have to work together. It's the only way we're going to survive."

"I can't believe what you're saying. This isn't you, Tara. He's brainwashed you."

She smiled at Bethany's dramatic statement. "I'm thinking quite clearly for myself. I'm sorry, Bethany, but you're not running this show anymore. Now, why don't you give me the drive and go to bed?"

"We need to keep talking."

"You look like you're about to pass out."

"Tara—you have to help me save Michael."

"I'm going to do everything I can, Bethany. I promise. But this is bigger than all of us. And I don't want any of us to die over this flash drive. I almost lost you to that hit-and-run driver. I've just gotten you back. You need to work with me. You're not in this alone, even if you'd prefer to be. I'm a target now, too. So is Diego."

"I get that, but I need to have a say in what we do."

"Of course you'll have a say. We all will." She held out her hand.

Bethany reluctantly handed over the drive. "I am exhausted."

"I know," Tara said, as she helped her up from the couch. "We'll talk again in the morning."

Diego moved back into the kitchen as Tara led Bethany down the hall to the second bedroom. He smiled to himself as he poured a cup of coffee. He'd been about to offer the women something to drink when he'd heard Bethany demand Tara's allegiance.

He'd wanted to hear what Tara would say. There was a part of him that had wondered if she'd give in to Bethany. Tara had a lot of love for her friend, as evidenced by everything they'd been through. But she'd said no. She'd told Bethany in no uncertain terms that she would not sneak around behind his back.

He'd been surprised and pleased by the fervor of her response, the way she'd stood up to the woman she'd considered a sister. And she'd done it for him.

He knew there were feelings between them, but he hadn't had time or the desire to define those feelings. They were too caught up in everything else.

But hearing Tara put herself on his side had touched a part of his heart that he'd locked away a long time ago. His father's anger, resentment, and ultimate rejection—and his mother's unwillingness to come back for him—had hardened him. The word *love* had lost all meaning. He'd stopped looking for it, stopped wanting it. And he hadn't thought he'd missed it—until now.

That thought hit him like a sucker punch to the gut.

He wasn't in love with Tara, was he?

He really shouldn't be. He'd hurt her. She'd want more from him than he could give.

A dozen reasons why they couldn't work ran through his

head.

But he knew it wasn't about what she wanted from him; it was more about what he felt he could give, whether he could open himself up enough to be the kind of man she deserved.

He'd asked her to trust him with her life, and she had. But could he ask her to trust him with her heart?

"Diego?"

He spun around at the sound of her soft, hesitant voice and forced a smile onto his face. "Do you want coffee?"

"No. I'd like to get some sleep tonight."

"How's Bethany doing?"

"She was nodding off before her head hit the pillow."

"Are you sure she's not pretending to sleep until we go to bed? I wouldn't put it past her to sneak out of here."

"You heard our conversation."

"Some of it," he admitted.

"I have the flash drive, and I also took her shoes and hid them away, just in case."

"So, my concern is not unfounded."

"No. It's not. She's worried you're going to put Michael in jail. She wants to warn him. She wants to do what she set out to do—show him the flash drive, so he can see that the Salazars are trying to take him down. Then she would like to convince him to run away with her. She thinks they could disappear. Michael could get out of that life, and they could live happily ever after."

"That's one plan."

"Do you have another one? Because I'm thinking that you probably don't relish the idea of putting your little brother in jail or watching the Salazars destroy him."

"Neither scenario is good."

"Is there another way out of this for Michael? Or is this going to come down to brother against brother, good against evil?"

"I honestly don't know. That depends on several factors, including whether or not Michael wants a way out. Talking to him earlier didn't give me a lot of hope."

"But Michael doesn't know the Salazars are setting him up. That might change his perspective. Bethany didn't think he would believe her if she just told him what she'd heard. She thought he needed concrete proof."

"I think he does, too. Otherwise, he'll find a way to dismiss everything. I wish to God I could have protected him from all this. I wish I'd found a way to go after my mother earlier."

"None of this is your fault, Diego."

"Logically, I know that, but emotionally…"

Her gaze softened, and she walked across the room, sliding her arms around him, as she rested her head on his chest. "Is there anything I can do?" she asked.

He set down his coffee and pulled her into a tight embrace. "You're doing it."

He loved how well they fit together, his chin resting on the top of her head. Instantly his body hardened. He wanted another night with her. He didn't know how many more they would have, but he wanted at least one more.

She looked up at him, her eyes filled with emotion. "Let's go to bed, Diego."

He gazed down at her. "To sleep?"

"After," she said. "But let's make sure we have the car keys, and our phones in the room with us."

He smiled. "I like that you can love Bethany and still know her for who she is."

"I've had a lot of practice. You're only seeing the worst side of her, but she can be really kind and thoughtful, caring, too. I know it feels like you and Bethany are at odds, but you're actually on the same side. You both care about Michael. You want him to find a way out. You just differ on how to do that. But we can talk it all out in the morning."

"We can do that," he agreed, as he put his arm around her shoulders and walked her down the hall to the bedroom.

They closed the door behind them and undressed each

other with loving, restrained purpose. But all that restraint went out the window when they fell into bed together. Then there was only passion—wild, consuming desire that drove everything else out of their heads.

Tonight he just wanted Tara. He wanted her softness, her strength, her generosity—all the things that were uniquely her. And he wanted to take away her worries, free her from the fears of tomorrow, of the future. The only moment that mattered was the one they were in, and he was going to make it as good as he possibly could.

—➤◄—

Diego jolted awake. He'd heard something.

Sliding out of bed, he grabbed his briefs off the floor, pulling them on along with his jeans as he reached for the gun by the bed.

"What's wrong?" Tara whispered.

"Not sure yet. It could be Bethany sneaking out."

"Or someone sneaking in," she said, as she scrambled for her clothes.

He moved toward the door. Then he heard a scream. And he moved faster.

He threw open the door and saw Bethany being dragged down the hall by Pablo. She was kicking and yelling, but Pablo was almost to the front door. "Stop," he yelled. "Or I'll drop you where you stand."

Pablo froze, then put his gun to Bethany's head, as he kept his other arm around her neck.

"Let me go, you bastard," Bethany hissed, as she tried to pull herself free, but she was too weak to get away.

"This is between her and me," Pablo told him.

"Wrong. It's now between you and me. Let her go."

"I'd rather kill her."

"And then I'll kill you. Is that the way you want this to go down?"

The door behind Pablo flew open. Pablo looked like he'd been expecting someone else, his jaw dropping as Michael strode through the doorway, weapon drawn.

Diego sucked in a breath. He had the terrible feeling his worst fear had come true. It was going to be brother against brother. And at the end, one of them could end up dead.

Twenty

—➤➤◄◄—

"Michael," Bethany cried out in relief. "Thank God you're here. Pablo is setting you up. I have proof. I've been trying to get it to you."

"The bitch is lying," Pablo told Michael. "She's the one setting you up. She's been working with Pedroza. You can't trust a word she says."

"It's not true," Bethany protested. "I love you, Michael. You have to believe me. I heard all about Pablo and Rico's plan when I went to Cascada for Vanessa's birthday. They were drunk; they didn't know how much they were saying. They had everything on a flash drive, and I stole it, so I could give it to you."

"That's a lie," Pablo began.

"Shut up," Michael barked. He gave Diego a quick look, then turned back to Pablo and Bethany. "Let her go."

"She can destroy all of us," Pablo said, refusing to loosen his grip on Bethany. "She knows too much. Ask Rico. He's in the car."

"Rico is unconscious," Michael said coldly.

Pablo blanched at those words. "What did you do? Are

you crazy, Michael? You're turning on your family for this bitch?"

"I'm not betraying you, Michael—they are," Bethany said. "It's all on the drive: photos of you and Alan Pedroza together, inventory from your bar, financial records. They want to take you down because Caleb loves you too much, and you're not blood. They're jealous."

"I know," Michael said. "I figured it out."

"You did?" Bethany asked in amazement.

"Yes. I did a lot of thinking today, a lot of talking to people who are actually loyal to me. I know what Pablo and Rico have been doing. Let her go, Pablo."

"No, she's coming with me. She knows too much, with or without the drive. I'm just looking out for you, Michael. You have to believe me."

"I don't believe you," Michael said coldly. "And, you, of all people, Pablo…"

Pablo paled. "It was Rico's idea. He forced me into it. He's the one who came up with the plan. He's the one who talked other people into it. Rico—"

A shot rang out, followed by screams—Bethany, Tara, Pablo.

Diego instinctively pushed Tara back into the bedroom, as Pablo sank to the ground, clutching his bloody shoulder, and Bethany crawled away from him, crying in terror. He thought for a split second that Michael had shot Pablo, but there was another man in the doorway—Rico!

"Rico?" Pablo asked in shock. "You shot me."

"I'm protecting Michael—my brother," Rico said harshly. "I heard what Pablo told you, Michael, but it's not true. I had nothing to do with this. I didn't even know about the flash drive until this afternoon when Pablo asked me to help him find Bethany and get it back. I was curious to see what was on it, so I came with him. You didn't have to knock me out, Michael."

As Rico turned his head, Diego saw the blood on the

back of his scalp.

"I'm not your enemy," Rico continued. "It's Pablo and your bitch."

Michael's jaw tightened at Rico's words. And Diego realized that his brother did actually have feelings for Bethany.

"She's going to ruin your life—all these people will," Rico added, his gaze sweeping the room. "They have to die tonight. We clean up and we start over."

At Rico's words, Diego's hand tightened on the trigger of his gun. He was prepared to take out Rico, Pablo, and Michael if he had to. He'd kill all three of them to protect Tara and Bethany. But he was terribly afraid that Michael felt the same way in reverse, that he'd be willing to kill all of them to stay in the Salazar family, to protect his lifestyle, his job, his criminal brothers.

"You don't have to do it," Rico told Michael. "I will show you my loyalty by taking care of this problem for you."

Rico took aim at Bethany, but before he could fire, Michael shot him in the heart.

Rico stumbled back against the wall, blood spurting from his chest, shock in his eyes. Then he fell to the floor.

"Fuck, man, you killed Rico," Pablo said in shock, still clutching his shoulder as he tried to get to his feet.

"He just shot you. What do you care?" Michael asked coldly. "He was trying to pin everything on you."

"He was lying," Pablo said quickly. "I told you it was all Rico's idea. If you want to shoot someone else, shoot him. He's FBI," Pablo said, waving his good hand toward Diego. "I found out tonight. I have a source at the bureau. She told me they had Bethany. That's why I came here."

Michael's head swung in Diego's direction, and as they faced each other once more, with guns drawn, love and hatred burning between them, images from a lifetime ago flashed through his head. He and Mateo building a fort in the living room, playing on a Slip-N-Slide in the backyard on a hot day,

building war machines out of blocks, eating popcorn in front
of the TV. He remembered Mateo crawling into his bed when
he had a nightmare or when their parents were fighting. He'd
always told his little brother that he would be all right, that
everything would be fine.

But now he was out of promises and out of time.

He had a responsibility to protect Bethany and Tara. But
he didn't know if he could pull the trigger on his brother. He
wondered if Michael had the same doubts. After what he'd
just witnessed, he doubted it. He wished for another way out,
but there was no one coming to their aid. The building they
were in was empty. No one else would have heard the shots.
No one would know they were in trouble. He had to settle this
now—with his brother.

"Diego is your blood, Michael," Tara said from behind
him.

"Get back in the room," he told her, not trusting that his
brother wouldn't shoot at her first.

"Diego is more your brother than these men, Michael,"
Tara continued, as she ignored his plea and moved into the
hallway. "And if you're going to shoot him, you'll have to
take me out, too, and Bethany as well. Diego loves you and
so does Bethany. Are you really going to kill the two people
who actually love you? Because clearly these men have no
feeling for you. They wanted you dead. They wanted to
destroy you. But Diego remembers the little boy he used to
play with, the kid he can't imagine being cruel and heartless.
Bethany has somehow decided you are worthy of her love.
She has risked her life for you. She had absolutely nothing to
gain and everything to lose when she stole the drive from
Pablo. And she did it for you—so you would believe her."

Michael's gaze flickered toward Bethany, who was on the
floor crying.

"I do love you, Michael," Bethany said. "Everything I did
was for you. What Tara said is true. And I know you feel the
same way about me. We have something special. Please don't

let it die here tonight."

As Bethany spoke, Diego saw Pablo sidling back toward his gun, which had fallen on the floor.

"Stop," he ordered.

Pablo made one last lurch toward the weapon; it was his last move. Michael fired another shot—straight through the heart.

Tara and Bethany screamed once more. He shoved Tara back behind him, not sure who Michael would go after next.

Michael stared at Pablo, watching the blood gush from his chest wound. Then he tossed his weapon onto the floor and gave Diego a challenging look.

His lips tightened, but hope ran through him now that Michael had released his weapon.

"Your turn," Michael told him. "If you want to take me out, do it now."

He didn't want to take the shot, and thankfully he didn't have to.

Michael looked away from him, his gaze moving to Bethany. Then he walked over to her and dropped to his knees. He opened his arms, and Bethany crawled into them.

"I love you, too, Bethany," Michael said.

"You believe me?" she asked through her tears.

"I do," he said, kissing her with passion and love.

Diego let out a breath and lowered his weapon as Tara joined him in the hallway.

"It's over," she said, a bright light in her still terrified blue eyes. "He chose Bethany over his brothers. I didn't think he would."

"I didn't, either."

He walked across the room, keeping his gun at the ready, as he kicked various weapons out of reach in case Michael decided to make another move or someone else came through the door. He also checked on the two men. Both Pablo and Rico were dead. His brother had shot the two men he'd considered his brothers.

Had he done it out of love for Bethany? Or out of hatred for their betrayal?

Michael got to his feet and helped Bethany over to the couch, where they both sat down.

His brother didn't seem to be at all concerned that Diego still had a gun on him.

"What now, Diego? You want to arrest me?" Michael challenged. "My FBI brother?"

"You knew that before Pablo told you."

"I did a little research after you showed up at the golf course. It's been a busy day."

"And your research also revealed that Pablo and Rico were plotting against you?"

"Unfortunately, yes. I knew they would lead me to Bethany. And they did."

There was a note of detachment in Michael's voice. He was putting emotional distance between himself and the men he had grown up with. Diego recognized that trick. He'd done it dozens of times. It made him feel like he still had a connection to his brother.

"You have to let Michael go, Diego," Bethany pleaded. "He saved our lives."

"He also killed two people right in front of me."

"So they wouldn't kill you or Bethany or your blonde friend," Michael returned. "It was self-defense."

"Was it? Or was it payback for what they were trying to do to you?"

"They deserved what they got. They weren't who I thought they were, but then most people aren't," he said bitterly. "It's a lesson I keep relearning."

"Help Michael," Bethany pleaded. "He's your brother."

"Do you want to play that card?" he asked Michael.

"No," Michael returned. "Do what you want to do. It's your choice."

"A choice you gave to me. Why?"

Michael stared back at him. "Because I wanted to."

He didn't quite know what to make of his brother's answer. He knew what he wanted to make of it—he wanted to believe there was still love between them.

"Help both of us, Diego," Bethany continued, unwilling to stop fighting for Michael, for their love. "Let us go. We'll disappear. We'll leave all of this behind. We won't do anything criminal ever again. We'll live good lives. We'll be the best people in the world if you just give us a second chance."

He wanted to help them. There was even a part of him that wanted to let them both go, but that wasn't the right decision. He glanced at Tara, who hadn't said a word, but there was encouragement in her eyes. She wanted him to find a way out of this. And there was one possibility...

Clearing his throat, he said, "You'll never be safe if you try to disappear, not with the Salazars still in control. They'll hunt you down, Michael. There's only one way for you to change your life. You need to take the Salazar organization down—all of them—the entire operation from top to bottom. The government can put you in witness protection. Once the cartel is destroyed, you and Bethany will be safe."

"You want me to turn on the people who took me in, who raised me when no one else would?" Michael asked. "It's a lot to ask."

"Is it?" he challenged, meeting his brother's gaze head-on. "I'm sure there are still people in the family you care about, but you killed Pablo and Rico. No matter what your relationship was in the past, the family will now see you as their enemy. You turned against them. And you're not their blood." He took a breath, feeling a knot of emotion in his throat. "But you are my blood, my brother, and I don't want to see you in jail or dead. What's it going to be?"

Michael gave him a long look, then his gaze moved to his fallen brothers. "I never thought they would betray me. We grew up together. I never took anything from them. I tried to help them. I knew they wanted more, but they made mistakes, bad decisions. Caleb didn't trust them. He trusted me. He gave me money and power. He made me feel like I was in control of my life for the very first time."

Michael's words sent a wave of pain through Diego. "I know you had a rough childhood."

"You don't know anything, Diego."

"I know you have a choice to make now. One that could change your life for the better, give you real control."

"Real control? While I'm hiding? While I'm testifying against the people who took me in?"

"Yes," he said flatly. "Because going forward it's not about them; it's about you. Your life has changed. You can never go back. You have to accept that."

A small smile played across Michael's face. "I actually like your honesty. It reminds me of when you told me to toughen up and take that nasty cough medicine, because it was good for me."

"I'm still trying to look out for you."

Michael gave Bethany a quick glance. She was snuggled up against him, her eyes filled with adoration and love. Then he turned his gaze back to Diego. "Can you guarantee witness protection for both of us?"

"That depends on what you're willing to give up, how cooperative you'll be."

Pounding footsteps drew his attention to the door. He raised his gun once more, but this time it was Wyatt who strode through the door, followed by Bree. "What the hell are you doing here?" he asked in surprise, lowering his weapon.

"Tara texted me," Bree said.

Tara gave him a shrug as she lifted the phone in her hand. "I had to do something while I was hiding in the bedroom."

"Who do we have here?" Wyatt asked, tipping his head toward Pablo and Rico.

"Salazars," he replied. "They tried to kidnap Bethany. Michael stopped them. He prevented them from killing any of us." He paused. "This is my brother."

"Okay," Wyatt said slowly. "How do you want to play this? Or maybe Bree and I need to step outside and let you handle things?"

His gaze moved to Bree, who had the same question in her eyes. He knew they would go along with whatever he decided. But he would never put their jobs in jeopardy. There was only one decision, and Michael had to make it. But even if he didn't choose to cooperate, he would be taken into custody.

"Michael?" he asked, his gaze returning to his brother.

Michael didn't answer right away, conflict in his dark eyes, but Diego sensed his brother was getting to the inevitable conclusion.

"I know you'll put me in jail, Diego. You always had a sense of justice, even when you were a kid. You knew what was right and what was wrong."

"You used to know that, too."

"All right," Michael said. "I will help you to rip the organization apart. I have all the knowledge and the evidence you need to take down the Salazars." He blew out a breath at the end of his statement, as if he couldn't believe what he'd just said.

Diego felt both relief and concern at Michael's decision. It was the only choice, and he was glad Michael had made it. But the personal cost of taking down the family who had raised him would be high for Michael. Once again, his brother was alone. But not really alone—he had Bethany. That was something. And he suspected Michael was making this decision for Bethany as well as himself.

"In that case, I'll call this in," Wyatt said, as he took out his phone.

"Bree, would you mind taking Tara and Bethany into the other room? I need a minute with my brother," he said.

"Of course," Bree said, urging Tara and Bethany down the hallway.

"Michael." He tipped his head toward the kitchen, and his brother got up and followed him into the adjoining room.

They stood on either side of the kitchen island, which seemed like the perfect metaphor for their relationship.

"You called me Michael," his brother said, folding his arms in front of his chest.

"That's what you wanted, isn't it?"

"I did. Maybe not anymore."

"You said you followed Pablo here. Do you know how he figured out our location?"

"I assume he got the information from the woman he met on the Santa Monica Pier about an hour ago."

His heart jumped at that piece of information. "A woman? What did she look like?"

"She was blonde, wearing big sunglasses, tight jeans, and short top. Her hair was in a ponytail. Her posture was forceful. She and Pablo had an intense conversation."

His gut tightened. Michael's description sounded like Tracy. *But that was a crazy thought—wasn't it?* Tracy couldn't be involved with the Salazars. Although, she was the one who had given him the first tip.

But why would she have sent him to the church in Cascada? Why would she have wanted him in the middle of whatever deal she was running with the cartel?

Bree's words rang through his mind. *It feels like it's your turn, Diego, like someone is pulling the strings, and you're dancing on hot coals, running for your life, like I did, and Wyatt did—Parisa and Damon, too. You're the only one who hadn't had a secret from his past come back to haunt him— until now.*

Bree had been talking about Vincent, but maybe it had been Tracy all along.

But what did it mean? Was all of this a setup? For what purpose? To pay him back for dumping her after their one night together? That seemed way too extreme.

"You think you know who she is," Michael said.

"I can't imagine that I do. That would make her a traitor."

"Maybe that's what she is. This is an FBI safehouse. And she gave it up. That must mean she either works for the bureau or she was paid by someone who does to deliver the information."

"He said he did, but we can't ask him."

"You seem unfazed by the fact that two of your family members are dead, and that you killed them."

"They betrayed me." Michael's eyes blazed with fury. "I devoted my life to the Salazars. I did whatever they wanted me to do. I was so grateful that they had taken me in, shown me love, paid for my education, that I gave them all of my loyalty. We were family. But when Pablo told me a bullshit story this morning about Bethany stealing from him, I knew something was up. And I knew Rico had to be involved."

"You sent us away, so we wouldn't be there when Rico came back."

"Yes. Rico acts first, thinks later. I knew he would try to take you out, and I needed more information before I could act. So, I started digging into it. Pablo told me about Vanessa's birthday party in Cascada. I spoke to Vanessa. She told me that she thought Rico had convinced Pablo to do something he shouldn't do, and she was worried about her brother's part in it. She suggested that Rico was trying to set me up, but she didn't know why." He paused. "I had no idea Bethany had gone to the compound. I had deliberately kept her away from the estate. I didn't want her to get swept up in anything. I wanted our relationship to be separate from all that. When I heard she'd gone there behind my back, for a moment, I thought maybe she was playing me, too."

"She wasn't. She heard Pablo and Rico plotting against you. And she stole the drive with their manufactured evidence. I saw everything on it. They were setting you up, making it look like you were skimming off the top. They had photoshopped pictures of you and Alan Pedroza together. They were going to show everything to Caleb. I'm sure they thought he would take you down for them."

Michael's jaw tightened. "I've never met with Pedroza."

"They were very believable photos."

"They were faked. And I never took money off the top. I was loyal."

"Their proof was convincing. It was quite a plot, but it was foiled by Pablo's inability to hold his liquor and keep the drive safe."

"He's always had a problem with drinking too much. Both Pablo and Rico make terrible decisions. That's why they haven't been promoted, why they haven't been given more responsibility. I knew there was dissension, bitterness. I tried to give Pablo jobs that would help him gain Caleb's respect, but he always screwed something up. Still, I never imagined they would go as far as they did. Now who's the idiot?" Michael uttered a harsh laugh. "I don't know why I'm surprised, though. I should be used to it by now—my life changing in an instant. People I love turning on me, disappearing. It's the story of my life."

"It doesn't have to be going forward. Bethany wants to go into hiding with you. She wants to be with you. She loves you."

"I love her, too. She's the real reason I killed them. They would have made sure she died for what she did."

"I thought that might be part of it."

"But the reality of changing names, having no money, starting over—I don't know how long she'll stick around."

"She might surprise you. She took a huge risk trying to save you."

"I still can't believe she did it. But then Bethany is impulsive. She's driven by emotion. She reminds me of who I used to be."

"She definitely pushes the envelope. But in this case, she acted out of love. I like her—for whatever that's worth." He paused, needing to bring up the past even though Michael probably didn't want to hear it. But he had no idea if they'd ever have the chance to talk about it again. He couldn't let this moment slip away. "I know my father's rejection was incredibly painful."

"You don't know anything," Michael said flatly.

"That's not true. I'm sure it felt a lot like our mother's rejection of me."

Michael's gaze narrowed. "She didn't reject you; she was kicked out of the house."

"But she never came back, not even to see me for a brief moment. She got married. She changed her name and yours. She had another life. She never looked for me. She was my mother for thirteen years. You think I don't know what it feels like to have a parent reject you? To lose one of the two people in the world who is supposed to love you and protect you?"

Michael's lips drew into a hard line as he stared back at him. "She did try to see you in the beginning, but your father had you hidden away, and she couldn't get to you. She wasn't a very strong person, you know. She was caring and loving, but she was weak. She needed someone to take care of her. That's why she married Tomas. She didn't want to be alone."

"Was he good to her? To you?"

"I think he loved her. He treated me well enough. I didn't care that much about him one way or the other."

"I met Irina. She said she tried to take you in after Tomas died, but you wanted to be with the other kids at the Salazar compound."

"I did want that. Irina was a nice woman, but I didn't belong with her. The Salazar estate was where I felt at home. Caleb and Sophia treated me like a nephew, as did Juan Felipe and Santoro. Their kids were my cousins. We were a tribe. I thought it didn't matter that I didn't share their blood, but it always mattered. It mattered with your father. And it mattered with my cousins, when they thought I had too much."

There was a bleakness to his brother's eyes that tore at his heart. "It matters to me that you're my brother; you're my blood. Does it matter to you?"

Michael thought about that, then gave him a hard smile. "I'm a criminal. You're an FBI agent. Our blood doesn't matter. We're on opposite sides."

"That may be true when it comes to the law, but not when it comes to us. We are still brothers. And I never stopped looking for you. I don't want you to die, Michael. I want you to live. But you're the only one who can make things better. It's just like when I gave you a push on your bike and told you to pedal as fast as you could, so you wouldn't fall. I could only take you so far then; the rest you had to do by yourself. The same is true now."

A light flickered in his brother's eyes. "I remember that. I crashed into the bushes."

"Not before you rode a good ten feet. You were proud. You wanted to do it again."

"I wanted to impress you."

"You did."

"Was your father good to you after we left?"

"No. He was terrible. He was angry, bitter. He took me for revenge, not for love. In reality, he was done with all of us. I hated him for sending you and Mom away. We fought all the time. He forced me to go to military school. He wanted to straighten me out. At first, I was resentful, but then I was happy that I was away from him. I found a new family in the service. It felt good. I can understand why you felt like you belonged somewhere when the Salazars took you in."

"Mom never liked the family. She hated when Tomas took us to the compound. She didn't like that he did anything for Caleb and his brothers, but Tomas knew what it meant to be loyal."

"So loyal that he didn't question how our mother fell off a mountain during a solo hike?"

Something flickered in Michael's eyes. "I wondered about that, too, but it was wet that day. The rocks were slippery."

"Mom didn't even like to take walks. I can't imagine her hiking in the mountains by herself."

Michael shrugged. "She used to walk when we went to Cascada. Like I said, she didn't like to be around them."

"I want to find out more about her death, but that's for another day. What about your biological father? Are you sure you don't know who he is?"

"I don't. Do you?" Michael challenged. "You were older than me. You were more aware of what was going on."

"I've been thinking about it. There was a doctor at the hospital where Mom worked. He drove her home one night. I saw them out my window. She looked happy—happier than she had in a long time. But when she came in the house, Dad started yelling at her. He said she needed to quit her job before she did something stupid with that doctor. I don't know if his last name was Winters, but we could find out."

Michael gave a negative shake of his head. "No. I'm done looking for someone to belong to. I'm sure that man didn't want me, either. So, what's next? I go to jail until you round everyone up? That could take years, and I'm sure I'll die in custody. The family has a long reach."

"You won't go into custody; you'll go into witness protection. But we do have to process you through the system. Wyatt will take you into the detention center at the field office. You'll be isolated and protected there. Then you will be taken somewhere safe."

"And Bethany will go with me?"

"Not tonight. You need to show the bureau how much you're willing to give up. Tomorrow, once protection is set up, Bethany will join you."

"She's in as much danger as I am. You know that, right?"

"I do. And I will protect her with my life until I turn her over to the US Marshals. Once you and Bethany go into protection, you can't have any contact with anyone in your life, not one single person."

"What about you?"

He held his gaze for a long minute. "I'll keep an eye on you both. I couldn't protect you when you were a kid. I'm going to do my damndest to protect you now."

"It will be a challenge."

"It will be less of one the more you share with the bureau. The only way you'll really be safe is to completely destroy the cartel, to bring down the big hitters."

"Caleb never leaves Colombia."

"Once we cut off his network, his money, his power, his reach will diminish."

"And then another cartel will step into the breach—the Pedrozas, no doubt."

"We're going to look into them, too, especially the connection to Allende Tours, which is a US-based operation." He let out a breath, hearing more voices in the apartment. He had no doubt that at least a half-dozen agents had arrived. "There's so much I want to talk to you about, but we don't have time."

"You and Tara—is that something?" Michael asked, surprising him with the question.

"It might be," he admitted.

"She really fought for Bethany. She was fierce. It was her words earlier today that made me question Pablo's story. Tara was convinced Bethany was in trouble, and she was right."

"Tara has the biggest heart of anyone I've ever met. And she fights for people she loves." He paused, as Wyatt came into the kitchen.

"We need to move things along," Wyatt said shortly. "I'll take Michael down to the office. Bree is going to take Bethany and Tara somewhere else, so the agents can work. What do you want to do?"

"I'll go with Bree and Tara."

Wyatt pulled out handcuffs and faced Michael. "Turn around."

Watching his brother put into cuffs felt as surreal as

everything else that had happened. "Michael, I'll see you tomorrow," he said, as his brother met his gaze.

"I hope so," Michael said. "And call me Mateo. I think it's time I became him again."

He appreciated that Mateo was choosing the name he'd been born with, but he knew that with tomorrow would come a new identity. "Mateo," he said, savoring the word for a long second. "But it's not your name that defines you; it's your choices. Make the right ones."

Twenty-One

Tara was getting used to waking up next to Diego—the weight of his arm over her waist, his head snuggled into the back of her neck, his breath brushing her cheek. Squinting her eyes at the clock, she was happy to see it was only seven thirty. She didn't mind having a few more minutes of sleep before facing whatever was to come.

After Michael had been taken away by the feds, agents had swarmed the apartment. Bree had taken her, Diego and Bethany to another two-bedroom apartment a few miles away. According to Bree, she was the only person who knew where she was taking them, so there was no way their location could be compromised.

Bethany had crawled into bed and fallen instantly asleep. She and Diego had not been far behind, with Bree insisting on taking the couch in the living room, just to be sure there were no more surprise visits during the night.

Diego had tried to fight her on that, but Bree had been as strong-willed and determined as Diego, and in the end, she'd won out.

When they'd gotten into bed, she'd thought Diego would want to talk about everything that had happened, but he'd simply pulled her into his arms and told her to sleep, that there was time for everything later. She'd been too tired to argue.

But today was a new day—and sure to be a long day.

She didn't know when the FBI would want to hide Bethany and Michael away, but she was guessing it would have to be soon. Once family members realized that Pablo and Rico were dead, they'd be after Michael and his girlfriend. The fact that Pablo and Rico had found them at the safehouse meant that there was a leak in the FBI, which also meant that Michael might not be as safe as Diego thought he was.

He'd promised Bethany that Michael would be all right, and she'd backed him up. She really hoped that hadn't been the wrong decision.

Bethany was in love with Michael, and she didn't want her friend to lose him. On the other hand...

She breathed in deep as she thought about the fact that Bethany was going to have to disappear. After today, she might never see her again. That realization brought a deep ache to her heart. Bethany was her sister. She was supposed to be her maid of honor, the aunt to her children, the best friend of her life. How could she go years without ever seeing her again?

Diego shifted his weight, brushing her hair off her face, as he placed a kiss on her jaw. "You're thinking very loudly."

"Am I?" she murmured.

"You're worrying about Bethany."

She rolled over to her other side, so she could face him. "Actually, I was feeling sorry for myself. I just found Bethany. Now I have to say good-bye, maybe forever."

Diego's gaze filled with compassion. "Forever is a long time. I don't think it will be that long."

"But you don't know how long the Salazars will be a

danger to them. Will they ever really be free?"

"That's a fair question. I guess you have to focus on the fact that she'll be safe."

"Is that what you're telling yourself about your brother? You just found Mateo, too. Are you ready to let him go?"

"No, I'm not ready. But I'm certain this is the only path where both Mateo and Bethany get to live. And we take a lot of bad guys off the street at the same time. We break up a huge drug network. There are a lot of wins here, Tara. And you should feel incredibly proud of yourself for not only finding Bethany but helping to destroy the Salazars. We did this together."

"I'm happy about most of it. I just don't like the part where I don't get to see Bethany again. I'm going to miss her so much. She's been my confidant my whole life."

"I understand. I know it's different for me and Mateo. I've had a lot of years to get over missing him. But it still sucks. I wish there was a different way to end this." He slid his hand through her hair. "But they do get to live. And that's something. We get to live, too."

"Do you think we'll still be targets?"

"No. The Salazars are going to be very busy trying to stay out of prison. And you and I were minor players. However, I still plan on keeping my eye on you for a while."

His words were both touching and depressing, because she didn't know what would happen at the end of *a while.*

Diego stiffened at the sound of voices. "I'm going to check on that."

"It sounds like Bethany is talking to Bree."

"I'll make sure." He gave her a kiss. "One of these days, we're going to spend a luxurious morning in bed together."

"That would be nice," she said, but she wasn't sure she believed it.

After Diego left the room, she went into the bathroom to take a shower and once more put on the clothes she was getting really tired of wearing.

When she entered the kitchen, she found Bethany and Diego having breakfast. Someone had run out and picked up muffins, croissants, and fruit.

"This looks good," she said.

"Bree picked it up for us. She headed home to change and get some sleep," Diego added. "Coffee?" He got up and moved toward the coffeemaker.

"Thanks." Turning to Bethany, she said, "How are you feeling today?"

"Relieved, scared, happy, sad..." Bethany gave her a helpless smile. "I don't know what's coming next."

"You love it when you don't know what's coming next," she said, as she sat down across from Bethany. "You've always told me that's what makes life exciting."

"How unlike you to throw my own words back in my face," Bethany said dryly.

She grinned. "Just saying."

Diego set her mug of coffee down in front of her. "I'm going to take a shower if you ladies can do without me for a few minutes."

"I think we can manage."

"Flynn has two guys watching the building, so there shouldn't be any problems," he added.

She frowned at the reminder of the danger they were in. "Two guys? Are you still worried, Diego?"

"We're all being extra cautious until we can get Mateo and Bethany into protection. I won't be long."

As Diego left, she looked back at Bethany. "Are you sure you want to give the rest of your life to Michael? You haven't known him very long."

"I know it must seem impulsive to you, Tara, but I love him. He's done some bad things. But he's changing his life now. He's doing what's right."

"Because he has to," she couldn't help pointing out. "I'm not sure he would have changed anything if his family hadn't come after him."

"But he didn't even see the flash drive before he took Pablo and Rico out. He did that for me."

"I can't argue with that. But when he shot those men that he used to consider family, there was a cold ruthlessness about him that makes me worry."

"But Michael has never treated me that way. He doesn't even yell when I'm being annoying."

She smiled at that. "Well, that's something."

"It's not like I have a real choice, either," Bethany added. "I'm a target, too. What I did eventually led to Pablo and Rico dying. The family will come after me."

"I know. I wish it was different."

"The worst part of all this is that I won't be able to see you, Tara. That's going to hurt."

"Maybe we'll find a way."

"I hope so. I also hope you won't continue to be in danger after we're gone."

"Diego thinks we'll be fine. They only wanted me because they thought you'd given me the flash drive or that I could tell them where you were."

"I still can't believe you went to Colombia to find me. That is not the Tara I know and love."

"I guess your adventurous spirit rubbed off on me."

"And maybe some of Diego's spirit as well?" Bethany teased.

"Well, I must admit that stealing an airplane with him and crash-landing it in the jungle was quite an experience. Not that I did much more than cling to the arms of my seat and try not to throw up."

"You'll probably never get airsick when you fly commercial again."

"Probably not."

"He's good for you, Tara."

"Maybe. But I don't know if I'm good for him. I'm such a cautious person—a worrier. And I don't make bold choices. I'm not as spontaneous as he is. I'm not that fun. I'm afraid once we get back to our real lives, I'll feel like a dead weight to him."

Bethany laughed. "You are nuts. You have made nothing but bold choices. You have been nothing but spontaneous."

"Only because of the danger. I could go back to who I used to be."

"I don't think you will. You've changed. I can see it. But even if you did go back to who you were, that wouldn't be bad, either. You've never seen your own strength, your kindness, your amazing traits. You're a great person—you're the whole package. And you are fun. Maybe not crazy fun, but definitely fun. Diego has fallen for you. I can see it in his eyes when he looks at you. It's why he's trying so hard to take care of me. Because you love me. That's the reason. He's doing everything for you."

"He wants to help his brother, too."

"I know. But he also wants to help me because of you."

"I do love you, Bethany. And I know that this isn't the end of us. We'll figure a way to see each other. Maybe it won't be right away, but some day."

"What will you tell your parents?"

"That you've fallen in love and you're moving away with an incredible man. They'll miss you as much as I will. But I'll tell them stories every now and then and maybe at some point you'll call them."

Bethany nodded, then got to her feet. "I'll certainly try. I need to take a shower before we go."

"I wish you were feeling better before you had to deal with all this." She rose to her feet. "I'm still not sure you shouldn't be in the hospital."

"I'll be okay." Bethany opened up her arms. "A hug for the road?"

"Definitely," she said, giving her a tight squeeze. "But that's not the last one. I'm coming with you until I can't."

"Thanks, Tara. You're the best."

As Bethany left the room, Diego came back into the

kitchen, his hair damp from his shower, his cheeks smoothly shaven. He looked good and smelled even better. He gave her a smile. "Everything okay?"

"Bethany and I had a good talk. It's going to be hard to say good-bye to her, but I'm at peace with it."

"Good."

"How soon will it happen?"

"Today."

She sucked in a breath. "That is fast."

"It's crucial we protect them, and with yesterday's apartment location being compromised, we can't take any chances. There's a leak somewhere and until it's plugged, we have to be extra cautious."

"Well, I guess it doesn't matter, because today or tomorrow or next month—it still wouldn't be long enough. I'm really going to miss her." Her eyes blurred with tears and Diego's arms came around her. She rested her head on his chest. "Sorry, I'm being a baby."

"You don't have to apologize."

"I keep thinking about all the things she's going to miss."

"But she won't miss them because she's dead." He cleared his throat. "Sorry, that was too harsh."

She lifted her head to look at him. "No. It was honest. You and I have always been honest with each other."

"We have," he agreed.

"So, can I ask you a question?"

"No."

"No?" she echoed in surprise.

"I don't have an answer yet."

"You don't know my question."

"I have a good idea. You want to know what happens with us after we say good-bye to Mateo and Bethany."

"Okay, you did know my question." She licked her lips. "You have to report to DC for your next assignment soon, right? Where will that take you?"

"I'm not sure. I was supposed to be in DC tomorrow, but

that's not going to happen. I need to talk to my boss today, let him know what's going on. Even with Mateo and Bethany in protection, there's a lot to do to take down the Salazar organization, and I want in on that."

"But eventually you'll go to DC?"

He stared back at her, his eyes dark and unreadable. "That's the plan. When do you have to go back to work?"

"I guess as soon as I can."

"I don't think long distance works, Tara."

"I don't, either. And it would be crazy to change our whole lives for a relationship that's been going on less than a week."

"That doesn't seem smart," he said slowly.

"I usually do the smart thing."

"Me, too."

Their gazes clung together, heated emotions flying back and forth between them.

And then Diego's mouth was on hers, and they said everything else with a series of scorching kisses that were far more honest and open than any words they'd just exchanged.

It was only the sound of a ringing phone that broke them apart.

Diego picked up his phone from the counter. "Rivera," he barked out. He listened for a moment and then said, "Got it. We'll be ready."

"Ready for what?" she asked.

"Our ride. Wyatt is on his way. He's going to take us down to the LA office."

"Is that different from where we went before?"

"Yes, it's the official field office for this area."

"Am I going to be interviewed? Do I need to think about what I'm going to say?"

"You will be interviewed, but all you have to do is tell the truth, all of it."

"And Bethany?"

"After she gives her statement and the agents are satisfied

with whatever information Mateo has turned over, they'll be picked up by the US Marshals Service. They handle witness protection."

"I'm afraid to let anyone protect them but us," she commented. "But I know you're doing your best."

"I just hope it's good enough," he said tightly.

Twenty-Two

——➤➤◄◄◄——

Once they arrived at the field office, they were all separated. Tara was put in a conference room, where she remained for almost three hours while two FBI agents she didn't know asked her a litany of questions. She didn't know where Diego and Bethany were, or Mateo, for that matter, but she was ready to be done. And, finally, so were the agents. They told her to stay where she was and left the room.

She picked up the bottle of water they'd provided her and took a long sip. She checked her watch. It was two o'clock. She wondered if she was completely finished, or if there was going to be a round two.

The door opened, and she straightened, relieved to see Diego come through the door. At his warm, intimate smile, her heart skipped a little beat.

"How did it go?" he asked, giving her a kiss before sitting down next to her.

"I told the truth. It sounded like a crazy story when I was telling it. I can't quite believe everything that happened."

"I know the feeling."

"What's happening with Bethany? I know she's still pretty weak. If she's going through what I just did, I'm worried about her health."

"The marshals picked her up a few minutes ago."

Her heart sank, and anger ran through her. "Really? I thought I would get to say good-bye. This isn't right, Diego. You shouldn't have let them do that. You must have known I would want to say good-bye."

"It was Bethany's choice, Tara. She said it would be too difficult, too painful, for her to say good-bye to you. She said you'd already had the conversation she wanted to have."

"You should have told her that I would want to see her."

"I did, but she refused. And, honestly, Tara, I think it was the right decision."

"Are you going to feel that way if Mateo suddenly vanishes?"

He stared back at her. "I know it's going to hurt—both of us—a lot. But this is what has to happen. It would never be a good time to say good-bye. I hope this won't be forever. But it's going to be for a long while. Michael will eventually have to testify at many criminal trials. And it will take the bureau, in conjunction with every other government agency, a long time to take down the Salazar network."

She let out a sigh, knowing he was right, but it didn't make her feel better. "And when that's done?"

"Maybe."

"I want a better answer," she complained.

"I wish I had one. But for now, that's all I've got."

"Do you think the Salazars know that Pablo and Rico are dead?"

"Yes. We already picked up six individuals working here in the LA area, and agents are preparing other raids and arrests throughout the country. Word will travel fast."

Diego stood up as the door opened. Damon and Parisa entered the room.

"Well, you both have been busy," Parisa said, giving

Diego a hug and offering Tara a smile. "Wyatt filled us in on everything. I'm sure dealing with your long-lost brother in this complicated situation has been very difficult."

"That's an understatement."

"We need to have a meeting," Damon said. "With our team—just the five of us. I hope you can excuse Diego for a few minutes," he added to her.

"Whatever you all need to do."

"Someone will be in shortly with food," Diego said. "You must be starving."

"I could eat."

"I'll be back as soon as I can."

Parisa lingered at the door as the men exited. "I'm glad you're okay, Tara. And I'm really happy your friend is, too."

"Thanks. I appreciate that."

As Parisa left, she took out her phone and turned it on. Her voicemail and text messages lit up. She'd read through them later. Instead, she punched in her favorite number.

"Tara," her mom said. "Where have you been? I've left you a half-dozen messages. I know you're on vacation, but you can call your mother."

Her heart swelled with love at her mom's familiar and loving voice. "Is everything all right?" she asked. "Are you and Dad okay?"

"We're fine. How are you?"

"I'm great. It's all good."

"What have you been doing that's kept you so busy?"

"Oh, just sightseeing."

"You sound a little funny. Did you meet someone? Is that why you suddenly got so busy?"

"Actually, I did meet someone. His name is Diego, and he's an amazing man."

"Well, that sounds promising. Where does he live?"

"That's the tough part. He lives in DC. I'm not sure if it's going to go anywhere, but even if it doesn't, I'm really happy I met him."

"Oh, honey, don't let distance get in your way. You can teach anywhere."

She was shocked by her mom's words. "But you and Dad are in California."

"So? There are airplanes. DC isn't that far away."

"You're suggesting I change my whole life for a guy I met less than a week ago?"

"Not exactly. I'm saying that real love is worth the effort. Only you can decide if this guy fits into that category. I've never heard this tone in your voice before. It reminds me of when I fell in love with your dad, which was also fast and furious, by the way."

"You didn't get married for two years after you met," she reminded her mom.

"No, but I knew two days in he was the one for me. We just had to get through school and get our first jobs before we tied the knot. But we both saw right away that we had a forever kind of love. How does this guy make you feel?"

"Happy, loved, protected."

"Then he sounds like he has a lot going for him."

"I think he's a little scared of love."

"Most men are, honey," her mom said with a laugh.

She smiled. "Probably true."

"Tell him we want to meet him. You can bring him home for dinner. Your dad will test his barbecue skills and see if he's worthy to spend more time with."

"Very funny. I don't know, but I'll think about what you said."

"Good. Are you home now?"

"Not yet. But soon. I'll call you when I'm back."

"Okay. By the way, have you spoken to Bethany?"

"I have. She's doing well. She's also in love."

Her mother laughed. "Bethany is always in love."

"I think this is also different for her."

"Well, then I'm happy. Is he the man in London? Because I got a text from her a few minutes ago, and she said she was moving there, and that she wouldn't see us for a while, but she wanted to let us know she was happy and would miss us."

She smiled to herself, happy that Bethany had found a way to talk to her parents. "I'm going to miss her, too, but she's making the right move. I'll talk to you later, Mom."

"I love you, Tara."

"Love you, too," she whispered, as she put the phone back in her bag.

The conference door opened, and a blonde woman wearing navy-blue slacks and a white dress shirt under a blue blazer walked inside. She was carrying a bag of food that smelled delicious.

"Hello," the agent said with a friendly smile. "I heard you need some lunch. I hope you like pad Thai."

"I love it, and I am starving."

"They're going to use this room for a meeting, so if you wouldn't mind coming with me, I can take you down to the kitchen snack area."

"Sure," she said grabbing her bag off the floor. "I was getting kind of tired of this room anyway."

She followed the woman out of the conference room and into the elevator. She was surprised when the agent pushed the button for the garage level but maybe that's where the kitchen was.

"How did your interview go?" the woman asked.

"It was fine. I'm happy to be done. Do you know Diego?"

"I do. He's a good agent. Very smart, sometimes a little too smart."

She wasn't sure what that meant, or why there was an odd tone in the woman's voice. "What did you say your name was?"

The agent smiled as the elevator doors opened. She put her hand in front of the door. "After you, Ms. Powell."

She stepped off the elevator, confused by the fact that they were in the parking garage.

"Where are we going?" she asked, then gasped for a

breath as a strong male arm came around her neck and some material was pressed against her nose that had a strong, sickening scent. Her head spun. She couldn't breathe. Everything was going black.

She'd thought she was safe now. She'd been wrong.

—➤➤◄◄—

"I figured out who met with Pablo," Wyatt said, as Diego, Bree, Parisa, and Damon huddled around a table in a conference room on the top floor of the building.

Diego's pulse jumped at that piece of information.

"You're not going to like it," Wyatt added. "It was Tracy Cox."

His stomach turned over. He'd had that suspicion, but now it was confirmed. "Are you positive?"

"Yes. We reviewed cameras all around the pier." Damon pointed to the monitor behind him and hit a button on the computer.

Tracy's image appeared. She was walking down the pier while talking on the phone.

"I don't have a picture of her and Pablo Salazar," Wyatt said. "But the fact that she's there, in the same location—it can't be a coincidence."

"Where is she now?" Diego asked.

"She's in the building," Parisa said. "I saw her a little while ago in the restroom. She didn't act like she was worried or agitated about anything. She was putting on her makeup."

"She doesn't know we're on to her," he said. "We need to find her. Let's shut down the building." He paused as his phone buzzed. "Or maybe we don't have to. This is her." He connected his phone and put it on speaker. "Tracy. I'm glad you called. We need to talk."

"It's a little late for that, Diego. Things are unraveling fast."

"What the hell are you talking about?"

"Are you with your pals—with Wyatt and Bree, Parisa and Damon? I saw you all heading into the conference room before I went to see Tara."

"You went to see Tara? Why?"

"Because she's part of this."

"Part of what? Where is she?" His gut tightened with fear.

"That's a good question, but not one I can answer. You know it's not an accident you're all here, right? The funding of the medical center wing was a ruse to get Damon and Sophie, Parisa and Jared into town. Tonight, you're all going to pay for leaving Jamie behind."

His pulse jumped into his throat. "Are you working with Vincent?"

"Yes. Vincent is a master manipulator and a blackmailer, but he pays well in both cash and connections. He hates you all. He's been torturing you for the past few years, and today is the grand finale. You could still win, but the cards are stacked against you. Everyone you love has been taken, and that includes Tara. It was actually quite easy to have her walk downstairs with me."

He never should have left Tara alone. "Where did you take her?"

"I didn't take her anywhere, but she's going to be where it all began. If you can figure it out in time, maybe you can rescue her—rescue all of them."

"Where's Vincent?"

"He's waiting. He's watching. It's been a long time for him. He wanted you to each know what it's like to lose someone you love. All the other stuff he did was a warm-up—a way to torment you, see if you could survive your secrets, your pasts. Of course, you all did. I think Bree started to guess in Chicago that Vincent was involved, but she couldn't get the rest of the way. Isn't that right, Bree?"

"Help us," Bree pleaded. "You're not Vincent, Tracy. You know we didn't kill Jamie."

"What I know is that all of you always come out on top. And people like me get screwed. I won't be seeing any of you again. I'm going to disappear, start over."

"Vincent won't let you do that, Tracy," he said. "You know too much."

"He's going to kill you," Parisa interjected. "Just like he killed every other agent he used to get to us."

"I've done everything Vincent asked me to do—in Chicago with Bree, and then by sending Diego to Colombia."

"That was Vincent's lead," he muttered.

"Yes. He was disappointed that you and your brother didn't end up killing each other. He thought that would have been a fitting end, but since you now have someone else you care about, it's just as well."

"Vincent knew my mother was dead? That Mateo was a Salazar?" He'd wondered who Tracy's source was, and now he had his answer.

"Vincent knows everything. He has connections everywhere. You have no idea how powerful he is, how many people he can use to get what he wants. You'll never be free of him."

"We can all be free of him if we take him out," he argued. "You can help us, Tracy. Tell us where everyone is."

"If you remember that training mission, you might be able to discover their location. Oh, and Vincent said come alone. Or a lot of people will die. Good-bye, Diego. I thought at one time we might have something. But you didn't want me."

"So, this is revenge?"

"Actually, it's survival for me. Good luck."

"Tracy, wait—" he shouted, but she was gone.

As he looked around the room, he saw Wyatt on his phone. Then Wyatt swore and said, "Avery missed her show at Nova Star. Her assistant says no one knows where she is."

"Nathan isn't answering," Bree said, her phone also at her ear.

"Neither is Jared," Parisa put in, a grim look in her eyes.

Damon was still on the phone, but he gave a furious shake of his head. "I'm getting voicemail for Sophie."

Guilt swept through him. "I never thought Tara would be in danger here."

"You couldn't have predicted this," Bree said, giving him a pained look.

"You tried to tell us, Bree. You tried to warn us," he said. "Why didn't we go after Vincent?"

"Because he was smart enough to always look like he was helping us," Parisa said.

"Okay, let's think," Damon said, crossing his arms. "Vincent is using the people we love as hostages, which is the same setup as the training mission where Jamie lost his life."

"Which means they're in an abandoned, condemned apartment building," Bree said. "It has to be here in Los Angeles." She sat down at the table and jumped onto her computer.

"It will be as close to the building used in our training mission as possible," Damon continued. "Vincent is meticulous. We've seen that all along, in every step he's made. He's conniving, manipulative, and incredibly clever. Look at how he's played us. My God, it started with Sophie's father, Alan, Jamie's teacher at Quantico. And then Vincent went after Sophie and me and blew Wyatt's cover in New York, almost getting him killed."

"And he figured out how best to get to me," Bree said. "By digging up my long-lost child and kidnapping her."

"Then it was my turn again," Wyatt continued, a hard edge to his voice. "I knew Vincent's relationship with the Nova Star founder was no coincidence, but I couldn't prove anything."

"I thought his relationship with my friend's fiancé was also an odd coincidence," Parisa said. "But he had such a plausible explanation. One thing is clear—Vincent likes a show. Tracy said he would be nearby, waiting and watching."

"We need to find the building first," Bree said, her attention back on the computer.

"I'm going to call Flynn, get the team in on this," Wyatt added.

"They can do the groundwork, but the rescue is on us," Diego told them. "You heard what Tracy said. We're the ones who have to play this out."

"Got it," Wyatt said tersely. "Let's get to work."

Thirty minutes later, with Flynn's task force and an entire building of agents working on the parameters they'd been given, they zeroed in on a possible location—a ten-story apartment building in Long Beach that had been condemned within the past week. It was currently empty and awaiting a teardown by an out-of-state owner.

Donning bulletproof vests and wearing their FBI jackets, the team took a black SUV to Long Beach. They were followed by Flynn and four other members of his task force in a second SUV and five additional agents from the LA office in a third SUV. The latter two groups would set up a perimeter around the apartment building, evacuate any neighbors in possible peril and provide backup if needed.

Diego's heart was pumping hard as they drove across town, every red light, every bit of traffic making him want to throw open the door and start running. But that definitely wouldn't be smart, and if there was ever a time to exercise his brainpower, it was now, because Vincent was playing a mind game, and they had to figure out how to beat him at that game.

He was sorry that Tara had gotten caught up in this. He couldn't lose her now, not after everything they'd been through together. She had to be terrified. And she'd been kidnapped right under his nose. He'd let her down. And even worse, he'd never told her how he felt about her. He'd resisted answering any questions about what was next, because he'd been afraid to commit, to make a promise he couldn't keep.

But what the hell had he been so scared about? Loving

her? Living with her? Spending the rest of his life with her?

What a fool he'd been. He was in love with Tara. He had to get her back, so he could tell her. There was no other option.

Twenty-Three

———→⇒≫⇇←———

It was five o'clock on Tuesday evening when Diego and his team pulled up in front of an abandoned ten-story apartment building, which was on a corner in a lower-income neighborhood. There was an empty lot next to the building that was filled with weeds and surrounded by a chain-link fence. On the other side of the building was a three-story apartment building.

Flynn's group parked near that building and would evacuate any residents at that location and keep them at a safe distance until they could ascertain if the abandoned building had been wired with explosives as it had been in the training mission.

The third SUV took a position at the other end of the block and on his command, they'd take the necessary steps to lock down the buildings on the opposite side of the street, which included two buildings that appeared to belong to the same apartment complex, a laundromat, and an insurance office that appeared to be closed for the day.

Vincent was somewhere nearby, but at the moment their

priority was on rescuing their loved ones.

He followed Damon up to the front door of the building. There was a chain padlock on the door, which they used a tool to break through, and then stepped inside.

The building smelled like rotting garbage, and there was the sound of rats scurrying away from the sound of their footsteps. There was an elevator, but he doubted it was operational. The stairs looked suspect as well. Apparently, the building had been condemned after several pipes burst, damaging the apartments so badly the owner had decided to tear the place down and start over.

"Okay," Damon said, as they huddled around. Damon had taken command of that training mission, and they had decided to play this out exactly as they'd done before. Damon's eyes were cold blue steel, but Diego knew that Damon's heart was pounding a million beats a minute as he thought about Sophie. "Remember the obstacles we ran into before."

"Shooter came in at the third-floor stairwell," Bree said.

"Top floor stairwell door was booby-trapped," Wyatt put in.

"Another shooter when we got through that door," Parisa said.

"Then we deal with the explosive device on the apartment where the hostages are being held," he said. "Hopefully, we won't need to call in a bomb squad."

"I think I can handle it," Wyatt said. Out of the group, Wyatt had the most experience with explosives.

"Once we open the door, we pull out the hostages and we leave as fast as possible," Damon continued. "I have no doubt Vincent intends to play this out to the last detail, which means there will be a blast somewhere, fire, smoke, debris. No one stays behind. No one goes back in. No one falls out a window. We do this together."

"Together," they echoed, and then they headed up the stairs.

Damon led the way, followed by Bree, Wyatt, Parisa, and himself at the back. It had been almost five years since they'd met, since they'd done a mission together—all five of them in the same place, but it felt like they'd worked together yesterday. They'd always had the ability to read each other; it was what had made them a strong team.

When they hit the third floor, the door flew open, and shots rang out. Damon ducked, then fired, as they all dropped back, weapons drawn, waiting for a shooter to appear as had happened in the training mission.

When the shots ceased, Damon said, "There's no one in the hallway. There's a gun rigged to fire, probably a pressure sensor on the floor." He walked into the hallway and examined the gun. "It's empty. Let's go."

They continued up the stairs until they reached the top floor. As expected, the door was wired with explosives.

He kept an eye on the stairs behind him, while Wyatt and Parisa worked on dismantling the device.

"We'll get in," Bree said with confidence. "Vincent would never want it to end here in this stairwell. It's not exciting enough for him."

"Good point."

A moment later, Wyatt said, "We've got it. The door is disarmed. But there's probably another gun waiting to be triggered."

Damon grabbed one of the backpacks they'd brought with them and tossed it through the door. When it hit the hallway floor, more shots rang out. They waited until the rounds were spent. Then they moved through the door and down a dark hallway that was lit by the beam of Damon's flashlight.

"Anyone here?" Damon yelled.

"We're here," a male voice called out.

"Jared?" Parisa said with relief. "Are you all right?"

"We're okay, but the door appears to be wired with explosives," Jared replied. "Don't get too close."

He was immensely relieved to know they were all right. "Is everyone there?" he asked, impatient to hear Tara's voice.

"It's me, Sophie, Avery, and Nathan," Jared replied.

His heart stopped. "What about Tara?" he yelled.

"We haven't seen her," Avery called back. "She's not with us."

Tara wasn't there? Where the hell was she?

"We'll find her," Bree assured him.

"Okay, I think I've got this one disarmed," Wyatt said, dismantling the device connected to the door. "Everyone move back as far as you can." He turned to look at the rest of them. "Are we good?"

He trusted Wyatt, as did everyone else. If he was ready to open the door, then they were all ready.

He held his breath as Wyatt turned the knob and the door opened.

But as they ran into the room, a blast knocked them to the ground, chunks of ceiling falling down around them in the smoky darkness. The explosion hadn't come from the device on the door. It was somewhere else. And he doubted it was the only bomb set to go off.

He scrambled to his feet, as the others reunited with their significant others, exchanging desperately grateful hugs.

"Everyone all right?" he asked, fighting back the urge to start running wildly through the building. He couldn't act without thought. That's exactly what Vincent wanted.

"We're okay," Jared said, although as Damon flashed a light on Jared's face, Diego could see a multitude of cuts and bruises. "I got those when they grabbed me," Jared said in reply to Damon's unspoken question.

"Let's get out of here," Damon said.

"You're sure no one has seen Tara?" he asked.

"Maybe they didn't take her," Avery said hopefully.

"No, they took her. She's here somewhere."

"Let's get everyone out and then we'll look for Tara together," Wyatt said. "We'll find her."

They'd no sooner left the apartment when another blast sent them sprawling once more. Vincent was definitely teasing them, like a cat with a mouse.

Scrambling to their feet, they ran down the stairwell that was now thick with smoke and heat from fires burning somewhere in the building.

Finally, they reached the ground floor, and rushed through the front door. The cold evening air was a welcome respite. Flynn's team was now right outside. The other team was keeping back interested, curious neighbors.

"Everyone out?" Damon asked.

"I'm the last," he said, meeting Damon's gaze. "But I have to go back and find Tara. She's probably in another apartment."

"You can't," Bree said. "It's what Jamie did."

"I think that's the point," he said grimly. "One of us has to go back, and it has to be me, because it's Tara, and it's because I didn't stop Jamie."

"Jamie went back in because he thought he heard someone, but there was no one there," Parisa reminded him. "Tara might not be there, either. It's a trick."

"It might be, but I can't take the chance that it's not."

"Firefighters are on their way," Wyatt said, as the sirens split the air.

"They can't go inside," Diego argued. "We know there are more bombs. It has to be me."

"We'll all go," Damon said.

He turned toward the door, took one step inside the building, and then was knocked back off his feet by a rolling blast of fire that landed him on his ass.

"Tara," he yelled, scrambling to his feet.

Wyatt and Damon held him back.

"You can't go in there," Damon said. "The stairs will be gone now."

He fought his way out of their grip, but the fire coming through the doors told him they were right. He couldn't get back in. The building was ripping apart, much like his heart.

Another explosion rocked the ground beneath her feet. Tara could feel the heat. She could smell the smoke. She had to get free, but she was trapped in a chair, her hands locked behind her back by a plastic tie. She'd been struggling to get off the chair for the last half hour, ever since she'd woken up, strapped to it in the middle of some dark, almost empty apartment. She had no idea where she was or who had brought her to this place, but she knew she was in trouble.

The Salazars must have had Tracy on their payroll. She'd betrayed her own agency in God knew how many ways.

But who else was involved? Had Bethany and Mateo also been kidnapped? What about Diego? Where was he?

The frustrating, agonizing questions ran through her head as she fought not only the chair but the desperate panic rising inside her.

Wrenching her arms first one way and then the other with as much energy as she could knocked her off-balance, and she crashed to the floor. More pain swept through her shoulder as she landed hard, and for a second, she thought the crack she heard was her arm breaking, but as she moved again, a piece of the wood on the chair came loose.

Joy swept through her. She turned on to her side and finally managed to get her arms free of the wood. They were still behind her back, but now she could get to her feet.

Once she was up, a bout of dizziness hit her. She didn't know what she'd breathed in earlier, but she was still feeling the effects of those fumes. She blinked several times, focused her gaze on the front door of the apartment. When the lightheadedness passed, she moved around the small room.

As she'd thought, she was in a studio apartment that had a bath and a small counter area serving as a kitchenette. The only furniture in the room was a card table and two wooden chairs, including the one she'd been sitting in. There was a bucket on the floor near the front door. Moving toward it, she saw more plastic ties, duct tape, some kind of metal device that she couldn't identify, and a packet of wires. They looked like the kind of items you would use to make a bomb.

That sent another chill through her.

Turning around, she moved toward the window that had seemed so far out of reach just minutes before.

When she got to it, the scene across the street took her breath away. The building was completely on fire, flames shooting high in the sky, and down below were a crowd of onlookers, many of whom were wearing FBI jackets. She couldn't make out who anyone was, but she thought she saw Bree, maybe Wyatt…Diego had to be there, too.

As she squinted, she saw a blonde hug a taller man, and she realized that was Damon. There were other civilians, too.

Was one of those Avery? Was she with Wyatt?

Why was everyone down there and she was up here?

And then it hit her. This whole scene reminded her of Diego's story of Jamie's death. The abandoned building, the hostage rescue—the explosions. Jamie had gone running back into the building, searching for one more person, sure there was a hostage in trouble. But then the building had blown up. And Jamie had fallen out of a window and died.

Her heart stopped as she saw a man pacing in front of the building across the street.

It was Diego. She was sure of it. She could almost feel his fear. He was looking at the flames like he was seeing a ghost.

It suddenly made sense. He thought she was inside. He was going to go back in—exactly the way Jamie had done. He would die trying to rescue her.

She had to stop him. She ran to the door and tried to open it with her hands still behind her back, but there was a bolt, and after a few frustrating minutes, she gave up.

She returned to the window. If she could break the glass,

maybe someone outside would look up and wonder what was going on. Although there was so much noise with the fire and the crowd, it was possible no one would notice. But she had to try.

She ran toward the bucket on the floor. She managed to grab the handle and carry it toward the window. She angled one way and then the other, trying to hit it against the glass, but she couldn't make it happen. She needed to use her hands.

Tears of anger filled her eyes. She blinked them away. She couldn't quit. She had to stop Diego from going into that building. She also needed to save her own life, because clearly no one knew where she was. And it was quite possible there were more explosives, and this building was blowing up next.

She took a deep breath and squatted a little lower so she could raise the bucket high enough to hit the glass. She swung it as hard as she could back and forth, trying to get momentum, and then it struck the glass. The first hit only broke one or two pieces. She tried again until glass rained down in a shower on her head. Cold, smoky air hit her in the face. She stuck her head out the window screaming for help.

Finally, one head turned. Someone pointed in her direction.

Relief ran through her. They'd seen her. She screamed again.

And then the door to the apartment burst open.

She whirled around, hoping it was someone who had come to help her.

But cold fury came off the man striding into the apartment. He was an older man with pepper-gray hair and dark eyes, and he was, oddly enough, wearing a very expensive suit.

And then she realized who he was.

"Vincent," she said. "You're Vincent Rowland—Jamie's father."

"I see you're up to date." He grabbed her by the arm.

"And you're trying to mess up my plan with your scrappy attempt to get some attention. But it doesn't matter. They might have saved each other, but they won't save you." He hauled her toward the window, and at that moment, she realized what was going to happen next.

She could not let him push her out the window. She tried to butt his chest with her head, but that didn't seem to make a dent in his intent to shove her through the shredded chards of glass. She was running out of time, so she made the move she'd made a few days earlier. She kneed Vincent in the balls.

Vincent let out a groan of rage as he instinctively doubled over. She kicked out at him again, freeing herself from his grip. She took one step toward the door, and then Vincent grabbed her arm once more.

She screamed as she struggled to get away from him again.

But he was pulling her closer and closer to the window.

And then a shot burst out and his weight on her arm dragged her down to the floor. She pushed Vincent aside as blood poured out of the hole in his head. His eyes were shocked wide open, as if he couldn't believe his plan had failed.

She stared at Vincent in confusion. And then Diego pulled her up and into his arms.

"Diego," she breathed.

"You're all right," he said, hugging her tight. "You're okay now. God, Tara, I was so scared."

"I was, too."

She heard more footsteps, more voices, and lifted her head to see the room filling with Diego's team: Wyatt, Bree, Damon, and Parisa. They were all there. They hadn't let Diego come in alone. She should have expected nothing less.

"Are you all right?" Bree asked with concern.

"Diego shot Vincent." She looked back at Vincent sprawled on his back, his leg twisted awkwardly beneath him, his gaze fixed on the ceiling. "He is dead, right?"

Damon was checking Vincent's body. He gave a nod and said, "He's dead. He's never going to hurt anyone again. This is finally over. His revenge is done."

She looked back at Diego. "I was so afraid you would go into that burning building to find me. He was playing out the scene from the training mission, wasn't he?"

Diego nodded. "Yes. And when you weren't in the room with the other hostages, I knew he'd stashed you somewhere else, but I thought it was in that same building. I thought the bombs going off..." His jaw tightened. "I didn't know how to get to you."

"I wasn't there."

"Thank God."

"But you said there were other hostages? Who?"

"They kidnapped everyone we love," Bree explained. "Nathan, Jared, Avery, and Sophie. They were in an apartment across the street."

"Thank God you broke the window," Diego said, drawing her gaze back to him. "It was genius."

"It was desperate. Luckily, Vincent had left me alone. I guess he figured I couldn't do anything. My arms were tied around the chair, but I managed to break the chair and get free. The window was tougher."

"You're amazing."

"No. You're the one who is amazing. You saved my life again."

He gave her another fierce hug and then said, "Let's get out of here."

When they got down to the street, she was enveloped in more hugs from Avery and Nathan and two people she was meeting for the first time—Sophie and Jared. The women looked fine, as did Nathan, but Jared looked like someone had beaten the crap out of him.

"You're hurt," she said.

"I've been knocked around worse than this," Jared said

lightly.

"You fought hard to get away."

"Not hard enough. I'm glad you're all right, Tara. Diego was going out of his mind."

She smiled back at Diego, as he put his coat around her shoulders.

"You're an honorary FBI agent now," he said.

She gave him a shaky smile, feeling a bit weak now that the adrenaline was wearing off. "I think I'll stick to teaching high school Spanish."

He smiled back at her. "The bureau's loss."

"I think the bureau is probably going to be happy to see the end of me. When I woke up in the room alone, I thought it was the Salazars, because Tracy came and got me out of the conference room. It wasn't until I heard the explosions and I saw the fire across the street that it clicked, that it was the story you'd told me playing out again." She paused. "Where is Tracy?"

"I don't know," Diego said grimly. "But the entire bureau is going to be hunting her down. If she's still alive, we'll find her."

"Why would you think she wasn't still alive?"

"Because Vincent has made a habit of getting rid of the people he's used in his plans. But we'll see if Tracy was smarter than he was."

--->>><<<---

With Flynn's team and a team from the field office cleaning up the scene, Diego and his group were free to leave. There would be more interviews in the morning, more official statements to make, but for the moment they could take a minute to catch their breaths.

He took Tara back to the apartment they'd spent the night in. The rest of the team followed shortly thereafter, bringing pizzas, salad, beer, wine and soft drinks with them.

Sitting in the living room with chairs from the dining room table set up around the couch, the ten of them were quite a sight, covered in dust and soot, but they were all alive, and that was something. He felt incredibly lucky.

"I think we should have a toast," he said, raising his beer bottle. "First—to Jamie, our fallen teammate, one of the best guys any of us has ever known. He was not his father, and I won't have his memory tarnished by Vincent's actions."

"Here, here," Wyatt said.

"Second," Diego continued. "To all of us, for stepping up when it counts, for having each other's backs, for never being unwilling to break a rule or make a bold choice. I know I missed a few important moments, but from here on out, I promise to step up."

"We all step up when we can," Bree said. "We don't judge each other, Diego."

"I know. But I still want to do better. So, to us. Cheers."

"To us," the rest of the group echoed, as they clinked glasses and bottles.

"Well, I'm glad Vincent is dead," Bree continued. "I think it was probably the only way we could have stopped him."

"But it will take some time to unravel all the people he used along the way," Damon put in. "He had connections in every office. We might have taken down one of the most conniving and evil moles the bureau has ever seen."

"We'll get all of his friends," Wyatt vowed. "The rats will scurry into hiding, but we'll drag each and every one of them into the light of day."

"Now that we've exposed Vincent for who he is, the entire bureau will be dissecting every move he made in the last five years," Parisa put in. "I'm just sorry so many people had to die in his quest for revenge. He always had a fall person, someone who was allegedly the bad guy. And he was so normal at times. I think back to the memorial services we attended. I thought he was a grieving father, who actually seemed to care about us."

"It was a pretense," Sophie said. "I feel bad for Cassie—for Jamie's sister. She's now lost her father, too, and I know she wasn't a part of this." Sophie paused. "I'd like to make a toast as well—to my dad. He was the first of Vincent's victims. He wasn't completely innocent himself. He made mistakes, but he didn't cause Jamie's death, and he was torn apart by it, just as we were."

"He was a good teacher," Damon said. "And he'd be proud of us for taking Vincent down." He put his arm around Sophie and gave her a hug. "To Alan," he said.

They toasted once more.

"Well, it's finally over," Diego said. "Reliving the scene tonight reminded me that Jamie's death really was an accident. Whatever he heard that day, whatever reason made him go back inside when the drill was already over, was just part of who Jamie was. He always pushed the envelope, and he always jumped when someone was in trouble. He was a hero. He was born one, and he died one."

"I think you're all heroes," Tara put in. "And I can see why you were some of the best trainees who ever went through Quantico."

As Tara finished speaking, the doorbell pealed. He got up to let Flynn in. The agent had texted him earlier that he'd be coming by so no one would get jumpy and shoot him.

"I hope you saved me some pizza," Flynn said with a grin. "I've worked up an appetite."

"There are still plenty of slices," he replied, waving him inside.

"Great." Flynn nodded to the others. "Before I eat, I have big news. Tracy got in touch with me."

"What?" Diego asked in surprise. "Seriously?"

"Yes. She wants a deal. Immunity for turning over everything she has on Vincent and his operations. She already sent over recordings that she made of some of their calls. The higher-ups are considering her offer."

"No way," Wyatt said furiously. "She is not getting immunity."

"I don't think she'll get immunity," Flynn said quickly. "But she may be able to reduce her sentence if she has what she says she has. Also, according to Tracy, she's one of Vincent's victims as well. He was blackmailing her."

"Who cares?" Diego asked. "She could have turned the tables on him by coming clean earlier. Now she knows she's cornered."

Flynn tipped his head. "Probably. At any rate, her information should be able to reveal Vincent's entire network. The bureau can clean house, start over." Flynn paused. "Diego, I have an offer for you. If you decide you'd like to stay in LA, my task force will be expanding in the next few months. We've been given additional funding to take on some interesting assignments. I'd like to have you on my team. In fact, I'd like to have all of you on my team. Damon and Parisa, that includes you. What do you say to bringing the band back together? I know I wasn't your original leader, but I do respect all of your skills. And I think I can offer you some fun challenges."

"I'll think about it," Diego said, wondering if Flynn's task force wasn't exactly the change he needed.

Damon and Parisa answered in a similar fashion, saying it was definitely something to think about. And then Flynn dove into the pizza, and their conversation turned to more personal topics and some surprising announcements. Sophie announced that she and Damon had snuck off a few weekends earlier and gotten married at Niagara Falls. With her parents both deceased, she'd decided she didn't want to have a big formal wedding. But the more exciting news was that they were going to have a baby in October, and she was planning to take a year off work.

There were congratulations all around, and now Diego knew why Damon had been more emotional than usual when he'd found out Sophie had been kidnapped. He'd been worrying about his wife, and his unborn child.

Wyatt also announced that he and Avery were setting the date for next Christmas. And with Bree and Nathan already set to wed in August, Diego thought it was going to be a busy year. Parisa and Jared also looked pretty cozy, too. He suspected they wouldn't be far behind in making it to the altar.

Which left him. He looked over at Tara's pretty face, hating the bruises that marred her beauty, but loving the fight and the fire still lingering in her gaze. She was not a woman who would ever quit, and hadn't that been exactly the kind of woman he'd been looking for his entire life?

"What?" she asked curiously, catching his gaze on her.

"I'll tell you later," he said, grabbing another piece of pizza.

The party finally ended around midnight. And he wasn't sorry to see his friends go; he wanted to spend time alone with Tara.

"That was fun," she said, as he settled back on the couch next to her. "I like all your friends. Actually, they feel like your family."

"They are my family." He turned to face her. "So are you, Tara."

"You think of me as family?" she asked tentatively.

"Also, as a friend." He paused, seeing the uncertainty in her eyes. "And as a lover."

The shadows lifted from her gaze. "I think of you the same way, Diego. I can't believe we've known each other for less than a week. It feels like a lifetime."

"It does. And I can't imagine waking up and not seeing your face."

"But that's going to happen soon, right? You have to go back to DC and I have to go back to San Clemente."

"What if I stayed in LA, worked for Flynn? Would that be close enough?"

"It would be even closer if I got a different job next year, somewhere around here."

"Would you want to do that?"

"Would you?" she countered.

He smiled. "Okay, I'll go first. I've fallen in love with you, Tara. I want to keep seeing you. I want us to have a relationship that goes the distance. I want that more than anything. I know I have a difficult job. I may travel. I may disappear for days at a time, but I will always come back to you."

Her gaze grew a little teary. "If you didn't, I would come and find you."

He laughed at that comment. "I don't doubt that for a second."

"I love you, too, Diego. And I would like the chance to see what could happen between us. I would probably worry like crazy about you when you do disappear, but having met your friends, your team, I would have confidence in your ability to get the job done and come back to me."

"I would do my best. And I would never leave again without you knowing how I feel. When you went missing today, I thought about how I'd been too scared to have the conversation I knew you wanted to have."

"No, you were right; it was too soon."

"It wasn't too soon. The first time I saw you in the church, I knew you were going to be important. I just had no idea how much you would come to mean to me."

"Thank goodness you saved my life so many times so we could find out. I wanted to save yours tonight. I was terrified you were going to go back into that building for me, because I knew that's what you would do. It's who you are. You risk your life for the people you love."

"So do you. We make a good pair."

"We do. I want you to meet my parents. I told my mother I met someone on vacation. She's dying to meet you. She wants me to invite you to dinner. She promised my dad would grill something special, while he's checking out your barbecue skills, of course."

"I'd like that. And I hope I can pass your dad's test."

Tara licked her lips. "But I still feel like I have to ask…"

"What? Ask me anything."

"A lot has happened. We found Mateo and Bethany, and hopefully they are going to be safe for a long time. Are our feelings colored by adrenaline and relief? Joy at being alive? Is this love we feel real?"

"I think it's real. In fact, I have absolutely no doubt how I feel about you, Tara. I always shielded myself from love, from relationships. I didn't know if I had it in me to give my heart to anyone. It was so painful when my family shattered. It was easier not to care, not to get in too deep, but with you there was no choice. We were in deep and fast and I found myself telling you things I'd never told anyone. You're an amazing woman, and I would count myself lucky to be with you."

"That's a really nice thing to say. Unlike you, I had great role models for love and marriage. My parents are awesome, and I was raised in a wonderful family, but the men I've met over the last decade have never measured up. I've never felt like I could count on them or that I could really be myself. I know I've been too cautious, too sheltered, too unadventurous, but going to Colombia changed all that. It made me realize I could be anything I wanted to be. Actually, it wasn't just Colombia that made me feel that way. It was you, Diego. You had confidence in me. You saw my strength and my intelligence, and through your eyes, I saw myself."

"Then I have an idea. Why don't we tell each other how we feel every day for the next fifty or sixty years? And if at any point it doesn't still feel like love, we'll reassess."

"I could do that," she said, giving him a sweet, hot kiss that lighted the spark within him.

As he looked down into her beautiful, shining blue eyes that now glittered with happiness, he felt overwhelmed by emotion. "How did I get so lucky?"

"I was thinking the same thing," she said with a laugh. "And now, I really think we've done enough talking for tonight."

"See—we're always on the same page," he said, pulling her to her feet, and taking her into the bedroom.

Epilogue

Five months later

"Nathan and Bree chose a hellishly hot day for their wedding," Diego said, tugging at his tie, as they walked into the garden patio at the Drake Hotel in Santa Monica. The chairs were lined up for the small, intimate wedding.

"It's August in Southern California," Tara said with a laugh, loving how handsome Diego looked in his dark-gray suit. "And stop pulling on this," she said, fixing his tie.

He grinned back at her. "I've never been a fan of suits. I only wear them at work when I have to. Thankfully, that isn't often now that I'm working for Flynn."

Diego had officially made the move to Flynn's task force two weeks earlier, after wrapping up his previous position in DC and then helping the LA office compile multiple cases against Salazar cartel members. Mateo had been very helpful, providing an enormous amount of information to the bureau and other various government agencies.

The Salazar organization had been completely

dismantled, their assets in the US frozen and their distribution network ripped apart. Fighting among family members had scaled to new heights with Juan Felipe and Santoro being killed by Caleb as punishment for them taking out Father Manuel, a fact that had come out during the course of the investigation. Shortly thereafter, Caleb had suffered a debilitating stroke. They might not get him out of Colombia, but his criminal days were done.

With trials still to get through, Mateo and Bethany were hidden away somewhere in the country, but according to what Diego had heard, they were remarkably happy in their new life. For Mateo, there was no pressure to live up to anyone's expectations, no name to honor, and for Bethany, it was a chance for her to start over with a clean slate, something she'd been wanting to do for a long time.

"There's Damon and Sophie," Diego said, drawing her attention to the now very pregnant Sophie.

They exchanged hugs, and then she said, "Sophie, you are glowing."

"And huge," Sophie said with a laugh, but there was pure joy in her eyes. "I can't believe I still have six weeks to go. By the way, we have news." She glanced over at Damon. "Or did you already tell Diego?"

"I did not," Damon said. "I thought we'd tell everyone today."

"Well, don't leave us hanging," Diego joked.

"I have decided not to join Flynn's task force," Damon said.

Diego frowned. "I thought this was going to be good news."

"It's pretty good," Damon said. "I'm being promoted to special agent in charge of the Los Angeles field office."

Diego grinned. "So, you're going to be our boss's boss."

"I'd like to think of it as being a great supporter for your activities."

"Well, I'm glad you're coming to LA. When are you

moving?"

"We're closing on a house on Wednesday, and our things will be shipped out next weekend," Damon replied. "We want to get settled before the baby comes."

"I'm thrilled you're going to be in town," she told Sophie. "And, Damon, congratulations."

"Thanks," he said, pausing as they were joined by Parisa and Jared, Wyatt and Avery.

"How's everyone doing?" Wyatt asked.

"Damon has news," Diego said.

"Yeah, I already heard," Wyatt said. "Flynn told me earlier today that you're heading up the LA office. We're going to miss you on the task force, but it will be nice to have you as backup."

"I live to be your backup," Damon drawled.

Wyatt laughed. "Don't I know it."

"What about you, Parisa?" Tara asked. "Are you also coming to LA?"

"Not at the moment," Parisa replied. "But maybe in January. Jared has some Langley cases that he's involved in that preclude us moving out of DC right now. But down the road, I'm definitely interested. My mom and stepfather are actually moving to London, so I won't have any family ties in DC after Christmas."

"It would be good to have you on the team," Diego said.

"Hopefully, it will work out. We better sit down. Looks like the ceremony is getting ready to start."

They settled into their seats as Nathan stepped up to the front with another man, who Diego told her was Nathan's brother-in-law. And then the music started, and a little girl came down the aisle, wearing a pretty pink dress, a crown of flowers around her dark hair.

Bree had told them a week ago that she and her daughter's adopted parents had decided the time was right to tell Hayley that Bree was her biological mother. Hayley had been thrilled and had immediately asked if she could be the flower girl at Bree's wedding.

As the little girl reached the front and turned around, she gave the audience a big, happy smile, and Tara thought how much Hayley looked like Bree.

"At least Vincent did one thing right," Diego muttered. "He brought Hayley and Bree back together. Actually, he did three things—he led me to my mother's grave and he brought my brother into my life."

"Because he was hoping you'd kill each other," she said dryly.

"True. But it still got us together."

Avery walked down the aisle next as Bree's maid of honor. And then it was time for the bride. They rose to their feet. Bree gave them a smile as she walked by, her eyes brimming with happiness.

Tara had gotten to be pretty good friends with Bree and Avery over the last few weeks, since she'd moved from San Clemente to Santa Monica, and she now counted both of them as very good friends.

"Bree looks beautiful," she whispered to Diego, as they resumed their seats. "She and Nathan are really in love."

He took her hand in his and gave her a sexy smile. "So are we."

She smiled back at him. "Yes, we are." And then she sat back to listen to the minister.

The ceremony was friendly, intimate, with laughter and smiles. Afterward, the guests were treated to champagne and appetizers while the bride and groom took plenty of photos.

"Let's take a walk," Diego said. "The sun is setting over the ocean, and I know where there's a better view."

"All right," she said, curious if Diego wanted to get her alone for a kiss or really wanted her to see the sunset.

They walked around the edge of the building along a narrow path above the ocean.

"This is nice, isn't it?" he asked, an odd note in his voice.

"Yes. It's beautiful. But we live near the beach, and we

see the ocean every day, so is there something else going on here?"

"Yes." He pulled out his phone.

She gave him a confused look. "Who are you calling?"

"Someone who wants to hear from you." He punched in a number, then handed her the phone.

"Diego, what's going—" She stopped abruptly as a familiar voice came on the line. "Oh, my God, is it really you?"

"It's me," Bethany replied. "How are you, Tara?"

"I'm great. How are you? I can't believe we're talking." She gave Diego a questioning look. He simply smiled and leaned against the nearby rail, looking out at the ocean. "I know I probably can't ask you anything, but are you happy?"

"More than I ever thought I could be. It was scary at first, but we're getting used to being new people, living in a new place. We've even made a few friends. I'm working for a party planner. We do birthday parties for kids. It's actually fun."

"You've always been great at parties. What about Michael—Mateo—I don't know what you're calling him now."

"He's good. He has a job, too. It's nothing like what he was doing before, but he says it's honest work, and it feels right. I know you probably don't have the best impression of him, but he had to grow up and survive in the Salazar world. Now, he's finally free to be his own man, and he's flourishing. It's like a weight has been lifted off him. He's so much more relaxed. He's funny. He's creative. And he gets me."

"I'm so glad." She was very happy to hear that Michael was doing well, not only for Bethany's sake but also for Diego's."

"We've gotten super close, Tara. This is where I was meant to be. Michael really is my soulmate. I know you've never believed in soulmates..."

"I actually do believe in soulmates now."

"Because you're in love with Diego."

She could hear the laughter in Bethany's voice. "Yes. I'm in love. Diego and I moved in together a few weeks ago. I'm going to be teaching at a new high school in LA starting next month. My mom and dad love him, too. Diego lets my dad teach him about grilling meat, even though I'm sure he's perfectly capable of barbecuing steaks on his own."

"I'm not surprised your parents love him, because he's crazy about you. And that is what they've always wanted for you. Diego is a good guy. He set up this call, because he said you needed to hear my voice. It was incredibly thoughtful. I needed to hear your voice, too."

"I told him that the other day, but I didn't want to put anyone in danger."

"The marshal said it was okay. We're actually not in the town where we normally are right now. It's all good."

"I wish I could see you. I think about you all the time."

"I think about you, too. It's all going to work out, Tara. One day…"

"One day," she echoed, tears coming to her eyes. "Until then, be happy."

"You, too. Don't do anything I wouldn't do."

She laughed at Bethany's teasing comment. "That gives me a lot of latitude."

"I know. It's funny. I thought travel and living large were what would make me happy, but it's not that at all. It's the little things, the quiet, intimate moments. It's trust and connection."

"It is all that," she said, Bethany's words echoing exactly how she felt.

"I'll be thinking about you, Tara."

"And I'll be thinking about you."

She gripped the phone as the call disconnected, wishing they could have spoken a little longer. On the other hand, she should be grateful they'd had any contact at all. She blinked some tears out of her eyes.

Diego gave her a concerned smile. "Did I make a mistake?"

She shook her head. "No. These are happy tears. Thank you for setting that up."

"I wish I could have done it sooner."

"I know. I'm really grateful, Diego. I miss her. But she sounded happy. She said she's exactly where she wants to be, that Mateo is her soulmate. Who would have guessed that your brother and my best friend would end up together?"

"It was fate—not just for them, but for us."

"I think so, too. We were meant to be together. I can't wait for the rest of our lives."

"We don't have to wait. We're living our love and our lives right now."

"That's true," she said. "You taught me to stay in the moment, and this moment is lasting forever." She framed his face with her hands and pressed her mouth against his. Kissing Diego was her absolute favorite thing to do, and the fact that she could do it whenever she wanted made it even better.

He lifted his head and gave her a blazing look. "We better stop, because we have a reception to get to."

"I just wanted to give you something to think about," she said with a laugh.

"Oh, believe me, I won't be thinking about anything else." He put his arm around her shoulders, and they walked back to the reception.

Flynn gave them a nod, as he grabbed a beer from the bar. "How's it going, Tara?"

"It's good," she said. "Did you bring a date?" The very attractive Flynn seemed to also be very single, and she was curious about that.

"No, I'm flying solo."

"His favorite way to go," Diego drawled.

"I like to travel light," Flynn continued. "Where did you two sneak off to?"

"Just wanted to look at the view for a minute," Diego said.

Flynn laughed. "I'll bet. I'll see you inside. I think we're sitting together."

"What's his story?" she asked Diego, as Flynn disappeared into the restaurant.

"I'm not entirely sure. Flynn has his secrets."

"I thought your team knew everything about each other."

"Flynn wasn't part of the original team."

"But now he's your team leader. Seems like it's time for the secrets to come out."

"I'm sure they will at some point. That's the deal with secrets. They are always revealed, even when you think there's no way anyone will ever find out."

"You're talking about your family now."

He gave a nod. "I suppose I am. I wish you could have met my mother."

"Does that mean you're not as angry with her as you were for not coming back for you?"

"Let's just say I've made my peace. I think that she did what she was capable of doing. Mateo told me she wasn't a strong person, and maybe I need to stop blaming her for her weaknesses and appreciate the years we had together."

"Just when I think you can't get any better, you do." She put her arms around him. "I love that you can forgive, even if you can't forget."

"You showed me what it means to love unconditionally when you chased your impulsive friend around the world."

"We've both inspired each other."

"Let's keep doing it," he said.

"Absolutely. You and I don't quit."

"We don't quit," he echoed.

"Not ever," she said, giving him a long, loving kiss.

THE END

Want more
OFF THE GRID: FBI Series?

Coming soon!
Ruthless Cross (#6)

Also Available
Perilous Trust (#1)
Reckless Whisper (#2)
Desperate Play (#3)
Elusive Promise (#4)
Dangerous Choice (#5)

About The Author

Barbara Freethy is a #1 New York Times Bestselling Author of 66 novels ranging from contemporary romance to romantic suspense and women's fiction. Traditionally published for many years, Barbara opened her own publishing company in 2011 and has since sold over 7 million books! Twenty of her titles have appeared on the New York Times and USA Today Bestseller Lists.

Known for her emotional and compelling stories of love, family, mystery and romance, Barbara enjoys writing about ordinary people caught up in extraordinary adventures. Barbara's books have won numerous awards. She is a six-time finalist for the RITA for best contemporary romance from Romance Writers of America and a two-time winner for DANIEL'S GIFT and THE WAY BACK HOME.

Barbara has lived all over the state of California and currently resides in Northern California where she draws much of her inspiration from the beautiful bay area.

For a complete listing of books, as well as excerpts and contests, and to connect with Barbara:

Visit Barbara's Website:
www.barbarafreethy.com

Join Barbara on Facebook:
www.facebook.com/barbarafreethybooks

Follow Barbara on Twitter:
www.twitter.com/barbarafreethy